FEVER OF LOVE

Ross stood up, smiling. As she passed him, she stopped and pressed a kiss on the fair attractive head. But when she was in the cool bungalow, her smile vanished. Her brows knit. She wondered what Bill had said or done to annoy Clive. Surely nothing to do with her ... and yet ... she could not forget the Bill of last night, who had stood on the veranda, covering her hand with kisses — a revelation of his love, his wish to protect her. Perhaps he had roused Clive's jealousy. That was possible. Ross almost found pleasure in that thought. If Clive were jealous it must mean he still loved her ... in spite of Valmy.
If only she had known what really lay behind Clive's attitude.

**Also by the same author,
and available in Coronet Books:**

The Cyprus Love Affair
Forbidden
House Of The Seventh Cross
Gay Defeat
Do Not Go My Love
I Should Have Known
The Unlit Fire
Shatter The Sky
The Strong Heart
Stranger Than Fiction (Autobiography)
The Secret Hour
Nightingale's Song
It Wasn't Love
Climb To The Stars
Slave Woman
Second Best
Lightning Strikes Twice
Loving And Giving
Moment Of Love
Restless Heart
The Untrodden Snow
Betrayal (previously, Were I Thy Bride)
Twice Have I Loved

Fever of Love

Denise Robins

CORONET BOOKS
Hodder and Stoughton

Copyright 1931 Denise Robins

First published in Great Britain by
Mills and Boon 1931

Coronet new edition (Reset) 1964

Second impression 1969
Third impression 1976
Fourth impression 1977

---

*The characters and situations in this book are
entirely imaginary and bear no relation to any real
person or actual happening*

This book is sold subject to the condition that
it shall not, by way of trade or otherwise, be
lent, re-sold, hired out or otherwise circulated
without the publisher's prior consent in any
form of binding or cover other than that in
which this is published and without a similar
condition including this condition being
imposed on the subsequent purchaser.

Printed and bound in Great Britain for
Hodder and Stoughton Paperbacks, a
division of Hodder and Stoughton Ltd.,
Mill Road, Dunton Green, Sevenoaks,
Kent (Editorial Office: 47 Bedford Square,
London, WC1 3DP) by
Cox & Wyman Ltd., London, Reading and Fakenham

ISBN 0 340 00745 1

CHAPTER I

ROSS DERRELL moved softly round the bedroom. She hummed under her breath. She was very busy. She was laying a man's dinner-jacket out on one of the twin beds; black tie, collar, white boiled shirt, all that a man would need for dinner in the hotel tonight. They were for her husband and she fingered everything lovingly, obviously a woman in love. Happy to render small services such as these.

The radiators gave forth delicious warmth and bright lights dispelled the gloom of a March day in London. A pleasant glow was cast upon the rose pink satin eiderdowns, the pink carpet, the stereotype mahogany suite. Now and again mirrors reflected Ross Derrell and showed her as a very charming woman, still a girl for all her twenty-six years, with a full beautiful figure curving under the blue kimono which she was wearing.

Ross had never been pretty in the ordinary sense of the word, but her skin was exquisite — a clear warm tan — and she had a delightful mouth. She was a Rhodesian — born and bred — and looked it. She radiated good health and good humour. She had warm brown eyes — almost chestnut in colour with a frank innocent expression. Curiously innocent eyes for a married woman. Clive Derrell, who had married her three years ago in South Africa, had told her then she was quite the most innocent creature he had ever met. She retained a strange aura of virginity which clung to her and looked straight from the clear serene eyes.

There was an almost old-fashioned atmosphere about Ross, with her long brown rope of hair hanging to her waist. She had not yet conformed to the prevailing fashion and cut that satiny hair. At home on the Ranch near the Zambesi, fashions did not matter. One wore a print overall or riding-kit. One's few party dresses were out of date and nobody minded. Ross was the daughter of a South African farmer and had never belonged to the smart set. Clive, although a Londoner and not so much part of Rhodesia as Ross, never bothered about Ross's appearance, and Ross took it for granted that he was satisfied with her.

This was their first visit to London together and Ross's very first glimpse of England. London seemed to her a wonderful, awe-inspiring city. The vastness of it — the ceaseless noise — the traffic — the great shops — had interested and thrilled her when they first arrived. She had also enjoyed their week's visit to Clive's uncle and guardian, in Richmond. Everybody had been very kind to her and made her feel welcome. But she herself felt awkward — even nervous. Out in Africa — mistress of Swallow Dip — the big, flourishing ranch left to her by her father just before her marriage — there was nobody more self-reliant than Ross. There she was entirely at home. A splendid housewife, a capable manager, and quite a stern disciplinarian of the Kaffirs on the Ranch.

She was a little afraid that Clive might have found her dull and stolid, here in the land where he was so much at ease. But he seemed quite pleased with her. Dear, wonderful Clive! Ross thought that there was nobody in the world quite so splendid. She had thought so when she had first met him in Rhodesia. She still thought so after three years of marriage and she had never loved any other man, although a good many men at home had wanted to marry Ross. There was an undeniable, quiet charm about her that drew man and woman alike to her.

Modesty and a complete lack of self-consciousness being intrinsic parts of her nature — Ross never ceased to wonder why Clive had married her. The rapture of his wooing and their first passionately happy days together was still upon her. It had been a brief, tempestuous courtship on Clive's part. He had come out from England, after leaving Oxford, where he had wasted both time and money, to try his luck at farming near the Zambesi. He was, and even Ross had to admit this, hopeless at farming.

He had only tried the Colonies to please his uncle, who had wondered what to do with him. A handsome, attractive boy with no particular talents except for playing a ukulele delightfully and drawing women to him like a magnet.

His laziness and incompetence were too hidden behind his superficial attractions for Ross to see them. Her men friends were the rather quiet, stolid farmers round about her home. She had never met anybody like Clive. She could not resist him. Did not want to. The fact that he was a year younger than herself had been of no account. Neither did it matter that he had no money. Ross had means and Swallow Dip. A good many hundreds of acres, splendid herds of cattle, a flourishing farm, in fact.

She would not allow him to hesitate because she had everything and he nothing. She was crazily in love with him and if he loved her that was enough. Besides, when his Uncle, Thomas Derrell, died, Clive would inherit his money, so there was something coming to him.

He had made her terribly happy so far. She took it for granted that he, too, was happy and had settled down to life on a Rhodesian farm.

It had taken all Clive's power of persuasion to make her leave her beloved farm and venture to England. And she would never have left Swallow Dip but for the fact that Bill McCrayle, her manager, was there to look after things for her. A thoroughly reliable fellow, Bill. During the lifetime of Ross's father he had been junior assistant at Swallow Dip. After the old man's death he had taken over the management with Ross. There had been a time when McCrayle had been very much in love with Ross. But she had not cared that way. Only liked him immensely as a friend. So he had remained her friend. Bill was like that. And he had even deceived Ross into thinking that he was no longer in love with her.

If her marriage to the young Englishman had been a bitter blow Bill had not shown it. And when Ross had asked him to remain in management at Swallow Dip, after her marriage, he had not refused. He loved that Ranch as though it were his own. His work was his life to him now. And Clive had agreed that he was much too good a man to lose.

As Ross moved about the bedroom, so happily and busily, her thoughts would keep winging back to Rhodesia. It seemed the furthermost ends of the world now. So utterly different was the life here to life at Swallow Dip. And she was bound to admit that she was homesick even though she was here with the husband she adored.

They were going back at the end of the month. A little uneasily Ross remembered how Clive's face had clouded when she had reminded him of this fact at breakfast. Did Rhodesian life bore him? He was so amusing – so fond of dancing – theatres – and London was his home.

Ross was a woman – a woman in love. All other things faded into insignificance beside this love. And not being very experienced with men she supposed that it was the same with Clive. Of course he would not mind going home — Rhodesia was his home now as well as hers.

A voice sounded outside the door.

"Let me in, darling."

Her face coloured with pleasure and holding the wrapper about her, she ran to the door and opened it.

A slimly built man entered, carrying an overcoat over his arm. He pitched the coat on to a chair and looked at Ross with a careless smile.

"Getting dressed already?" he asked. She put two bare sun-browned arms about his neck and held up a glowing face.

"My darling!" she murmured.

He kissed her. Her lips clung to his and she was unconscious of the fact that all the warmth and passion was on her side. She was too blinded by the physical ecstasy which her husband's embrace always roused in her. She looked at him with adoration, frank and unstinted, in her warm chestnut eyes. Clive strolled to the dressing-table and lit a cigarette. Very good to look at, was Clive Derrell; smooth fairish hair, brushed to one side, with a golden glow on it under the electric light. Skin burnt rather a reddish hue and very blue eyes with long fair lashes which gave him a boyish and even appealing look. The worst feature of his face was his mouth. Sulky, sensual, selfish. He looked spoiled. And of course he had been spoiled from his babyhood. The good things of this life had spilled into his lap. He had reached a stage where he took people and things for granted. His wife, her love and her possessions he took entirely for granted. He had not meant to marry so young, but when he had met Ross at the bungalow of a mutual friend near the Zambesi, he had been desperately bored. The Colonies bored him, and having to work for his living was very disagreeable to one of his luxury-loving nature.

He had never met a woman quite like Ross before. She was so innocent and entirely natural and rather refreshing to a young man who had had many promiscuous and not very savoury affairs. Her money attracted him as much as her personal charm though at the time he deceived even himself into thinking that it was Ross only that he wanted. Anyhow he married her and for three years he had made quite an astonishingly good husband. Then had come nostalgia for London and the old smart set, and he had made his wife come over with him. He might have known that it would be disastrous; that Ross who was a little queen in Rhodesia would be a nonentity here. It had struck him as soon as they had landed. She was dowdy. She had absolutely no idea how to dress.

The slender, fashionable girls over here who were a product of the day — with their smart hairstyles, cleverly made-up faces, chic clothes — put Ross in the shade for Clive. And when, tentatively, he had suggested she should use a lipstick, she had laughed at him and said: "Don't be silly, darling. Just imagine me painting my face!"

Not that she was a prude. She admired all the smart London women but she had no intention of competing with them.

Clive had persuaded her to buy one or two fashionable dresses. But they did not really suit her. She looked her best in her old corduroy breeches and a riding shirt, on the farm.

It was too late for Clive to wish he hadn't come to England with his wife. The harm was done. Ross no longer satisfied him and he knew it.

"What are we doing tonight?" he asked her, seating himself on the edge of a bed. Ross, brushing her long thick hair, smiled at him in the mirror.

"Don't you remember my little English cousin, Valmy Page, is coming to dinner with us?"

Clive Derrell frowned.

"Oh, Lord, yes," he said. "I'd forgotten. Will she be very dull?"

Ross looked at him quickly.

"Darling, would you rather have spent the evening alone with me?"

It was on the tip of Clive's tongue to say: "Oh! heavens, no!" but he desisted.

"No, that's all right," he said. "I only wondered what your cousin was like."

He knew what most of Ross's Colonial relations were like. All farmers; unimaginative; heavy, with only one topic of conversation. Farming.

"Valmy," said Ross, "is supposed to be the very reverse of dull. Her mother was my mother's sister who married an Englishman and settled in London here. Her people are dead now. I've only heard once or twice from the child in my life. But I understand she has had a very hard time of it since she has been on her own. She does shorthand-typewriting in some office in the City. Not much fun for a girl of nineteen."

Clive regarded the tip of his shoe moodily. The girl didn't sound very interesting.

"Rather a pretty name, Valmy, isn't it?" murmured Ross.

"Sounds like a new kind of chocolate to me," said Clive.

Ross had finished twisting her splendid hair into a coil at the nape of her neck. She slipped off her kimono. Clive glanced at the beautiful figure. Too fat, he mentally decided. Ross would never look *soignée* in the most expensive gown. The perfect glow of health and sunshine which radiated from her had ceased to attract him.

She came and sat beside him on the bed and looked up at him almost shyly. Even after three years she was a little shy of this delicious intimate life which she led with Clive.

"You've enjoyed our holiday here, haven't you?" she said.

"Frightfully," he said.

"But I am rather longing to see Swallow Dip again," she said.

He made no answer.

"Bill's letter, this morning, said that old Polly calved the day after we sailed and he had quite a business pulling her through," added Ross.

"H'm," was all that Clive had to reply to this. Details about the farm held no interest for him in these days. And never had held much.

He was thinking that it was a pity McCrayle couldn't go on managing the farm without them. With Ross's income and his own small allowance from Uncle Thomas, they might have quite a decent home in London. But he didn't dare suggest to Ross that they should leave South Africa for ever. He could imagine Ross's horror.

"You'll be quite glad to see Rhodesia again, won't you, honey?" said Ross, putting her hand over his.

Mechanically, he squeezed the slim strong fingers. He knew that his answer was a lie.

"Of course."

But he dreaded the very idea of the voyage home. And he wished that his wife was not so much in love with him. It made him feel a swine. He didn't like being made to feel that. It irritated him. So far he had managed to conceal his irritation and his boredom but he wondered how long he could continue the deception.

Ross looked at her wrist-watch.

"Good heavens! It's half-past seven and we are dining at eight. You haven't had your bath yet, Clive."

He stifled a sigh and rose to his feet, yawning.

CHAPTER II

"You don't know what it means to me to come out and have dinner like this!"

Valmy Page punctuated this speech with a long sigh of pleasure. She looked round the hotel restaurant where she was dining with her cousin, Ross, and the husband, Clive Derrell, who she was meeting for the first time. Her eyes rested enviously on a particularly well-dressed girl at a neighbouring table. Finally they rested on the cousin beside her with even deeper envy.

It wasn't Ross's dress that she envied. Although expensive, that red lace was a hopeless choice for a woman with the chestnut tints that Ross had in her eyes and hair. She didn't know in the least how to dress, thought Valmy, who at nineteen was sophisticated and very much *femme du monde*. But she did envy her this attractive young husband of hers. What luck! He was so frightfully good-looking and amusing and obviously Ross was very much in love with him. One could tell that from the way she looked at him and hung on his words. Ross was awfully nice, thought Valmy, but rather dull. She wondered if Clive Derrell minded that his wife was badly dressed and had so little to say for herself.

Valmy and Clive held most of the conversation. If Clive was witty, Valmy was quick with repartee and had plenty to say for herself. She knew how to be bright and amusing with men. The black velvet dress she was wearing was a year old. But Valmy had lengthened it cunningly and, greatly extravagant, bought a couple of orchids for her shoulder-strap; pinned them there with a paste brooch. Before she had left her 'digs,' her mirror had told her that she looked her best. It wasn't difficult for her to be *soignée*, because of her exquisite little figure. She was shorter than Ross and as slender as a boy with just the loveliest curves here and there to make a man's pulse beat faster.

Every time she caught Clive's eye she smiled and he smiled back at her. Oh yes, she could see that he was attracted by her and drank in his admiration with a thrill. Insatiable for men's admiration was Valmy. It didn't matter whether the man belonged to another woman or not.

"I do love this hotel, Ross," she murmured to her cousin. "It is frightfully sweet of you to ask me."

"My dear," said Ross, "I love having you. I've always wanted to meet my little English cousin and I'm sure Clive did too."

"Yes, indeed!" said Clive.

And he repeated inwardly, 'yes, indeed'. He had cheered up ever since Valmy Page arrived at the hotel. She had both surprised and enchanted him. Here was no unimaginative stupid creature. Valmy was altogether charming both to look at and talk to and a little devil, too, he reflected.

She had full red lips — reddened by lipstick, of course — accentuating a voluptuous bow. Her prettiness was not of the chocolate-box quality which her name suggested. It was too vital and, he thought, there were brains behind that white forehead, too. Hers was a fascinating face — creamy skin without much colour to it — long narrow eyes — the greenest eyes he had ever seen, between very thick black lashes. Her hair, closely shingled, was black as a raven's wing with a tight wave in it, and brushed back from her forehead, like a boy's, showing the tips of small ears in which she wore two large imitation pearls.

A provocative face — particularly when she smiled and narrowed her eyes until they were like green slits. She had rather a low-pitched, husky voice and laughed a good deal with a flippancy which made Ross's gravity and quietness all the more outstanding. She was a finished and attractive product of the day, thought Clive, and if a trifle audacious she intrigued him very much. One could, he told himself wryly, get tired of a good, serious-minded woman like Ross. And he forgot how madly he had been attracted by Ross when he had first met her in Rhodesia. How enchanting it had been to break through the veil of her shyness and ignorance.

He felt that he and Valmy met on common ground. It amused him to joke with her and they talked incessantly. Ross listened to them, a little bewildered. Cocktails, dance-steps, modern art and music, horse racing, poker-parties, these things were a little out of her depth.

Of course Clive understood these things. He was a Londoner born. He had been at Public School and the Varsity. And Valmy, although she earned her own living now, had been the daughter of a jockey. Ross remembered her father telling her of the aunt — Valmy's mother — who had left the Colonies for love of the rather gay young man who had finally broken his neck steeple-chasing, and left a sea of debts behind him.

Ross, who was the most generous of creatures, was quick to admire her pretty little cousin and to be sorry for her. It was too bad that she was alone in the world, typewriting for her living. She seemed so fond of life and fun.

"You don't know how I envy you people living in Rhodesia," said Valmy while they were drinking coffee. Clive, in the best of spirits, was sipping a cognac and Valmy had been persuaded to have a Cointreau. Ross, as usual, drank nothing but water. Not that she disapproved of alcohol but she didn't like it. It made her sick.

"It is rather lovely in South Africa," said Ross.

"The more I think of it," said Valmy, "the more I envy you. The glorious sunshine, the freedom! Think of me, in digs in Battersea and typing all day in an office!"

"It certainly sounds horrid, you poor little thing," said Ross.

"You weren't cut out for that sort of life, either," said Clive.

"What was I cut out for?" asked Valmy, catching Clive's eye.

"Love," was on the tip of his tongue. But he said: "Oh something more entertaining. You ought to get married."

"I haven't met the right man yet," said Valmy. "I've had one or two proposals, but —" she shrugged her shoulders and made a *moue* with her mouth. Clive looked at that fascinating mouth and thought:

"I wonder how many men she has kissed. I'd rather like to kiss her myself!"

"I think we shall have to take her back to South Africa with us as a secretary," he said aloud. "Somebody to keep all the books and do all the correspondence. Eh, Ross?"

He spoke jestingly. He was altogether surprised and curiously pleased when Ross took him seriously.

"I don't see why she shouldn't come back to Swallow Dip with us. For a few months anyhow. It would be a wonderful change for her and there are so many nice men she might meet. We must talk it over, Clive."

She turned with her charming, sympathetic smile to the girl.

"How would you like to come to Rhodesia?"

Valmy's cream pale face had flushed for an instant. Her greeny eyes sparkled with excitement. She felt rather than saw Clive's gaze fixed eagerly upon her. She answered with discretion.

"It sounds too wonderful to be true, cousin Ross. But you can't mean it."

"Why not?" said Ross.

"It isn't a bad idea," said Clive.

Ross began to rhapsodise on life in her beloved Rhodesia. Clive allowed her to talk. He had lit a cigar and was content to sit back in his chair and watch Valmy.

Her beauty was of such unusual and captivating quality he felt that he would never get tired of looking at her. The idea of taking her back to Swallow Dip — having her as a travelling companion on the boat going home — made his heart miss a beat. Of course, he was a swine and he knew it. He had no right to let his heart-beats quicken at the thought of a pretty girl of nineteen when he had a wife like Ross, who was an absolute dear and who adored him. But he was only human and there you were!

He had always been a lover of women, of beauty, of sensation. Valmy Page came into his life just when he was badly in need of a new sensation.

He did not want to show any undue eagerness over this business, but he counted on his wife reopening the discussion about Valmy after dinner.

Later, the three of them sat comfortably in arm-chairs in the lounge, listening to the orchestra. They were all smoking. Ross liked a cigarette now and again. Valmy had hers in a little jade green holder. Clive was almost ashamed of the thrill it gave him to see her small white teeth bite on that narrow jade holder.

Valmy was very graceful and always knew how to adopt the most attractive poise. She had arranged the long black velvet dress so that Clive could see her ankles. They were very exquisite little ankles and her feet in the black satin slippers seemed to him tiny. They made Ross's feet look large. But then somehow one always thought of Ross wearing her stout boots down on the farm. Certainly she was not at her best in this sort of atmosphere.

It had been the greatest surprise to Valmy to find that cousin Ross had married such an intriguing person as Clive. Within ten minutes of meeting him she had read the sex-hunger in his eyes. She responded to it immediately. She felt exactly like he did; bored. She was bored by the drudgery and loneliness of an unmarried business girl whose nature craved for the luxuries she could not afford. He was bored with matrimony. He wanted to flirt with her. Well, she was ready. To plunge into a passionate affair with Ross's husband would be most thrilling. She didn't bother her head about Ross's side of it.

"He's tired of her, I can see that," thought Valmy as she watched the couple. "She's too worthy — too quiet for Mr. Clive. I must see what I can do. If only Ross means what she says about taking me out to Rhodesia —"

Through a cloud of smoke she studied the graceful figure of the man; the bright fair hair, the nervous, well-shaped hands.

"Just my type," she thought. "I should like to feel those hands on me. I'd bet he'd make a marvellous lover. I wonder if he ever makes love to Ross, these days?"

Aloud she said:

"Tell me more about Swallow Dip, Ross?"

"My dear, I've done enough talking," said Ross. "Ask Clive to describe the place to you."

"I'm no good at descriptions. Besides, the child will have to see the place to appreciate the beauty of it," said Clive with cunning.

Ross swallowed the bait.

"That's perfectly true, darling. And I think Valmy ought to see it."

Clive drained his brandy. He was flushed and his blue eyes were amazingly blue tonight. He looked very handsome.

"Well, I don't suppose I ever shall see Rhodesia," said Valmy's little husky voice.

"I don't see why not," said Ross, "and, my dear, once you do see it you will never want to leave it. Oh, those blue hills, the sweep of the veldt — the freshness and spaciousness of it all! We're not many miles from the Zambesi, Valmy. Those falls are the wonder and delight of South Africa. When I was very tiny I remember my dear mother taking me to see the Falls and I've loved them ever since."

Valmy stubbed her cigarette end in an ash tray. The thought of the Zambesi held no particular attraction for her. But she looked through her thick black lashes at Ross's husband.

"Ross, it sounds too wonderful! You're making me thoroughly dissatisfied."

Ross looked at the girl earnestly. For a moment — possibly it was sheer imagination — she fancied she saw a trace of her beloved mother in the child; in the delicate curve of black brows and the darkness of her hair. Ross's mother had been very dark — so, also, the sister who was Valmy's mother. Ross, although only seven years older than Valmy, felt a maternal affection spring in her. The child was alone in the world and her kinswoman. She must do something for her. The maternal instinct was so strong in Ross. She was never happier than when she was 'mothering' somebody—something—whether it was a little Kaffir baby or a stray dog. It had been a bitter disappointment to her that there had been no child of her marriage. She wanted to bear Clive a son. But he had not wanted children.

"Let's wait," he had said to her more than once. "Let's stay as lovers. Children bring such a thoroughly domesticated atmosphere—and away goes romance. Later, we'll have kids."

That had pleased Ross in a way. But she hadn't entirely agreed with him. She told herself, now, that she would be a fairy godmother to this pretty little English cousin.

"Will it really interest you—the sort of life we lead on the farm out there, Valmy?"

"Yes, terribly!" said Valmy. "I'd adore it."

"Then we'll talk about it—Clive and I," said Ross smiling. "Tomorrow is Saturday. Do you get a half day at the office?"

"Yes."

"Then come and lunch with us and we'll make our plans," said Ross.

Valmy's heart raced and she bit her underlip, nervous and excited. She looked at Clive. He was looking at her in a queer way. She thought: "I don't know what I'm letting myself in for—but it's going to be most intriguing. I've been aching for something exciting to happen to me and it looks as though something *is* going to happen!"

The orchestra was playing a fox-trot. A young man, with a saxophone and horn-rimmed glasses, was singing in a nasal voice:

> "My heart is saying
> Why not trust her, gentle stranger?
> My head is saying there is danger
> In love!"

"Just listen to those ridiculous words," said Ross, laughing.

Valmy laughed, too. But she went on looking at Clive. He flicked the ash from his cigar with his little finger and put his tongue in his cheek.

"I wouldn't trust Miss Valmy Page a yard, and I know there's danger in it," he thought. "But that's what is so amusing; after three years of Rhodesia."

He stopped himself from putting the word 'Ross' in the place of 'Rhodesia'. Ross was a darling. But there wasn't any doubt about it, he needed a little excitement and variation.

"Why don't you two dance?" said Ross, utterly unsuspicious of her husband's reflections. It would never enter her head to be jealous of Clive. Hers was too generous and fine a nature to harbour jealousy or suspicion. Besides, she was firmly convinced that her husband was still essentially her lover.

"Have the first one with me, Ross," said Clive.

Ross's wide mouth curved into that rather boyish grin which Clive had found very attractive when he had first met her. It was such a thoroughly frank, good-humoured smile.

"My dearest, you know what a clod-hopper I am! I've always danced badly. Besides, Valmy is our guest, and I'm perfectly certain she dances like a fairy. Off you go, you two!"

Valmy found herself on the dance floor with Clive's arm holding her — lightly at first and then a little more closely. Her dark, sleek head only touched his chin. She was amazingly small and light after Ross and as Ross had guessed — Valmy danced like a fairy. She was like thistle-down in his arms. She was so slenderly built he felt that if he held her too tightly he would break every bone in that small body. Seductive — oh yes! Just the faintest perfume from her hair and the eyes looking up into his so very green and bright. He had never seen such green eyes.

"You dance very well, Cousin Valmy,' he said.

"So do you, Cousin Clive," she said demurely. And added: "What a dear Ross is! Frightfully nice and kind."

Frightfully nice and kind, yes. That did describe Ross, but Clive was in the mood for something more exciting and he found it in this girl.

"Do you really want to come back with us to Rhodesia?" he asked her while they danced, their bodies graceful, lithe, merging into one.

"Won't I be *de trop* — wouldn't you rather be alone with your wife?"

Clive's eyes narrowed. Was the little devil trying to get a rise out of him? He didn't quite know. Valmy asked the question so innocently. He answered shortly:

"Ross and I have been married three years — we're over the honeymoon stage."

"Don't disillusion me," said Valmy, screwing up her pretty eyes alluringly. "I've always hoped that life would be one long honeymoon when one got married."

"Oh, did you!" said Clive grimly. "Well, I won't disillusion you. Go on thinking it. Ross and I are very happy. But one can't keep at fever heat."

Valmy lowered her lashes.

"It's the fever heat that makes life worth living, though," she murmured.

He knew that she was right and felt suddenly a savage desire to crush his lips down on that mocking little mouth of hers. What an upper lip! It would be any man's undoing. He wished he had never seen Ross's cousin Valmy. Then he was glad that he had. He said almost harshly:

"Well, you know nothing about it, my child. You're much too young. Nineteen. A mere baby."

"My mother was married at eighteen," she laughed.

"But you aren't."

"Haven't met anybody I've liked."

"What sort of man do you like?"

"Valmy prefers blonds," she said very naughtily.

Clive Derrell flushed to the roots of his hair — that hair which was so very blond — and told himself that this girl, child in years, was very much a woman. She worked a bit too fast for his liking. But there was something about her which attracted him vitally and he was both ashamed and excited by it.

He didn't dance with her again. And after that dance he paid a lot of attention to Ross. But Valmy was unperturbed. She knew exactly how much she attracted him. He took her outside and put her into a taxi. Her black velvet coat with its shabby white 'rabbit' collar suited her well enough. The white fur made a good frame for her piquant face.

"Good night, Cousin Clive," she said demurely.

"Good night," he said. "Ross expects you to lunch tomorrow."

"Shall I come?" The green eyes sparkled at him.

"Yes," he said abruptly, and slammed the taxi door.

She sat back, laughing softly to herself.

Clive thrust his hands in his pockets and walked back into the hotel. He hadn't noticed how cold the March night was, out there on the pavement. He felt as though he were burning.

"Damn that girl!" he muttered.

He thought of what she had said about fever heat. For the rest of that night he tried to get her out of his thoughts and couldn't.

Later, when Ross was in bed, he strolled about the bedroom smoking a last cigarette.

"Well, darling, what do you think of Valmy?" Ross asked Clive. "Isn't she pretty and fascinating?"

"Not bad," said Clive, carelessly.

"Surely you think she's lovely?"

"Y-Yes – quite," he said, taking off his tie.

"I think we've done the right thing in offering to take her abroad with us," continued Ross. "You don't mind having a third person with us, do you, Clive?"

"Oh, no!" he said hastily.

He undressed and slipped into bed, where he lay smoking in silence for a while.

Long after Ross slept, Clive was awake. It was annoying how the thought of Valmy Page disturbed him; how much he thought of her.

He lay there, in the darkness, smoking one cigarette after the other. In the morning he looked rather guiltily at the small pile of cigarette ends on the ash tray by his bedside. But Ross did not notice them.

CHAPTER III

Ross and Clive Derrell sailed for South Africa on the 2nd April and Valmy Page went with them.

They went by one of those small, pleasant lines, running between England and Natal without touching the Cape. The boat was not crowded and Clive had managed to secure the extra berth for Valmy without difficulty.

Clive never forgot the sight of Valmy when she joined them on the boat-train. She dazzled him – as she had intended to do – in her new, chic clothes. It was Ross who had bought her those clothes; bought her an entire trousseau for the Colonies, in fact. It had given Ross enormous pleasure to spend her money that way. It satisfied some of the starved maternity in her to play the godmother to her young cousin.

And it was Ross who generously exclaimed to her husband:

"Doesn't our little Valmy look a fashionable young woman? Isn't she lucky, Clive, to be so slim and small. Mine's the sort of figure that's such a bore – I can't get into these smart little dresses like Valmy!"

But she laughed quite happily and contentedly. And she did

not see what lay in her husband's eyes when they rested upon Valmy. Certainly, he thought, the child knew how to dress. There wasn't a girl to touch her on board. He liked that wine-coloured tweed jumper-suit, with beads to match, accentuating the marvellous cream colour of her throat. A little red beret was crushed at a jaunty angle on the smooth dark head and she wore a tweed travelling coat with a big brown fur collar framing her piquant face. He found it hard to keep his eyes off her — to keep them from wandering to the slim ankles in thinnest of brown silk stockings; the small feet in their neat brown Russian leather shoes.

Ross must have spent quite a lot of money on her. Good of her! So like her — and who should know better than Clive what a generous person his wife was? Yet he found himself wishing, secretly, that Ross knew how to put on her clothes. That blue felt hat was too much on the back of her head. Wisps of the red-brown hair blew untidily about her face when they stood on deck waving farewell to English shores. Comparisons were odious — and well he knew it. And it wasn't fair to compare an inexperienced young Rhodesian like Ross with a girl such as Valmy Page.

The *Capron Castle* sailed at three o'clock that afternoon. Ross went down to the cabin to unpack. Clive and Valmy walked up and down the deck and watched the white cliffs fade into the distance. A strong breeze was blowing. The sun shone fitfully. The blue sea was crested with white waves and there was a bit of a swell.

"Are you a good sailor, Valmy?" Clive asked her.

"I can generally keep my end up on a Channel crossing," she smiled. "What about you?"

"Never been sick in my life," he said. "But poor old Ross is always bowled over for the first day or two."

Valmy accepted this information gladly. She foresaw forty-eight hours *à deux* with this man who was attracting her quite shamefully.

"Good-bye to dirty horrid old London," she said, "and in three weeks' time South Africa — the golden land. Cheers!"

"What a kid you are," said Clive.

"Anybody would think you were old," she laughed.

"An old married man," he echoed with a laugh. "But I'm beginning to feel remarkably cheery — like I used to feel when I was up at Oxford."

She screwed up her eyes at him.

"Are you glad I've come?"

"What do you think?" he said meaningly. "Have a cigarette."

She took one and he lit it for her. Their little fingers touched. Their eyes met. They were conscious of something electric and exciting flowing between them.

Then Valmy drew away from him.

"I ought to go down and help Ross unpack," she said.

"Oh, right-o," said Clive, guiltily.

But he followed the charming figure with his eyes until she was out of sight. His heart was pounding fast.

During the next few days he saw a good deal of Valmy alone. They were thrown upon each other for companionship because Ross, not a good sailor, kept to her cabin until the *Capron Castle* sailed into calmer waters.

Clive—like a good many men—hated and resented the sickness of others. He was enchanted to find that Valmy was a perfect sailor, as ready for fun, and food, and laughter on board as she was on land. It was bad luck on Ross, who fought bravely, and alone, against the throes of that most lamentable of all maladies, whilst her husband gaily traversed the deck with Valmy.

Ross saw very little of Clive. Now and then he dutifully put in an appearance—called her "poor darling", sympathised with her, and hurriedly departed again. Valmy offered to remain in the cabin and nurse her cousin, but of course Ross would not hear of such a thing.

"You keep Clive company and don't worry about me, Valmy," she said. "Clive will be so bored—so do stay with him!"

Valmy did not need a great deal of persuading. Very successfully she prevented Clive from being 'bored'. They sat for hours side by side on deck, as the ship ploughed its way through the green-grey sea, finding intense interest in each other's company.

Clive was experienced enough to sense the danger in all this ... to know that he was feeling something much more poignant than 'cousinly platonic affection' towards Valmy Page. She knew it, too, and revelled in the danger of it.

The first day that Ross was well enough to leave her cabin and come up on deck, Clive and Valmy hovered round her, paying her great attention, making a charming show of pleasure that she was able to be with them again. She was touched by it—utterly unsuspecting of the real feelings under the surface —of the relief they felt when she went back to her cabin at sundown.

She lay in her berth, thinking tenderly of them both.

"What a dear Clive has been to me today!" she reflected. "And what a charming girl Valmy is! I'm glad I brought her along with us."

Up on deck, in the violet mist of twilight, Clive and Valmy walked up and down the deck, arm-in-arm.

"Do you know, Clive, I've been wondering why you married a quiet girl like Ross," Valmy was saying.

"Why?" he asked.

"Well — you always say you like a woman to be lively and entertaining."

"So I do," he said. "To be with you, for instance, is like drinking a bottle of champagne."

"Then what made you marry Ross?"

"I don't know —" Clive frowned. "I suppose a boy of twenty-two is attracted by rather a serious kind of woman. One changes one's views," he added.

They paused near the rails and looked down into the phosphorescent water.

"Of course, Ross is a dear," said Valmy.

"Of course," he echoed. "But I'm wondering if she oughtn't to have married a man like McCrayle — our manager."

"What's he like?"

"Oh — stolid — virtuous — what the world calls a white man."

"Sounds like you, Clive," she said with her husky little laugh.

Her mockery inflamed the man.

"I'm perfectly well aware that I'm neither stolid, virtuous, nor a film hero," he said shortly. "And you wouldn't like me if I were."

"Who said I liked you at all?" she teased.

He caught his breath and looked down at her with eyes that were a trifle bloodshot.

"So you don't like me, eh?" he said between his teeth.

She didn't answer but half closed her eyes and lifted her face. The invitation of her lips sent caution, reason, honour flying to the winds. For days this girl had been provoking all that was worst in Clive Derrell's nature. At the best of times it was a rather weak and sensuous nature. He looked round the deck. It was deserted. Most of the passengers had gone below to dress for dinner and it was a dark, moonless evening. But he could see the whiteness of the girl's face and throat and what lay in her narrowed eyes.

The next moment she was in his arms. He held her against him, his body shaking, and said in a suffocated voice:

"You don't like me, eh?"

It was the embrace Valmy had wanted, dreamt of, schemed for. Her pagan young body and mind rejoiced in it. She put one arm about his neck and gave a low laugh.

"Kiss me, and see," she whispered.

"Valmy!" he said, and took her lips like a man dying of thirst.

It was a long mad kiss. Ruin to both of them and ruin for Ross's happiness. But they neither of them thought of Ross in that moment. When Clive lifted his head again he was as white as death and breathing like a man who had run a race.

"You witch," he said. "You little witch—this is madness!"

"It's wonderful," she panted. "I love you, Clive. I'm frightfully in love with you. You know it."

"I'm a bit in love with you myself," he said with a short laugh.

"Only a bit?"

He caught her against him and another crazy moment passed. They kissed feverishly—recklessly. Valmy had indulged in one or two love affairs—but they were minor and trifling compared to this passion which Clive Derrell had lit in her. It was a fire she had invited and not tried to quench. As for the man, tired of the quiet serenity of Ross's beautiful pure affection—this was the zest in life which he had been missing for the last three years.

The fact that this girl was not yet twenty did not deter him. She knew what she was doing. That was obvious to him. Most modern girls knew what they were doing and could look after themselves. But he was certainly curious to know how far Valmy's experience extended.

He looked down into her eyes, still holding her close.

"Answer me this," he said. "How many lovers have you had?"

"I've never had a lover—a real lover. I've had two affairs—a boy in the office, and a captain in the navy who was old enough to know better —" She laughed brokenly, smoothing Clive's fair head with her small hands. "But they weren't more than flirtations, Clive. Just a few kisses. I swear it. You're the first man I've ever really seriously been in love with."

He let his arms fall away from her and looked over the rails at the waves. Where the lights from the portholes rayed down the waters were like black, glittering diamonds. Some decent instincts stirred in him.

"Then look here, Valmy," he said, "I'm not going to be a swine like this — I'm not going to have it on my conscience that I was any girl's first lover —"

But there were no decent instincts in Valmy. There had been bad blood in Willy Page, jockey, her father. And there was a big streak of it in Valmy's veins. She had had no good influences since her mother's death and since she was seventeen she had been a little pagan — ready to drift out on the first big tide of passion that carried her off her feet. She told herself that she was sincerely in love with Clive Derrell. She argued with herself that real love was sufficient excuse for breaking the Commandments. That this man was the husband of the cousin who had been so dear, so kind to her, was matter for regret. But she was much too selfish to let that worry her for long. The kind of love that Valmy knew bred both cruelty and greed. Scarcely had Clive made his rather feeble, worthy speech, than she flung herself into his arms again and put her lips against a corner of his mouth.

"Don't be an old fool, Clive. You're not to have qualms about me. I'm nearly twenty — I can take care of myself — and if you love me nothing else matters. I'm glad you are my first real lover. It makes it all the more marvellous. Doesn't it?"

"I suppose so," he said, his pulses racing at the warmth and fragrance of her in his embrace. "But I tell you this is crazy, Valmy. I haven't got a lot of control and you don't help me."

"I don't want you to be controlled," she whispered. "I just want you to love me."

"You're mad, my child," he said almost angrily.

"Well, do you love me?"

"Damn it, yes."

He gave a swift, even furtive look about him, as though he expected to see the figure of his wife appear there on the deck. This would absolutely break her heart. Poor old Ross and yet — one could only be young once and, hang it all, he couldn't face the prospect of another forty years or more of staid, dull matrimony.

"We must go down and dress for dinner, Valmy," he muttered.

She put her hand across his lips and instinctively he kissed it. She said:

"Before we go, tell me you're going to love me terribly — like I love you."

He could feel her heart pounding against his. It was rather intoxicating to know that he had the power to make Valmy's heart beat so fast.

"You're rather a darling," he said.

"Is that all?"

"I'm crazy about you — whether it's right or wrong," he said weakly. "I don't know what it is about you, Valmy, but you go to my head like wine."

"You go to mine," she said. "I haven't felt like this for any other man in the world."

"I haven't slept for the last week — because of you."

"Neither have I."

"Valmy," he said, a little hoarsely, "you know what this means — I'm not a monk or a saint and I've wanted you ever since that night we danced in town. Hadn't we better quit it right here and now? Otherwise, we'll find ourselves in the devil of a mess-up with Ross."

Valmy clung to him.

"We can't quit it now. Clive, you know we can't — say we can't!"

"I admit it would be difficult," he said. "I oughtn't to have let Ross bring you — I knew what it would be —"

"Aren't you pleased I did come? Yes, you can't deny it. And you aren't the first married man to fall in love."

His cheeks reddened slightly.

"I wish to God there wasn't Ross — she's so decent and I feel such a cad — but you're right, Valmy, it isn't much use trying to quit it now. I shan't be able to forget your kisses in a hurry. You're rather good at it — this love business — aren't you, you little devil?"

Her green eyes sparkled up at him, long, luminous, rather like a cat's in the darkness.

"You're rather a good lover, yourself, darling."

"'Good' hardly describes it," he laughed shortly. "'Bad' would be a better word."

"Clive, kiss me again and tell me you're going to be my lover."

"There won't be much chance of it, on this damn boat," he said, "but I dare say out in Rhodesia — well, yes, there'll be plenty of chances out there."

"Ross need never know," whispered the voice of his young temptress.

25

"Good God, she must never know," he said. "This thing has got to be a secret between us, whatever happens. You understand that?"

"Yes," she lifted her face up to him. "Darling —"

He forgot everything for an instant but the witchery of this young, beautiful girl. He covered her face and throat with kisses.

"You lovely little thing — I'm going to love you as you've never been loved before," he said, with his lips against her ear.

"But we simply must go down. Ross will wonder where the devil I am. I'm going to kiss you good night now. I don't suppose there'll be another chance. We've got to attend that cursed concert in the saloon. But one night, my child" — his voice sank to a caressing whisper — "one night in South Africa perhaps we shan't have to say good night or good-bye."

Valmy's heart leapt.

"Clive, what do you mean?"

He told her, holding her in a tight embrace. The first officer, strolling along the deck saw the two figures — the tall and the short one — merging dimly into one shape. He grinned to himself. Another of these 'on-board flirtations'. Already, too! Fast work. But he had seen plenty of that sort of thing in his time. He walked past them whistling. He rather envied the man. It was against the rules for a ship's officer to indulge in flirtations on board ship.

"Lucky beggar," he thought, and strolled on.

Down in her cabin Ross Derrell lay on her bunk, resting, waiting for Clive to join her. For the last week, since she had found her 'sea legs' and been up and about again, she had been forced to notice that Clive paid Valmy a good deal of attention. But she was too broad-minded and unsuspicious to be irritated by this or to object to it. She knew that Valmy was amusing, could dance with Clive, share his taste in cocktails, and exchange flippancies.

She did not begrudge either of them the pleasure they found in each other's company. And Clive, who always acted a part when he was with his wife made her feel absolutely certain of him and his love.

When he came into the cabin, looking a bit flushed and excited, Ross, with her hands locked behind her head, gave him her boyish grin.

"Hullo, darling — the wind's got your face — doesn't it smart?"

He avoided her eye and the red deepened in his cheek.

"Does a bit," he muttered.

"What have you been doing?"

"Had a good stiff constitutional with Valmy," he still avoided her eye and fumbled in his case for a cigarette.

"Only a week more," said Ross dreamily, "and we shall be back. I expect poor old Bill will be pleased to see us."

"I dare say," said Clive.

She held out her hand to him. He glanced at it. It was well shaped but it looked brown, hard, capable and very unlike those velvet white fingers which he had just kissed so recklessly up on deck. He took Ross's fingers, perforce.

"Well, darling," he said with forced gaiety.

"Do you know," she said, "you haven't given me a really lovely kiss for a very long while?"

He glanced for the fraction of an instant into those warm hazel eyes which were so luminous with steadfast devotion for him. He knew that she was feeling in a mood for love making. It was going to be the very devil if Ross expected him to be demonstrative, now. She never demanded his caresses. But, of course, until Valmy came and shattered the really decent warm affection which he had had for his wife, he had given Ross his caresses unasked. Guiltily he reflected that it *was* rather a long time since he had played the lover to Ross. What was he going to do? He didn't want to hurt her but he knew that his love for her was dead. Valmy — the passion which had surged up between them so volcanically tonight — stood between them irrevocably now. He didn't want Ross any more.

"If only she didn't care so much for me it would be easier —" he told himself angrily.

Ross's tender arms were drawing him down to the bunk beside her.

"Sweetheart," she said with a faint lovely light of invitation in her eyes.

The man, irritated, chafing against it, bent and kissed her. Ross clung to him, suddenly very conscious of her immense love for him. Valmy could be his companion, his cousin, but she, Ross, was his wife and that fierce little feeling of possession was strong within her — curiously strong tonight.

When Clive drew back from her she whispered:

"I do love you so much, my darling. I'm the luckiest woman in the world."

It was as well that she was spared the bitterness, the humiliation, which would have been hers could she have read what lay in the man's mind when he stood up and turned away to light his cigarette.

CHAPTER IV

By the time the *Capron Castle* reached Natal, Clive Derrell was utterly in Valmy's power. Ross had become a nonentity. Valmy was the centre of his universe; his sun; his moon; his stars.

She had fallen in love with him in a wild, tempestuous fashion. She reached a certain reckless state of mind where she did not care how the 'game' ended, or who got burnt at the fire which she and Clive had lit between them.

Ross noticed nothing. She was so glad to reach home again. She had taken the holiday in England for Clive's sake; he had wanted it. But she — a true Rhodesian — was happiest in Rhodesia.

Bill McCrayle, manager of the Swallow Dip ranch — once Ross's suitor, now her loyal friend — met them at the station and drove them home.

McCrayle greeted Clive pleasantly, was introduced to Valmy whose presence was a distinct surprise to him, and then shook hands with Ross. His huge mahogany-coloured hand held hers in a grip that made her wince. Frank pleasure beamed in his eyes. He was extremely pleased to see Ross back again and looked it.

"Swallow Dip hasn't been the same without you," he told her. And added a trifle awkwardly: "It's nice to see you both again, I'm sure."

He used the word 'both' because he thought it the courteous thing to do. But in his heart of hearts he knew that it was Ross he was glad to see and not Clive. There was no spark of admiration in the grey eyes of Bill McCrayle for Ross's beautiful young cousin. He barely glanced at her. Ross Derrell with her healthy, tanned face, her splendid figure, her warm brown eyes, had always seemed, and seemed still, the most beautiful woman in the world to Bill.

When he had first come to her father, ten long years ago, as assistant manager of Swallow Dip, Ross had been a schoolgirl of sixteen. He six years older had thought then that there was nobody like Miss Ross.

From the beginning they had been friends. Bill was essentially a Rhodesian. His father had worked in the diamond mines. But Bill had preferred farming and at twenty-three — his parents dead — it had seemed to him a fine thing to become assistant-manager at Swallow Dip which was one of the biggest ranches in the country.

By the time Ross had pinned up her untidy mane of chestnut hair, Bill was firmly established at the ranch. He was part of the family. He and Ross called each other by their Christian names. They rode together, shot together, and shared an almost passionate love for the ranch. It was inevitable that Bill should fall in love with Ross, the woman of nineteen. There had never been any other woman in his life. But it was not to be. Ross loved him for her friend but did not want him for her lover. He accepted his defeat with a sort of stoic resignation that he showed over most of life's disappointments. But his love was deep rooted, for he was a quiet, reticent man and not one to form attachments easily. From the dark and bitter hour that he had attended Ross's wedding to Clive Derrell, he had known he would never love any other woman and would probably never marry, now.

Life was pretty lonely at times in the bungalow that Ross's father had built for Bill close to Swallow Dip. He was only human and he would have liked a woman in his life, in his home. Particularly he would have liked a son. He adored little children. Today, at thirty-three he was in the prime of manhood. It was impossible for him not to give way, at times, to an intolerable regret that he could not have Ross for his wife. There were many other women — nice Rhodesian girls whom he knew would have been glad to marry him. But there was nobody like Ross — for Bill — and there it was. He only hoped and prayed that she would find the happiness she deserved with the Englishman she had married.

At first he had feared for her. Young Derrell was altogether too good looking and suave and indolent — the kind to take everything and give nothing. However, three years had passed and Derrell appeared to make her very happy, so Bill came to the conclusion that his fears were unfounded. Clive Derrell was not the type of man whom Bill could ever really like or make a friend of — but he accepted him for Ross's sake. Moreover he accepted what was rather an intolerable position to him. Clive, with Ross, became his employer. From Clive he must take his orders. Clive, however, was not really interested in the ranch so Bill had his own way and there had been no friction between the men up to date.

Ross talked a good deal to Bill as they drove to Swallow Dip. She sat beside him. Clive and Valmy were seated at the back.

"England and London are amazing — and you ought to see them, Bill," she said, "all the same it's good to be back in South Africa. I love the very smell of it!" And she sniffed appreciatively.

McCrayle smiled down at her and then fixed his eyes on the sunlit landscape before them. He fancied somehow that Ross looked a little graver and older and he felt that years, instead of months, had elapsed since she went over to England with her husband. Was all well with her? Yes, of course. She was only tired. It had been a long journey from Natal and it was extremely hot.

"Tell me about everything, Bill," she bade him.

He gave her all the information that he could about the Ranch. Ross was absorbed. She hardly noticed that Clive and Valmy were very quiet at the back there, and of course she could not see that their hands were tightly locked and that they were looking at each other as though they were lost to the world.

Clive hurriedly loosened Valmy's hand when they came within sight of Swallow Dip. Ross turned round to them, smiling.

"Look, Valmy!" she said. "We are just coming to Swallow Dip . . . look!"

Valmy looked. But she was more interested in the man who sat at her side. Ross gazed through a mist of tears at the wide-spreading veldt: the spaces of cultivated land — the land her father had cultivated and which now belonged to her. She was so proud of it; proud of the splendid cattle, grazing in hundreds. They passed the kraals; the cattle-boys' huts; then came to the beautiful bungalow which she had had built when she had married Clive, and which had taken the place of the old ranch-house.

The bungalow, white, cool, spacious, stood in a garden that rioted with flowers — flowers of every glorious colour — and feathery trees.

"Look at that banana — there by the steps!" said Ross in an

ecstatic voice. "It's just the same as ever. Oh, Bill, I feel as though I'd been away years instead of three months!"

Bill McCrayle steered the car up to the steps of the veranda, where a couple of native servants in white kanzas and embroidered caps awaited their master and mistress. He switched off the engine, jumped out of the car and assisted Ross. His hand trembled a little as he took her arm. He dared not, must not say so, but he had missed her horribly; ached for the sound of her voice; for a sight of her face.

There was, however, only friendliness in his voice as he said: "It's good to see you back, Ross."

"Well, Bill — how are things?" asked Clive, finding it necessary to tear himself away from Valmy and pay some attention to his manager.

"Everything is in order," said Bill. "The cattle are fine."

Ross stood on the veranda, shading her eyes from the sun with one slender hand, looking out over the blue distant hills — the lovely sweeping hills of Rhodesia.

At length she turned her gaze to the two men who stood by the car, talking. For the first time in her life, perhaps, she was struck by the enormous contrast they made. Clive — slim, sleek, smart in his tailored suit; Bill McCrayle — a great, tall muscular figure, deep-chested, deeply-bronzed, with curly, rather untidy hair, rugged features, and steady grey eyes. Clive was a product of the town; Bill a son of the soil . . . a true son of Rhodesia, with a limitless love for her — for his work.

A sudden longing for Clive to come to her, to come and stand beside her here and put an arm around her, seized Ross. She wanted to call him, but could not; something kept her back. If only he would come . . . understand the emotion that welled in her, at the sight of home — of her Rhodesia —

Valmy, who had been peering inside the bungalow, alive with curiosity, danced out and down the steps, to the two men.

"Oh, what an enchanting place!" her gay young voice rang out — breaking the stillness of the African sundown.

Ross saw Clive swing round and face the girl.

"Do you like it? I'm so glad! Come and see the garden, Valmy," he said eagerly.

They walked off, side by side. Ross felt a queer little stab of pain. She had wanted her husband then more than she had ever wanted him; why she could not tell. Bill watched Clive and Valmy walk away. His lips were a trifle grim. He had been very surprised to find Ross's cousin with them when they had landed, and not over-pleased, for Ross's sake. He knew Clive's weaknesses so much better than Ross knew them. Was it not foolish of Ross to bring this young, extraordinarily pretty girl to live with them?

Valmy's beauty had not stirred Bill McCrayle to admiration, however. He turned and looked at Ross. How much more beautiful than Valmy she seemed to him! He walked up to her with a calm smile. And she did not guess the torment of longing within him to kneel at her feet; to kiss the hem of her dress; to tell her how he had missed her while she had been in England. But he must not. The gates of love's paradise were barred from him for ever. She was Clive Derrell's wife.

He stood beside her, talking to her, telling her of the affairs of the ranch; the recent sale of cattle. And while he talked, he watched her — saw her eyes wander towards the garden, seeking the figures of Clive and Valmy. He read anxiety in that glance. For the first time since her marriage he wondered if everything was right with Ross . . . if she had found all the happiness she had expected to find with Clive. And he felt, too, that if ever Clive did anything to hurt Ross, to break her faith in him — he, Bill, would kill him.

From the very beginning he did not trust Valmy Page.

On the second night of the Derrells' return home, Bill dined with them. His own bungalow which stood within sight of Swallow Dip, was run entirely by his faithful 'boys'.

It was a great pleasure and at the same time exquisite pain to him to spend an evening with the Derrells. He could never quite grow accustomed to the sight of Ross as Clive's wife.

Hitherto he had believed Ross was happy — that Clive returned her tender love. But now he was suspicious of Clive — afraid for Ross's happiness. He saw a new, worried look in Ross's eyes that troubled him inexpressibly. He believed that Valmy Page was the cause of that worry. But he did not think that Ross saw the state of affairs as he saw them. She was too trusting, too generous, too pure to suspect evil, since it was not thrust before her sight. Bill, however, was quick to perceive that Clive Derrell's attentions to his wife were purely forced . . . that his real absorbing interest lay in Ross's cousin. And the girl, Valmy, was obviously in love with Clive. She could not take her eyes off him. They exchanged frequent glances into which Bill read everything, whilst Ross remained blind.

Bill was forced to admit that Valmy was beautiful — even fascinating. At the same time he considered Clive a cur, a weakling to allow himself to be drawn into an 'affair'. How could he be so mad—he who possessed Ross, with all her nobility of character, her tenderness, her golden heart?

Bill McCrayle, who would have died for Ross, felt great bitterness in his heart when he left the bungalow that night to return to his own lonely home.

He felt restive, unable to sleep, so he remained in the Derrells' garden awhile, smoking, leaning his back against a spreading palm-tree, his rugged face upturned to the starlit sky.

Clive—who had managed to sneak out of the bungalow with Valmy for a few moments—failed to see his manager. Bill's tall figure was completely hidden behind the giant palm. Clive imagined Bill had returned home—that the garden was deserted. Mad for the touch of Valmy's lips, he had brought her out here, both of them in a reckless mood, for Ross had been with them all day, giving them no chance for a single caress.

Believing himself alone with the girl, he drew her into his arms and began to kiss her mouth, which was raised all too eagerly.

"I thought the evening would never end!" he said huskily. "I've been longing for this, Valmy."

Bill McCrayle heard the words ... recognised the voice ... knew that Clive Derrell was there, close to him, and that it was Valmy Page in his arms. His great body stiffened. He stood motionless, eyes full of fierce indignation.

Valmy's low voice reached him.

"Oh, Clive," she said, "kiss me again ... again! I'm mad for your kisses."

"And I for yours—for you, darling!" came the man's passionate response. "I think I shall go crazy soon if I can't be alone with you. This having to snatch a kiss here and there is sheer torture!"

"When shall we be alone?"

"I don't know. Ross seems to hang round us ... almost as though she were suspicious. But she isn't ... no, she can't be. Only she doesn't leave us alone much, does she?"

"She may be jealous without exactly knowing what for," said Valmy, with a short laugh. "But what about that man, Bill McCrayle? Do you think—he suspects?"

"He can't. He's a great fool."

Bill McCrayle bit his lip—clenched his hands by his sides. A fool, was he? Well, better to be a clean fool than a dirty clever scoundrel who lets his worst passions master him.

33

He heard Derrell's voice again, breaking the stillness of the African night.

"Valmy — Valmy — when are you going to belong to me altogether?"

"Soon, soon, I hope," came her reply. "We must go in now. Kiss me again!"

Came Clive's passionate voice. "Oh, your wonderful lips! Valmy! Good night, good night, you witch."

"Good night, Clive, darling . . ."

The voices died away. Bill knew that they had returned to the bungalow, afraid lest Ross should notice their absence and comment on it. He walked down to his own bungalow, his brown face creased with worry, his honest eyes full of shame . . . shame that Clive Derrell should so dishonour his home — and his wife.

In her bungalow, Ross was tasting for the first time of the cup of bitterness and sorrow which her husband and her cousin had mixed for her.

"Clive, where did you and Valmy go just now?" she asked, when he joined her in their bedroom.

He looked at her quickly — reddened.

"Oh, she wanted to see the stars! I told her what marvellous stars one sees in South African skies."

Ross, plaiting her thick brown hair in a long rope, secured the blind which was flapping in the cool night breeze, then turned to her husband, her eyes puzzled, distressed.

"Clive," she said in a low voice, "you seem to me to be paying a lot of attention to Valmy. You have hardly a word for me, these days."

"God!" he thought savagely. "She's going to be jealous . . . it's the very deuce . . ." Aloud he said: "My dear old Ross, don't be so ridiculous."

She came close to him, her sweet face flushed, her eyes very wistful.

"Am I being ridiculous? Perhaps I am."

He took off his collar and tie with an irritable gesture.

"I can't stand a jealous woman," he muttered.

Ross swallowed hard. Her pride, which was nearly as strong as her love for her husband, rose to her aid.

"Dear Clive, I am not exactly jealous. It is rotten — horrible — to suggest that I am jealous of you and Valmy. Only . . ." she paused, helplessly.

"All I have to say is, don't be stupid," said Clive in a short voice.

Tears started to her eyes. She held out a hand to him.

"Clive, what's happening to us? I can't bear this. Don't let us have any barrier between us."

"Don't be sentimental and idiotic!" he said. "There's nothing to be jealous about. Valmy and I are great pals – I dare say I do pay her attention. But you asked me to be nice to the poor kid," he added cunningly.

"Yes, I know. Only —" Ross's lips trembled into a smile. "Spare a few smiles and words for me, darling."

He moved away from her and went to his bed.

"By the way, old thing," he said in an indifferent tone. "Ask Sam to move my things into the next room tomorrow."

"But why —" she stared at him.

"I can't sleep in here," he said, keeping his face averted. "I'm getting very restless and I think I'd rest better in a separate room."

Ross's heart beat very quickly. Her cheeks retained the flush; her eyes that puzzled, hurt look. But she answered him with quiet pride:

"Of course – if you wish to sleep in the other room – I'll tell Sam in the morning."

After the lights were out she lay in bed, her eyes hot with tears, her face pressed against the pillow. She would not let Clive know that she was crying. She was suddenly terribly afraid of that happiness that had once been so secure. If only she had had a child ... a little son of Clive's. It was cruel of him to have refused her a child. Now her hopes of having a baby seemed more remote than ever.

She felt suddenly terrified of the future: a sense of impending disaster fell heavily upon her.

CHAPTER V

MORNING came.

One of the 'boys' brought Ross a letter whilst she was at breakfast. She opened and read it – then gave a little exclamation and glanced at her husband.

"This is from Elinor Feltham," she said. "Jack has had to go away to Durban and she expects to be alone all night except for the native servants. Her baby was only born three days, ago, so she must have someone with her. I'll ride over directly after breakfast, and stay with her the night."

Clive Derrell felt his heart leap. He dared not look at Valmy. He turned his eyes on his wife with well-simulated concern.

"But, dear, are you fit to ride all that way? You don't look very well this morning."

She smiled at him – a strange, sad smile that made him feel the beast he was.

"I'm all right, Clive. I shall go. I can't let Elinor be alone."

So, after breakfast, the stable-boy saddled her horse and brought it round to the bungalow. Clive and Valmy stood on the stoep, bidding her farewell.

She did not hesitate to answer Elinor Feltham's appeal. Elinor was an old friend – the wife of the Assistant-Administrator, and Ross – who adored babies – looked forward to seeing the new arrival as much as anything.

Clive Derrell kept away from Valmy until sundown. He pottered about the ranch – showing more interest in the farm than he had shown for months. But Valmy did not mind; she stayed in the bungalow idling away the long, hot hours, confident that Clive would return to her at sundown.

She put on the prettiest frock in her wardrobe to greet him when finally he came in for dinner. She looked lovely enough to drive any man, with Clive Derrell's nature, to distraction. The slim, small figure in a short dress of oyster grey chiffon. Pale arms and throat were bare; in the soft lamplight her dark hair gleamed like a raven's wing.

Clive tried not to look at her. But he made only a feeble effort. He left his dinner practically untasted – found himself staring at her across the flower-decked table in the cool dining-room. Her long green eyes laughed back into his – Eve incarnate; provocative womanhood, full of *diablerie*.

The thought of Ross in the Felthams' bungalow by the sick bed of her friend faded entirely from Clive's mind. He opened a bottle of champagne – drank heavily, and made Valmy drink with him. When the meal came to an end, he led her out on to the veranda. They sat there for a long time without speaking; the wide, untrammelled spaces before them – white in the clear moonlight. All the sounds and scents of the mysterious African night surrounded them. The sky was ablaze with stars overhead. A night for romance ... for beauty ... for love ...

Clive leaned forward in his chair and put a hand on Valmy's bare shoulder.

"Valmy," he said hoarsely.

She looked at him strangely.

"Yes – what is it?" she whispered.

"Do you realise that we're all alone, Valmy?" he said. "There's not a soul near us."

"Except Mr. McCrayle."

"His bungalow is a long way away. We're alone—absolutely alone, Valmy."

Her heart began to beat at incredible speed. She narrowed her gaze, thinking how attractive he was – his handsome face pale in the moonlight – his eyes blue and full of hunger ... a hunger which she knew was for her.

"Valmy," he said again.

And suddenly he rose and pulled her out of her chair into his arms. He stared down at her tantalising mouth. Her brilliant eyes were soft now – shadowed. The man – weak, tortured by desire – let loose his passion and his longing. He strained her small, graceful body against his. She yielded to the almost savage grip, putting one arm about his shaking form.

"Clive! ..." she murmured. And she closed her eyes languidly.

He crushed that maddening little mouth of hers in a kiss of fiercest passion. There was a long, long silence during which they stood there in the shadow of the veranda; their hearts beating one against the other to the same glad, mad tune.

"Valmy," he said, "how much do you love me?"

"With every bit of me – body and soul," she whispered.

He picked her up wholly in his arms and carried her into the bungalow, shutting out the starlit night behind him.

He switched out all the lights as he went.

A woman, riding across the starlit veldt toward the bungalow, saw those lights go out, one by one ... saw the solitary light that remained in the bedroom which she knew to be Valmy Page's.

She stared at that square pane of light that gleamed in the darkness, and a puzzled look came into her eyes. Valmy was going to bed ... of course, it was bedtime. Where was Clive? Perhaps he had gone down to Bill's bungalow for a chat.

That idea was dispelled by the sudden appearance of Bill McCrayle, himself. He was strolling over the veldt, bareheaded in the starlight, hands thrust in his tunic pocket. As he saw the horse with the familiar figure riding it, he stopped and waved a hand.

"Hullo, Ross — you back?"

"Hullo, Bill!" she called. "Yes. I've come back after all. Jack Feltham came home unexpectedly, so I had no need to remain with Elinor."

He looked up at her. She seemed tired, and in the clear light of the moon he could see shadows beneath her eyes.

"My dear," he said, "you're tired. You shouldn't have ridden all those miles back, so late."

"Oh, I'm all right," she smiled. "It's a perfect night, Bill."

He fell into step beside the horse and walked thus until they reached the gate of the Derrells' garden. Then Bill said:

"It'll be a surprise to Clive to see you home, Ross. He quite thought you were remaining with Mrs. Feltham."

"I thought for a moment that he was with you," said Ross, reining in her horse. "But I suppose he must be in bed and asleep. There are no lights on, except in Valmy's window."

Something — he knew not what — made Bill's heart almost cease beating for an instant. Then he recovered himself. He looked up at the face of the woman he worshipped, and took her ungloved hand, which was resting on the horse's mane.

"Good night, Ross," he said.

She detected unusual emotion in his voice.

"Good night, Bill," she said kindly.

Before she knew what was happening, he had raised her hand to his lips and kissed it. Then very quickly he walked away from her. He left her staring after him, her eyes troubled, her hand tingling from the warm pressure of his lips. Was it possible that after all these years Bill was still in love with her?

She touched the horse with her hand and it bore her swiftly to the stables. She handed the reins over to a sleepy 'boy'; then walked quietly up to the bungalow. The front door was unlocked. She pushed it open and walked through the hall toward her bedroom. She was conscious that her temples were aching and that she was very tired. She wanted Clive . . . Clive's arms . . . Clive to tell her how glad he was she had unexpectedly come home . . . Clive to kiss her hand as poor Bill McCrayle had kissed it out on the veldt just now.

Pushing open his bedroom door she was amazed to discover the room empty.

Where was he? What was he doing?

She turned back into the hall and paused outside Valmy's door. There was still a light shining through the cracks; Valmy must be still awake.

And then suddenly, with her hand on the door-knob, she paused, like a figure turned to stone. For she had heard a man's low voice issuing from that room.

"Darling! . . " that voice was saying — "darling!"

And she knew beyond any doubt that the voice was that of Clive — her husband.

CHAPTER VI

THE sound of Clive's voice, coming from Valmy's bedroom stunned Ross for the moment. With her hand on the door-knob, she stood there, rigid, incredulous. Then came Valmy's voice.

"Clive . . . I love you . . . Kiss me again."

Ross waited to hear no more. She turned and fled down the corridor into the lounge-hall of the bungalow, stumbling in the darkness against chairs and tables, bruising herself but not caring. She reached the front door, pushed it open and reached the moonlit veranda. Then a strange weakness seemed to attack her. Her knees trembled. She sank on to the steps, covered her face with both hands and sat there for a long, long time without moving.

The Rhodesian night was frosty, intensely cold after the burning heat of the day. Ross did not feel the cold. She was conscious only of horror. Clive, her husband, whom she had loved so deeply, trusted so implicitly, was unfaithful to her. She had come home unexpectedly tonight to find him in Valmy's bedroom. That it should be Valmy, her young cousin whom she had brought out here, from pure kindness of heart, increased the horror in Ross's heart — made Clive's conduct doubly inexcusable.

A girl — an unmarried girl, beneath his own roof — could anything be more disgraceful?

Ross did not pause now to consider Valmy's part in the outrage. . . . Her whole mind was concentrated on Clive — her husband. So many people blame the woman in a case of this sort, but it was typical of Ross — generous to her sex — to blame the man, whom she loved so much. For the man is the aggressor, and he has the final word — it is in his power to say 'yes' or 'no'.

How long had this been going on, Ross wondered. Had they been lovers for some time — on the boat — before reaching Rhodesia? Oh, it was horrible, and terrible — Clive, her husband, and Valmy, who was a mere child.

The agony of her thoughts, the sharpness of disillusion in her husband, became too keen for Ross to bear.

She said aloud:

"Oh, God . . . God . . . my God!"

Hot fury against the transgressors followed the first shock of the thing. How dared they commit this sin? How dared they destroy her peace of mind, the happiness of her home — the love which had existed between herself and her husband?

Almost she sprang to her feet and returned to Valmy's room . . . she would break open that door — face them, accuse them. But that feeling passed. She stayed out there on the steps of the veranda. Her head was bent, her hands twisted in her lap. Her eyes closed. No — she could not face them. She felt too ashamed — for them.

Obviously they had not heard her return. Engrossed in each other, they were still ignorant of her presence in the bungalow.

Ross shivered at the memory of Clive's low, husky voice . . . "Darling" he had called Valmy . . . and she — her voice warm with passion — had said: "I love you . . . kiss me again. . . ."

Within a few moments the happiness of a lifetime can be destroyed. Ross had ridden across the veldt back from the Felthams' bungalow, serenely happy; and ignorant; longing for

Clive's lips. That had been barely a quarter of an hour ago. And now she knew she would never be happy again, because she could no longer imagine he had any love left for her. He was in love with Valmy — infatuated by her beauty, her youth. That was why he had been so cool, so undemonstrative lately. Ross understood — understood why he had arranged to sleep in a separate bedroom. So many other little things he had lately done and said were now comprehensible.

She bowed her head until it touched her knees — she wondered what she was going to do — what she would say to Clive and Valmy ...

When she lifted her head again, she saw the figure of Bill McCrayle, standing beside her. She started and rose to her feet.

"Bill — you?" she stammered.

"Hello, Ross," he said. His voice was awkward. He looked harassed and troubled. "I had to see you," he added. "I watched you come out on the veranda and sit here. You're in trouble, Ross. I know it. I had to come and see what was wrong. Can I help?"

She looked at him without answering for a moment. Then she put out a hand and gripped the nearest veranda support, clung to it.

"You — saw me come out? You must have been watching me, Bill," she said.

"Yes," he said, without embarrassment. "I did watch. I felt somehow that something was wrong."

Ross felt a hysterical desire to laugh. Her lips twisted into a smile.

"Wrong? What do you think's wrong, Bill?"

"I don't know. I want you to tell me, Ross."

He did know — at any rate, he guessed, Ross was positive of that. But even now, though Clive had behaved so badly — insulted her by making love to Valmy under her own roof — she felt the desire to shield him. She was fine and loyal. Too proud to admit humiliation or defeat.

She flung back her head.

"Nothing's wrong, Bill," she said. "I — I just felt I needed fresh air — I came out here — sat down for a few moments. I'm tired — that's all."

"There's something more than that, Ross," he said. "Won't you tell me?"

She bit her lower lip. He saw that she was struggling to keep back the words that would have been such a relief to her; that she longed to tell him that 'something' and would not, for Clive's sake. He knew quite well what had happened. Ross had discovered the thing that he, Bill, had discovered last night. But she was not going to admit it. She was too loyal to Clive.

Bill's heart ached as he looked down at the woman he loved. The beloved face was white and haggard. There were dark bruises under her eyes. She was suffering—going through hell — he knew it. And mingled with his love and pity was rage against the man who was the cause of her bitterness.

"Ross," he said, "tell me—you know I—I'm your pal. Can't I help you?"

"No, Bill—nothing's wrong. Honestly."

"Ross, I know you so well, I'm sure that you've had some sort of shock—something's upset you."

She clenched her hands at her sides. For an instant her strained eyes sped to the door of the bungalow. In there was Clive—her husband—and in his arms, Valmy Page. Here, before her, stood Bill McCrayle, who had always loved her—was the most faithful and dependable man she had ever known. She had only to hint to him what she had heard tonight, and she knew he would want to murder Clive. She shivered and looked away from the door, up at Bill's face. No—she could never tell him. Whatever she decided to do, for the future, she must not tell Bill. She must talk it all over quietly, with Clive—first.

"Go home, Bill," she said, "forget it. Nothing's wrong. I—you have made a mistake. But thanks for coming, my dear. It's good to know that I've got a friend at hand."

"Dear old Ross," he broke out, losing his control for an instant. "God knows I'd cut off my right hand if I could save you a moment's pain."

She winced, thinking of the man whose name she bore and who had so wantonly and carelessly broken her heart. But she managed to smile at Bill. She gave him her hand.

"Bless you, my dear," she said. "I shan't forget."

He caught the hand—covered it with kisses. His big body was shaking.

"Ross, Ross! Tell me you'll send for me if you want me."

"Yes, of course I will," she whispered. "Now go—please go, Bill. Good night."

He turned and walked through the moonlit garden, down toward his own lonely home.

Ross stood where he had left her, leaning against one of the posts of the veranda, her hands pressed against her heart. She felt dazed, undecided. Within one short hour she had made such devastating discoveries — Clive's infidelity — Bill's love. The latter had existed, she knew, years ago. But she had not dreamed that he cared so much today. It being so, it was all the more necessary, she thought, to keep what Clive had done a secret.

She forgot Bill and began to think of Clive again. ...

CHAPTER VII

IN Valmy's bedroom, the light was still burning. But Valmy had flung a red silk scarf over it to soften the glow.

She stood by the window with her lover's arm about her waist. The moonlight, clear and white, fell on her face, making it radiant. There was no shame in the queer green eyes — only triumph. Her red lips were exultant, too; smiling.

But the man's face was a trifle pale and worried. It was typical of the woman to live only for the moment ... of the man to look ahead ... now that the first heat of the passion had passed. Clive's conscience was pricking him. There was Ross to be thought of.

Valmy read what was passing in his mind. She wound her arms about his neck and leaned against him.

"Clive," she whispered. "Darling, you're not sorry — already — are you?"

"Of course not," he said weakly. "But you —"

"I have no regrets," she said. "I love you too much."

"Yes, I know you do," he said. And deliberately shutting out the thought of his wife, he pulled Valmy roughly against him. He could feel her heart beating madly. With one hand he stroked her smooth bare arms from which the wide sleeves of the silk Japanese wrapper she wore had slipped. Bending his head, he put his lips to her soft throat.

"Rather a pet," he murmured.

"Swear you'll always love me, Clive," she said. "Swear you'll never stop caring —"

"Of course I'll always love you," he said.

"You'll never forget?"

"Could any man forget you?" he asked. "It's been perfectly wonderful, Valmy. *You* are so wonderful—you beautiful, passionate child!"

"I feel that I am your wife," she said. "Clive, Clive . . . I am —aren't I?"

The word 'wife' struck unpleasantly on his ears, but he did not let Valmy know it. He kissed her hair, her cheeks, her eyes until they closed languorously.

"Little witch," he whispered. "I must go now—back to my own room."

"I don't want to let you go," she said.

"You know I don't want to go, Valmy."

Regretfully he looked round the room in which he had spent an hour of such wild, sweet, wrongful passion. It was flooded with the African moonlight which drowned the lamplight. Through the half-opened casement window came the rich scent of flowers. A wonderful, starry night. He looked back at the girl in his arms, and her beauty went to his head like wine—drugging his sense of right and wrong once more.

"I'm absolutely mad about you, Valmy," he said huskily.

He kissed the warm nape of her neck and stroked the sleek black waves of her hair.

"Good night, darling child," he said. "My little lover."

"Good night, Clive darling," she said. "And tomorrow —"

"We'll fix something up," he whispered. "We will have to be careful of Ross—and McCrayle. But we'll fix something up. Good night, sweetness."

Reluctantly he left her—tip-toeing to the door and opening it very quietly—not because he thought Ross was back, but because he did not want to rouse Ross's young Boer-maid who slept at the back of the kitchen.

He walked into his own room and switched on the light. He felt wide awake—unable to sleep. With his mind still bemused with the thought of Valmy, he could not think very clearly. He was not sure that he wanted to . . . at any rate, he did not want to think too much about the wife to whom he had been so unfaithful this night. He fumbled in his coat pocket for cigarettes. Finding none, he walked out to the drawing-room where he knew he had left a box of Players.

At that precise moment, Ross dragged her tired limbs across the veranda into the bungalow. In the darkness of the lounge-hall, she ran straight into her husband.

The sudden contact of a soft body against his own gave Clive a violent shock. For the moment he did not realise who it was.

"Hullo – who's this?" he asked sharply.

Ross drew back from him, her heart pounding in her breast. The sound of his voice unnerved her. She lost her self-control. She burst into tears.

"It's – Ross," she said in an agonised voice.

Brushing past him, she stumbled along the corridor to her bedroom and flung herself on the bed, tearing down the mosquito-net as she did so. She lay there with her face pressed against the pillow, the scalding tears pouring from her eyes, her body shaken with wild weeping.

Clive – utterly taken aback – stood where she had left him in the darkness a moment. He wore an expression of almost ludicrous amazement. Ross – Ross in the bungalow. But he had imagined she was staying the night with the Felthams. When in God's name had she come back? He hadn't heard her. Of course, Valmy's bedroom was at the other side of the bungalow – her window faced west. Ross had come in from the opposite direction. But she had come in ... *and she must know*. Clive realised that fact at once. Her queer manner, her sudden fit of sobbing, the way she had run from him was proof positive of that.

"Oh, hell!" said Clive aloud.

He stood there, hesitating, the hand that held the cigarettes shaking.

The shock was considerable. All sorts of wild thoughts flashed through his brain. How long had Ross been in the bungalow? What had she heard? How much did she know?

He did not think of Valmy in this moment. His feelings toward her were purely passionate ones, and passion has no particularly loyal or protective instincts. The one idea in his mind was to save himself – to pacify Ross. If necessary he would talk till all was blue, in order to bring tonight's affair to a satisfactory climax. But first he must find out how much Ross knew – he must go to her at once. . . .

Clive turned and walked to Ross's bedroom. The man who had been on fire with love and desire for Valmy an hour ago, was now cool and calculating. He had risked everything in order to become Valmy's lover – but he had never thought the risk of discovery very great. He realised that the situation required delicate handling. At all costs he must satisfy Ross that nothing was wrong. He had ceased to love her, but he remembered that she owned this bungalow; the ranch, the farm, the money. To be divorced — flung out with Valmy — without a penny, was not what Clive Derrell wanted in the least.

He walked into his wife's room and shut the door behind him. By the light of the moon he found the lamp and lit it. Then he crossed to the bed and sat down on the edge of it.

"Ross," he said. "My dear —"

At the sound of his voice she swung round and raised her head — revealed a wet, flushed face.

"How dare you come into my room? Go out — go out at once."

Clive's heart missed a beat. Her words sent all hope flying from him. She knew — she must know. ... But he decided to fight her, in spite of it.

"My dear old girl," he said, putting a hand on her shoulder. "What on earth's the matter?"

"Don't touch me," she said. "How can you dare lay a hand on me, Clive, after — after —"

"Well, after what?" he asked coolly, as she paused and stammered.

"Oh, you know!" she said in an anguished voice. She felt overwhelmed by shame, by a horror of him. Looking through a mist at his handsome face, she wondered how he could be so calm; how those eyes, so intensely blue, so fatally attractive, could regard her so serenely. Had he no shame — no conscience?

"My dearest girl," he said. "I'm absolutely in the dark. Tell me, what is the matter? Why are you crying? What's this all about? To begin with, I thought you were staying the night at the Felthams'."

"I know you thought it," she said bitterly and turned her face from him. "That's half the trouble."

He was glad she had turned her face away. He felt his cheeks grow hot and red.

"Half what trouble?" he asked. "Do explain, please."

"Why force me to explain?" she asked. "It's all so beastly — so humiliating. Clive, Clive, how could you have done it?"

"Done what?" He pretended to be angry now, and he was a first-rate actor. He deceived even Ross. She looked at him again, astonished.

"But Clive — you can't say you don't understand what I'm talking about. I — I came back unexpectedly — because Jack Feltham got home and there was no need for me to stay with Elinor. I — I looked for you, and couldn't find you. Then I was just going into Valmy's room and I—I heard—your voice. You were in there—calling her 'darling' ... and she was saying 'I love you' ..." Ross broke off, swallowed hard; and buried her face in her hands. "Oh, Clive," she added. "I would never have believed it. You and Valmy—my little cousin. Clive—Clive—"

She began to sob again. Clive let her cry for a moment, without speaking to her. Like most men in the middle of a 'scene', he wanted a cigarette. He got up from the bed, lit the cigarette, and returned to Ross's side, smoking fiercely. He knew exactly where he was now. He knew just how much she knew. So he could deal with it.

The sound of Ross's pitiful sobbing jarred on his nerves, rather than moved him to remorse. He was the type of man that detests tears. Yet only a few short years ago he had loved Ross —carried her off her feet by his tempestuous wooing. Tonight he sat beside her, unfaithful to her, hotly infatuated with her cousin, a witness to the destruction of her peace and happiness —and felt no spark of love or tenderness. He was sorry—yes— but not sorry that he had made love to Valmy, or that he had been unfaithful to Ross. Only annoyed because he had been found out, because there was so much at stake—he had so much to lose, if he lost Ross. From a financial point of view, this thing spelt ruin unless he could patch it up. Something must be done about it.

After a moment he leaned forward and put an arm about Ross's shoulders.

"My dear," he said. "I don't know what to say to you. I—I'm rather shattered. But I think you might do me justice —Valmy too. You've rather jumped to conclusions, haven't you?"

His cool, measured voice had the required effect upon Ross. She stopped crying, sat up and dried her eyes. They were swollen and red. She looked at her husband in a dazed way.

"Clive, what do you mean ... that I've jumped to conclusions? There's only one conclusion to be drawn."

"Why?"

"You were in Valmy's room, just now. Isn't that so?"

"I don't deny it," he nodded, flicking the ash from his cigarette on to the carpet.

Ross flushed to the roots of her hair. The calm admission brought back all her former feelings of shame, of intense indignation.

"How could you do it, Clive? Oh, how could you?"

"Wait," he said, without looking at her. "I've just told you you were jumping to conclusions, and you are. You had better hear the truth before you think any more absurd things."

"Absurd?" she repeated.

"Yes," he said. "How long do you suppose I was in Valmy's room?"

"I know," she said. "I was riding back toward the bungalow and I saw all the lights go out, except one—which was in Valmy's room. You were in there with her—from then until now, which is an hour."

That staggered him for an instant. Then he said:

"That's wrong, to begin with. I had only just gone into her room a few moments ago. I suppose it was when you stood outside the door and heard me call her 'darling'?"

"Where were you before that?"

"In my own room," he lied. "I didn't put the light on—the moonlight was so bright and the damned insects are a perfect pest —"

"But at any rate you've been in Valmy's bedroom—no matter how long," she argued.

"Yes, I admit it, and I'm terribly sorry, Ross. I went in a moment of madness—I suppose I felt lonely and—and—"

"Oh, don't" she broke in. "It's all too horrible."

"But you must listen to me," he said. "Ross, I swear you're making a mountain out of a molehill. There's no need for all this awful fuss."

"No need!" she said. "When you were in Valmy's bedroom? Clive!"

"Oh, I know," he broke in. "There's a good deal of evidence against us, but I want you to believe me, Ross, when I tell you that I only kissed her good night—just that and nothing more."

Burning colour swept into Ross's face, and receded, leaving her very white. She stared at her husband and he looked back without flinching.

"I only kissed her good night," he repeated. "I lost my head —she's so pretty—so attractive. She lost hers for the moment— she said she loved me. But of course she doesn't and I don't love her. It was a momentary madness."

Ross breathed very quickly. She still stared at her husband —searchingly, almost desperately. She wanted to believe him. She did not want to think that the worst had happened—that he had been actually unfaithful. At first she had thought so. But now he was swearing that he had only kissed Valmy. That was bad enough—for him to go into her bedroom at night when she, his wife, was away, and kiss her.

"Clive," she said huskily. "Are you speaking the truth? Is there nothing more between you two than a—a kiss."

"Nothing," he said. "I swear it, Ross. And Valmy will tell you so, too. Bring her in—ask her."

"No, no," said Ross. "I don't want to ask her. That would be insulting you. If you swear to me that—it was just temporary madness—that you just kissed her—I—I'll try and believe you."

His heart leaped with relief. He shut his eyes, then opened them again, with a sigh.

"Thank God you do believe me," he said.

Ross, who had loved him so much, felt the tears rush to her aching eyes. She did not think he was a liar and a hypocrite. She knew his restless, moody nature; his love of sensation and of pretty women. She blamed herself for leaving him alone tonight, with Valmy. It was putting temptation in the way of them both—they were both so good-looking and charming—and hot-blooded. She was not like that, herself. Although she was deeply affectionate, passionate at rare moments, she had a great deal of self-control. But she was sufficiently generous to excuse weakness in others. She tried to excuse Clive's conduct—tonight. She could never forget it; never trust him again; never feel the same affection for the girl who had let him into her bedroom. But she would try and forgive them both.

The tears rolled down her cheeks. She looked at Clive, her lips quivering.

"I will believe you, Clive," she said. "It was a dreadful thing for you to do—when I was away. I simply don't understand how you could have let your feelings run away with you like that. Isn't your love for me stronger than that? We've been so awfully happy, haven't we, darling?"

He bit his lip. The pathos of that question stirred him to momentary remorse.

"I swear I'm sorry, Ross, old thing," he said. "You're a darling—much too decent to me. I suppose you can't understand men—what rotten beasts we are."

"Not all men, Clive," she said, thinking of Bill McCrayle—clean, honest, faithful Bill who had stood by her, offered her his service, tonight.

"Well, most men, anyhow," muttered Clive. "You can't understand."

"Perhaps not, but I'll try to, and try to forget what happened tonight."

He took her hand and pressed it between both his own.

"You're very decent to me, Ross," he repeated.

She wiped away her tears. His handsome face, flushed, remorseful, was so like the face of a boy who has been mischievous, rather than sinful, and is penitent. It roused all the mother-love, all the old tenderness in her. She loved this man, whatever he had done. He was her husband — he had once been her lover. Sudden sharp jealousy of Valmy stabbed her. Breathing quickly, she moved to Clive's side and leaned her head against his arm.

"Clive," she said. "What's happened to you? Don't you love me any more? Don't you care like you used to? I've guessed for some time that you've changed — you hardly ever kiss me — and you wanted separate rooms — oh, Clive, what has happened? Why are you tired of me?"

He would not have been human had he ignored her appeal. He looked down at her bowed head, guiltily. He began to stroke her hair, biting nervously at his lips. What a generous, magnanimous creature she was. Of course if she had known what *had* happened in that room, opposite — he grimaced to himself — there would have been awful trouble. Possibly Ross would have left the bungalow — gone to Durban — sued for divorce. Thank goodness he had managed to convince her that he had only kissed Valmy—she believed his word.

"My dear," he said. "I don't know what to say to you, except that I'm a brute and a beast."

"I loved you and trusted you so absolutely, Clive," she said. "I still love you — God knows I'm not the sort to change. Perhaps you are."

"Oh, I'm rotten — I know," he said. It gave him a certain amount of pleasure to scourge himself like this, in her hearing.

"Don't — I can't bear to think that," she said. "Clive — Clive — you aren't rotten. Oh, you will never, never be so mad again — will you?"

He moved his head rather impatiently.

"My dear, I know it was awfully wrong and foolish to go into Valmy's room — but it was only a kiss and —"

"That was enough," said Ross, drawing back from him.

"Yes, yes, I know," he said quickly. "And I'm devilish sorry. It won't happen again. I swear it."

Ross put up her hands and began to plait her tumbled hair.

"Oh, I'm only too thankful to believe that, Clive," she said with a long-drawn sigh.

"And will you forget it?"

"I don't know," she said in a low tone. "But at any rate I — I won't discuss it ever again with you."

"What about — Valmy? It was my fault and — don't be too angry with her," he stammered.

Ross's heart was stabbed with jealousy again.

"I don't know what to say about Valmy. But she ought to go away, at once, of course."

Clive frowned. He did not wish Valmy to go away. Now that he had secured Ross's forgiveness, he was busy with plots and plans for the future — and Valmy centred in them all. He began to think of Valmy again — to remember her with a wild thrill — that hour spent with her tonight — her soft, yielding body — her passionate young mouth. He certainly did not mean Ross to send her away.

"Look here, Ross," he said. "The whole thing was my fault. Don't blame Valmy. It isn't fair on the kid. She didn't want to let me into her room — I made her open the door. She isn't really a bit in love with me. I don't want to think that I've been the cause of ruining all her chances out here. She's so looked forward to living in Rhodesia — meeting some decent man and marrying him."

This cunning speech — so glibly spoken — swayed Ross to his way of thinking. It was quite true — the child had longed for Rhodesian life — for the chance to marry that she had never had at home. She could not be really in love with Clive. It was just foolishness.

"Perhaps it was all just the stupid folly of the moment — she's a romantic child," Ross thought. "It would be very unkind of me to send her away."

Besides, they were thousands of miles away from London now. And Valmy had no home save this one. The best thing to be done was to let her stay — to prove by this that she trusted them both again.

"Listen, Clive," she said at length. "I shan't punish Valmy by sending her home. She can stay. I'll tell her in the morning that I know about tonight and that I have decided to forgive and to try and forget it. And you'll give me your word of honour that you'll never kiss her again?"

"Yes, yes, of course," said Clive hurriedly.

He was enormously relieved to think that Valmy was not

going. But he must make some pretence of loving his wife. It was the devil, he reflected moodily. She would be suspicious now — always looking for trouble. He and Valmy would have to be very careful. In fact they would find it difficult to snatch a moment alone together in future.

He put an arm around Ross.

"Darling, try and forgive me," he said humbly. "The whole thing was most regrettable, and I was crazy."

She did not see into his heart — did not dream that he was even now aching to hold Valmy in his arms again. She yielded to his embrace — lifted her lips to his.

"My dear, my dear," she whispered. "It would have broken my heart if I had thought you had been unfaithful to me."

He did not answer, but kissed her with more warmth than he had known for months. She, loving him, forgave him for the 'folly' of tonight freely. She did not know that his were the kisses of a traitor and a coward.

Outside the bedroom door, Valmy Page had been crouching, shivering, listening at the keyhole. Now she crept back to her own room, slipped into her bed and lay there, shaking from head to foot, her cheeks hot, her eyes like hard jewels in the darkness.

So Ross knew . . . a little . . . but not all. That was a nuisance. And Clive had denied infidelity — pretended indifference to her — promised not to kiss her again.

Valmy clenched her small hands.

"He *shall* kiss me again," she muttered to herself. "He shall kiss me many times — as he did tonight."

She was no fool. She knew, from what she had just overheard that Clive was a coward; that he had no desire for a legal separation from Ross, because she held the financial reins. Everything belonged to Ross. Clive had no money of his own.

Valmy was wildly in love and she was not going to let Clive go. She did not think for a moment that he wanted to go. She must find some subtle way of separating him from Ross, without making him lose the money. There was Bill McCrayle. He was in love with Ross. Why not force Ross into the arms of Bill?

Callous schemes flitted through the mind of the girl as she lay there, shivering with excitement. She felt not a grain of pity for her cousin. She was utterly selfish, basely ungrateful toward the woman who had in all kindness clothed her and brought her out to Rhodesia. In the morning she would act a part — she would aid Clive in blinding Ross for the moment — if that was what he required. And later – Valmy shut her eyes and gave herself up to ecstatic visions of Clive, not only as her lover, but her husband. She longed to feel the strength of his arms around her again: his lips on her mouth.

"Clive – my Clive," she whispered.

The Rhodesian dawn broke over the veldt. It filled the Derrells' bungalow with pearly light. The fresh wind ruffled the curtains and sweetened the rooms with the fragrance of many flowers.

In his room, Clive Derrell slept; a pleased smile on his lips. In her room, Valmy also was sleeping. But Ross Derrell was wide awake. She could not sleep. She was too tired; her brain too active.

She had kissed Clive and forgiven him before he slept. She was going to try and forgive Valmy too. But it was impossible to forget what had happened. Depression weighed her down as she lay there in her lonely bed, wide-eyed, restless, in the dawn light. Her thoughts turned to Bill ... to the kisses he had pressed on her hand and the unmistakable love that had glowed in his eyes. Her cheeks flushed at the memory.

Poor Bill! Poor faithful, steadfast Bill! But thank God she could face him tomorrow with more control than she had had last night. She could assure him with truth that 'nothing was wrong'. She must show him that she still loved and believed in her husband.

CHAPTER VIII

BREAKFAST that morning was not a success. The atmosphere was strained. Clive was ill at ease – kept his gaze on his plate, and felt that two women were looking at him ... his wife with troubled hazel eyes – Valmy with a passion he dared not meet while Ross was present. And Valmy made a very poor pretence at eating.

She was almost relieved when – after the meal ended, Ross called her into the drawing-room. Just as Ross disappeared round a bend in the corridor, Clive managed to seize Valmy's hand and whisper:

"Be on your guard . . . she doesn't know much . . ."

Valmy squeezed his hand very tightly in response, gave him an ardent glance from her long-lashed eyes . . . a look that made the man's pulses leap . . . then walked sedately into the room where Ross awaited her.

Ross did not face her cousin. She felt very embarrassed . . . she dreaded opening up the discussion. But she knew it had to be done. She pretended to be busy with a bowl of blue, sweet-scented water-lilies which stood on an ebony stand before the window through which the sun was pouring. It was already hot.

"Sit down, Valmy," said Ross.

Valmy remained standing. She bit a trifle nervously at her lower lip. She had plenty of aplomb . . . of 'cheek', but she had the grace to feel a little guilty and ashamed before this cousin whom she had wronged last night.

"Yes — what is it, Ross?" she said.

"I want to speak to you about . . . last night," said Ross. A burning blush spread over her face, right down to her charming, sun-browned throat. "About Clive. Oh, Valmy . . . ." She broke off, agonisingly shy and distressed. She really did not know what to say to this young girl who was standing there, so calm, so unashamed. She looked at her, telling herself that, really, Valmy was distractingly pretty. The slender figure in a pale pink linen frock, with a belt about the small waist, was lovely enough to tempt any man. The sleek black head, the green eyes; the small, pearl-studded ears and creamy skin were definitely alluring. Ross realised for the first time how crazy she had been to bring Valmy to Swallow Dip and allow her to be constantly alone with Clive.

She reminded herself, however, that she had decided to forgive. She must place her trust in her husband and her cousin once more. She was too generous to go back on her word whether she doubted the wisdom of her decision or not. And after all, Clive *had* given his word.

"Valmy," said Ross in a halting voice. "I know that Clive came into your room last night. I came back from the Felthams' bungalow unexpectedly."

Valmy managed to start quite effectively and to hang her head.

"Oh, Ross!" she murmured.

"Yes. It was a dreadful thing," said Ross, pressing her hands together. "You and my husband. Valmy . . . how could you be so disloyal to me?"

"I . . . I know it was wrong . . . but just a kiss and . . . we both realised how wrong it was . . . he went away at once. I'm terribly sorry. Will you forgive me, or shall I go away . . . go back to England, Ross?"

Valmy spoke in a humble, distressed voice. Her face flushed, her eyes filled with tears. She was a clever little actress. And after a moment Ross walked up to her and took one of her hands – gently pressed it.

"My dear, I am sure you are terribly sorry and ashamed," she said. "You must have forgotten yourself . . . your upbringing – you shouldn't have allowed Clive – or any man – into your bedroom. What would your mother have said, Valmy?"

Valmy remained silent. But her lips curled a little. She did not appreciate the nobility, the generosity of Ross's nature. She saw only a 'fool' and a 'prude' – she laughed within her at the memory of the fires of passion into which she had thrown herself with Clive. Ross was thoroughly out-of-date – Victorian.

"No wonder Clive's sick of her," she thought. "She's much too worthy for him!"

"Valmy dear," said Ross. "Look at me."

Valmy unwillingly raised her head and looked into Ross's anxious eyes.

"Well?" she muttered. "Shall I go away?"

"No. I brought you out here to give you a chance to marry well. There are so many fine, splendid fellows in Rhodesia . . . men who have come here to fight their way . . . to do great things. I'm not going to send you home and rob you of that chance, because you're alone in the world and I'm your kinswoman. It is my duty to help you, to mother you, although I am not much older than you. I'm going to believe that last night you and Clive – were crazy – and lost your heads. I'm going to believe that you're sorry and that you'll never do such a thing again. Isn't that so, Valmy?"

"Yes," muttered the girl, longing to wrench her fingers away from Ross's tender hands.

"Then stay with us, Valmy, and we'll forget all about it."

"You're too good," said Valmy. "I *was* crazy last night . . . of course . . . but forgive me . . . and let me do all I can to show how ashamed I am."

Impulsively Ross leaned forward and kissed the girl's velvety cheek.

"That's all right," she said. "We won't ever talk of it again."

She turned back to the bowl of water-lilies and stared down at the exquisite blue blossoms, her sight blurred with tears. But there were no tears in the eyes of Valmy as she walked out of the drawing-room to her bedroom and put on her riding-kit and soft felt hat. She was smiling, rather a scornful, amused smile. She strolled out of the bungalow and down to the stables, and ordered the stable-boy to saddle a horse for her. She had received her first lessons in riding from Clive and was proving an apt pupil. She was one of those people who are born to the saddle.

She knew that for the next half hour Ross would be busy in the bungalow, giving Bimbo, the cook-boy, his orders for the day. Clive was nowhere in the garden or within sight on the surrounding land. But she was determined to find him. It was typical of her nature that she could go straight from that conversation with Ross to her lover. Ross's kiss of forgiveness was forgotten. Valmy was conscious only of her reckless, overwhelming feelings for Clive.

She rode out on to the veldt. It was cold and grey at home, in England. But in Rhodesia summer was at its height. The sparkling sun shone over a flower-starred veldt. The mysterious kopjes rose here and there like sentinels; heliotrope bell-clusters peeping from the stumps, and in between the iron-stones that were piled one on top of the other. For hundreds of miles stretched fields of rice and mealies; cattle-kraals; kaffir-huts like dark dots on the radiant landscape. The African sky was intensely blue; the earth red and dry.

But the beauty of Rhodesia did not grip Valmy as it gripped so many who look upon her landscape. She looked impatiently about her as she rode along. She wanted Clive. Wanted fiercely to see him — to make sure he loved her as much this morning as he had loved her last night.

When she had ridden a mile, she came within sight of a small shanty with corrugated iron roof, and a little tangled garden that boasted a gum-tree, a banana, and a glorious mass of blue convolvuli. Shading her eyes from the sun, she stared at this small rude dwelling. And suddenly her heart leaped and her eyes gleamed. For she saw a man's slim figure in a white suit, with a wide-brimmed hat set at a careless angle on his head. It was Clive. She would have known him from any distance. Who else had that graceful, lazy walk ... that fair, smooth head?

She galloped up to the shanty, reined in her horse and slipped from the saddle.

Clive stared at her in amazement.

"Valmy!" he exclaimed. "Where on earth have you come from?"

"From home, of course," she said. "I've just had a talk with Ross. I had to see you alone for a few moments, so I came to look for you, Clive."

"Mad child," he said. "If Ross finds out she'll kick up an awful row."

"She won't find out," said Valmy impatiently. "We can ride back separately. But whose place is this?"

"It belongs to a Boer who owns some land near ours. I came to see him on business, but he's out."

"Then it's empty," said the girl eagerly.

"Yes, it is," he nodded and smiled down at her eager face—so beautiful under the brim of the soft felt hat she wore on her dark, sleek head.

She gave a low, contented laugh and flung herself into his arms.

"Oh, Clive," she sighed.

He held her tightly and pressed his lips to her mouth. Then he drew her into the shade of the veranda which was sheltered at one side from the sun by a green-matting blind. For a moment he held her against him without speaking, drinking in the honey of her lips. She clung to him, satisfied that he was still as hungry for her kisses as she for his.

"Clive, my Clive," she murmured.

"Little witch," he muttered. "But what about last night?"

"It was rotten luck," said Valmy, leaning her hot cheek against his brown one. "Who'd have thought Ross would come home?"

"Not I," he said. "It was the very deuce. We had an awful scene, Valmy. She believed the worst at first but I managed to persuade her that we had only exchanged a harmless kiss."

"She must be a fool to believe it," said Valmy. "But all the better."

"It isn't that she's a fool ..." Clive frowned a little. "Only she's very innocent and unsuspicious. Although she's married, Ross has a most unusually pure sort of mind—she's quite unsophisticated, old-fashioned in a way. She'd never think the worst of anybody, unless she were forced to."

"She's forgiven us, anyhow," said Valmy. "She said in the drawing-room that she'd forgive and forget it."

"She may forgive but take my word she won't forget," muttered Clive.

"At any rate, we are all right for the moment."

"Yes, thank the lord. I don't want a divorce. I can't afford it, Valmy."

Valmy did not reply for a moment. Her thick lashes hid the curious expression in her eyes. She toyed with the lapels of his coat.

"I suppose you've promised never to make love to me again?"

He gave a sheepish laugh.

"Oh, yes. The promise was made to break though, Valmy. You know that."

"I made the same . . . and shall break it."

"Little devil," he laughed. "You know you *are* a little devil, Valmy."

"But you love me," she murmured, nestling close to him. "You love your little devil, Clive?"

"Yes, I do," he said. And he looked down at the red, dewy mouth upraised to his and was lost to all sense of honour or decency. Ross's generous treatment of the situation should have awakened some spark of respect and gratitude in his heart. But he was pitifully weak and no woman had ever appealed to his senses quite so strongly as Valmy Page.

He bent his head and their lips met and clung.

"Yes, I love you," he said, when that kiss ended, "and I'd risk anything for the sake of your kisses, Valmy."

She gave an exultant little laugh.

"I've already risked a lot—for you, Clive. Tell me you won't give me up."

"I won't—I can't— I want you too much."

"We must deceive Ross—see each other alone sometimes, Clive. We must or I shall go mad."

Suddenly the sound of a horse disturbed the lovers. Clive raised his head swiftly and looked out at the sunlit veldt. Two men on horseback were coming at a canter toward the shanty. Clive let go of Valmy and muttered an oath.

"What is it?" she asked breathlessly.

"Vandecken, the man this place belongs to, is coming," said Clive. "And Bill McCrayle is with him. Blast! Bill will see us here together. What the devil can we do?"

CHAPTER IX

VALMY gripped Clive's arm and stared over his shoulder at the approaching horsemen. He could feel her trembling slightly. He muttered another oath.

"Damn McCrayle! Why should he turn up just at the one moment he's not wanted!"

"It can't be helped," said Valmy. "We'll have to brazen it out, Clive. I don't suppose he'll carry tales back to Ross. He's supposed to be very keen about her — isn't he? I shouldn't think he'll want to worry her by telling her about us."

"I'm not so sure about that," said Clive with a short laugh. "He may want to separate Ross from me altogether and have her himself."

There was no time to discuss things further. The two men had reached the bungalow. Vandecken — a huge man with a flowing yellow beard and grizzled head — slid from the saddle, patted his horse's steaming flanks and advanced toward the veranda. Bill McCrayle followed. Bill had seen Clive and the girl beside him, and his lips had tightened. His grey eyes hardened till they looked like flint.

"Clive and Valmy — again." he said to himself. "What a swine the man is. Poor Ross —"

Clive came down the steps of the veranda and greeted his manager and the Boer trader with seeming nonchalance.

"'Morning, Vandecken ... I've been waiting for you.... I want to see you about sowing those mealies next spring ... suppose we crossed each other. You've been over to our place, have you?"

Vandecken raised his hat and bowed a trifle stiffly. He had no great liking for Clive Derrell, who was inclined to treat him as an inferior and patronise him. Ross's father, in the good old days, had been friendly — a true, open-minded, big-hearted Rhodesian. Vandecken had no use for men of Clive's type. They came out to this land with well-cut suits and Varsity drawls and imagined themselves vastly superior.

"Good morning, Meester Derrell," he said, speaking with a guttural Dutch accent. "Yes, I have already been over to the ranch and seen Meester McCrayle. He was returning with me to see my plans for turning that piece of land I recently bought from you into mealies."

"Ah, yes," said Clive. "Then we might both talk business with you. Miss Page — my wife's cousin rode over with me. She is a stranger to Rhodesia and anxious to see the country round Swallow Dip."

Vandecken bowed again. There was admiration in the eyes he turned upon Valmy, who stood beside Clive tapping her smart riding boots with a crop. She was very small and exquisite. There was a subtle 'something' in those eyes of hers that swiftly roused the beast that lies in men. Vandecken narrowed his gaze as he looked at her, and pulled slowly at his beard.

But there was no admiration in the eyes of McCrayle. Sternly he looked from Clive's flushed, handsome face, to the girl, who threw him a glance at once guilty and defiant. Her physical charms left him cold. He could think only of Ross, whose life's happiness she was doing her level best to ruin. What right had Clive Derrell to bring Valmy out here to Vandecken's lonely hut? How long had they been here, together? What would Ross say — if she knew . . .?

Bill drew his brows together in a fierce frown as he asked himself these questions. He looked away from Clive and Valmy, out at the sunlit veldt. This morning he had seen Ross — for a few moments, when he had gone up to the bungalow to ask for Clive. She had told him, smilingly, that Clive had gone to see Vandecken. She had seemed the old, contented Ross — very different from the pale, haggard woman who had come out on to the veranda last night to battle with some secret grief. She had had nothing to say to him about last night. But she had given him to understand by her manner, her smiles, that all was well with her again.

Bill was left to guess that Clive had 'patched up' the row. He was still in the dark as to how much Ross knew — as to how much actually existed between these two lovers who stood before him now, assuming an indifference they were far from feeling.

Bill turned his gaze from the veldt and looked at Clive. The man's good looks and attraction were undeniable, but it would have given Bill great pleasure in that moment to punch that handsome face with his fist — smash it into shapelessness. Ross loved him . . . but he was no more worth her love than a common jackal. Whatever had passed between husband and wife last night, it was obvious to Bill that Clive did not intend to mend his ways. He had started a new day by a clandestine meeting with Valmy Page.

"I'll ride along home and leave you men to talk business," Valmy said. "So long, Clive. Good-bye, Mr. McCrayle – good-bye, Mr Vandecken."

"So long, Valmy," said Clive carelessly.

McCrayle and Vandecken bowed. As Valmy passed Bill she threw him a swift, defiant look from her narrow eyes. He reddened – clenched his hands at his sides. The girl was a brazen little hussy, he reflected. She ought to have a sound thrashing.

And it was for her Clive Derrell was risking his whole future – for her that he was trampling Ross's devotion into the mud.

With a gesture of exasperation, McCrayle turned on his heel and walked into the shanty.

"Come on, Vandecken," he said.

They left Clive to help the girl mount her horse.

Clive looked up at Valmy and touched one slim booted leg with a caressing hand.

"Rotten luck – them turning up like that, sweetheart," he whispered. "But we'll manage something – some other time."

She leaned down to him.

"Clive – do you think Bill will mention this to Ross?"

"Be damned if he does, but I don't think he will. I'll say a word to him on our way back."

"Careful," said Valmy.

"No need to warn me," he said with a brief laugh. "Cut along now – I'll see you later, darling."

She detained him a moment – a hand on his shoulder.

"Tell me you love me, Clive."

"You know I do," he said. "Much too much. It's damned dangerous."

"I love danger – with you," she whispered, an excited little catch in her voice. "You darling – good-bye."

He kissed her hand. She touched her horse with the whip. Clive stood back, watched the animal and its rider until they vanished from sight, then turned and walked into the shanty. He felt moody and annoyed. He was angry with Bill and Vandecken for interrupting his tête-à-tête with Valmy.

"Now then – to work," he said as he joined the other men. "Let's see your plans for dividing up that land, Vandecken."

Bill McCrayle, sitting at the square wooden table in the centre of the roughly-furnished shanty – puffed silently at a pipe. But his gaze rested upon Clive. After a moment, against his will, Clive was mesmerised into looking back at Bill. He read the anger, the contempt in those eyes, and he flushed scarlet. He felt his heart leap in an uneasy fashion.

"Hang it—how much does Bill guess?" he said to himself. "What's he looking at me like that for?"

Later, when they left Vandecken and rode back together to the ranch, Clive decided that it was necessary to silence Bill on the subject of Valmy's presence in Vandecken's shanty, this morning.

Awkwardly he took the plunge.

"Look here, Bill," he said. "I want just to ask you as a favour to me not to mention to Ross that—er—Miss Page was at Vandecken's this morning."

Bill did not speak for a moment. He was looking ahead at the blue mountains on the horizon. The hand that held the reins of his horse clenched till the knuckles showed white.

"Rather a peculiar thing to ask me, isn't it, Clive?" at length he said. "Is there any reason why Ross shouldn't know that her cousin was with you?"

Clive inwardly cursed.

"No particular reason," he said with a shrug of his shoulders, "except that Ross has lately taken it into her head to be—er—jealous of me. Women get like that. It's absurd, of course."

"I see," said McCrayle.

He turned now and looked at Clive through narrowed lids.

"Women like Ross don't get jealous without cause, Clive," he added. "I've known Ross for years. I became under-manager of this ranch when she was still a little kid running about with her hair in plaits. Her nature is not a suspicious or jealous one."

"I'm afraid you don't know as much about my wife as I do," said Clive with an impudent laugh.

"No, but I know more about your feelings toward Miss Page than you think I do," said Bill with sudden cold fury in his voice.

Clive pulled in his mare with a violent jerk. He went red to the roots of his hair.

"By God, Bill, you'd better stop and explain those words," he said.

He was only blustering, trying to save his face, and McCrayle knew it. He also reined in his horse and faced the other man calmly. But white-hot rage was making his body shake.

"My words don't need much explaining. I happen to know

that you're carrying on an affair with Miss Page behind Ross's back."

"I see," said Clive. "And what the hell has it to do with you, in any case?"

"This much," said Bill. "Ross is a great pal of mine. Her father was also my friend. I don't intend to stand by and see you smash things up for Ross. Neither do I intend to be made an accessory after the fact by keeping quiet when you meet Miss Page secretly."

Clive bit his lips till they bled. He could willingly have murdered Bill McCrayle, there where he sat on his horse, calmly accusing him. After all, McCrayle was only the manager — he, Clive Derrell, as Ross's husband, was owner of Swallow Dip and Bill's employer. It was humiliating to have to sit quietly under his insults. On the other hand, what could he do? Bill held the trump cards.

"I am not a sneak and I don't want Ross to suffer — at least not as long as it can be prevented —" said Bill, breaking the pause. "So I'm not likely to tell her that Miss Page came with you to Vandecken's place. On the other hand, Clive, you've damn well got to put an end to this business."

"What do you mean by ordering me about?" blustered Clive. "Go to hell and leave me to mind my own affairs. And in any case why the devil are you insinuating that — that there is anything more than ordinary friendship between Miss Page and myself?"

"I do more than insinuate. I definitely state that there is more than friendship between you. I was in the garden two nights ago ... you and Miss Page did not see me. I needn't say any more."

That silenced Clive for the moment. He was staggered. He had not dreamed that McCrayle had been a witness to any of the love-passages between Valmy and himself. Then suddenly the cad in Clive flamed up. He looked at Bill with hot, sneering eyes.

"You're a nice one to preach," he said. "I'm not at all sure that it's all platonic friendship between you and Ross. You seem jolly anxious to champion her, anyhow and —"

But here he stopped, quailed before the look on the other man's powerful face. To cover his embarrassment he gave an uneasy laugh, pulled a cigarette out of his pocket and lit it.

"Oh, you needn't look like that, my dear fellow," he added. "You're not a plaster-saint."

It seemed to Bill McCrayle as he sat there, glaring with white-hot rage at this man who dared to desecrate the friendship that existed between him and Ross, that Clive was too mean, too lacking in common decency to deserve anger. He was beneath it. He called only for utter contempt. After a moment Bill controlled the longing to pull Clive from his mount and thrash him. He said in a short, savage voice:

"I've never liked you, Clive, but I didn't know you were a dirty cad. You carry on a love-affair with Ross's cousin ... and then ... because I say a few words to you — you suggest that Ross and I —" he broke off, then added: "You're a filthy swine!"

"Oh, come off your pedestal!" said Clive. "You were Ross's lover before I came out to Rhodesia and you know it."

"I may have cared for Ross, but it has no bearing on the present situation," said McCrayle, shivering with rage. "Whatever my feelings were in the past, I buried them on the day Ross became your wife. And they would have remained buried had you turned out the sort of husband Ross deserved — the sort she expected you to be."

"Oh — so you admit the feelings have revived now," sneered Clive.

"I admit nothing, but that your own conduct does much toward helping those feelings to revive. If you hurt Ross ... if you break her heart I swear before God I shall stand by her and offer her my love and protection. So now you know."

Again Clive lapsed into silence. He wanted to find fault with Bill McCrayle, to pick holes in his defence; to put his feeling for Ross on the same base level to which he, Clive, had sunk through his passion for Valmy. But he was unable to do so. There was something very frank and decent in Bill that Clive could not challenge.

He pitched his half-smoked cigarette on to the red, sandy soil and took up the reins of his horse.

"We'd better be going," he said in a low, sullen voice.

"Certainly," said McCrayle. "I have nothing more to say. We know exactly where we are now."

They rode back to the bungalow in dead silence — conscious of a new, deadly enmity.

They parted before Ross, who was sitting on the veranda, sewing, could see them. Bill did not want to face the woman he worshipped just at that moment. Without a word, he turned herself, hated things going wrong at Swallow Dip. The destructive locusts and the loss of the mules, however, did not affect Clive Derrell at all. Not only did he inwardly smoulder with resentment against McCrayle, but he chafed against the lack of opportunity to see Valmy alone. Ross was ever-present. If he and Valmy remained indoors, Ross remained with them. If they went out – she followed. They had not seen each other for more than a few moments, for two whole weeks.

Clive sulked, Valmy secretly fretted. She hungered for her lover's arms and lips. She began during those two weeks to hate Ross, the generous, kindly cousin who had brought her out to South Africa. Ross stood – an imperturbable barrier between her and Clive. If thoughts could kill, Ross would have lain dead at Valmy's feet.

To do Ross justice, she did not deliberately haunt the couple. She had decided to forgive and forget what had happened on the night she had gone to the Assistant-Administrator's bungalow, and she kept her word. She was with them only because she found it natural to remain with them. She had not the slightest idea that they were both hating her, wishing her out of the way and that they would soon reach breaking-point.

She herself was not very happy. Clive was so irritable. His smiles and caresses became less frequent every day. And Valmy was no companion to Ross. She even avoided her. Altogether there was an atmosphere in the bungalow that distressed Ross deeply. It also bewildered her. It was so foreign to her nature to be suspicious or to think the worst of people that she did not guess what was at the root of all the trouble. At the same time she was forced to realise beyond any doubt that her husband was no longer her lover, no longer even her comrade. He was a stranger, keeping his distance and forcing her to keep hers.

During this last fortnight, Bill McCrayle had not been near the bungalow. She had seen him in the distance, riding on the veldt, or working with his men, but he did not come to the house as he had always done in the past for a 'sundowner' or after supper, for a game of cards.

She began to miss him. She realised, with a queer little ache at her heart, how much dear old Bill's friendship meant to her out here. He had not spoken to her since that night of revelation on the veranda. She had never been able to discover the cause of the quarrel between him and Clive, but she presumed that the quarrel was the cause of Bill's present reluctance to come up to Swallow Dip.

A feeling of loneliness, of depression such as she had never felt before, gripped Ross these days. Her usual good humour was damped. The old spontaneous love which she had always given Clive was crushed. He did not want it. He made no effort now to be demonstrative. She did not understand it, but his attitude hurt her terribly. She realised with a sense of impending disaster that it was the coming of her cousin, Valmy, that had separated her from her husband. She had made a great mistake in bringing Valmy here. But it was too late to rectify that mistake.

One night, Clive lost his self-control badly. The three of them were sitting in the drawing-room after dinner. It was the first week in May. Clive, who had been out all day, supervising the sowing of mealies, trying to forget his mad hunger for Valmy and throw himself into work — was tired and surly. Valmy's long-lashed eyes were fixed on him with a hungry look of which he was only too conscious, and which he returned every now and then with interest.

She looked particularly pretty in the soft lamplight. She wore a dress of blue and green chiffon, fashionably long — with a diamanté buckle on the belt which confined the small waist. During these last two weeks her cheeks had grown a little thin; her long green eyes circled with shadows; as though the force of her longing for Clive were wearing her out. The very knowledge of this drove the man crazy. There was ill-concealed hatred in his eyes whenever he looked at his wife whose serene presence prevented him from taking Valmy in his arms and crushing her lips with kisses. Ross was plain, he told himself — badly dressed — dull — a dowdy, sunburned Colonial without charm, without 'sex-appeal'. He was sick to death of her.

Ross did not meet her husband's gaze. She was reading. The silence of the room was broken only by the monotonous sound of the tom-toms played by the boys down in the servants' compound.

The incessant droning of the tom-toms got on Clive's nerves until his patience snapped. Suddenly he got up, knocking his chair over violently.

"Damn those niggers!" he said.

Valmy dropped her lashes and her lips smiled a little. Ross looked up at Clive with surprise.

"Whatever is the matter, Clive?" she asked.

"Everything," he said. He was scarlet. He avoided her

reproachful gaze. "I'm sick to death of sitting in this damned bungalow doing nothing."

Ross laid aside her book and rose to her feet. Her lips tightened a little.

"You aren't very polite, Clive," she said, more sharply than she had ever spoken to her husband. "What you please to term the 'damned bungalow' was once a very peaceful home to you in which you were perfectly happy."

"If you don't find me polite, go down to McCrayle's bungalow and let him slop over you," said Clive, with a sneering laugh. He was in an evil mood and made no effort to control it.

Ross went crimson — then white as the linen dress she wore.

"Clive, you're crazy to say such a thing to me, and you ought to be ashamed of yourself!" she said in a gasping voice.

He looked at Valmy.

"You're too darn good to live, Ross — too darn good to live with, anyhow. Preach, preach — nothing but preach!"

"That isn't true," she said. Her throat felt dry. She was cheapened by this scene — a scene in front of Valmy. "Clive, I think you must be off your head to speak to me like this."

He swung round on her.

"If you don't like me as I am — I repeat — go and talk to McCrayle!" he said violently.

"Why drag Bill's name into this? It is the second time you have done it. What's he got to do with it?"

"Isn't he in love with you?"

Dead silence a moment. Valmy — shaking with excitement — looked from husband to wife. Ross was pale to the lips. She looked stunned. Clive in many moods she had known; but Clive in this horrible insulting mood, never. It astounded her and at the same time wounded her to the depths of her heart.

Then she said:

"I think, really, that you're off your head."

Without another word she turned and walked out of the drawing-room, closing the door behind her. The man and girl left behind heard a second door close; knew that Ross had gone into her bedroom.

It had not been a pretty scene, and it had not shown Clive Derrell in a very pretty light. But it in no way lessened the ardour of the girl who was infatuated with him. The instant Ross was gone, Valmy sprang to her feet and approached her lover.

"Clive, Clive," she whispered.

His evil mood rolled from him like a cloud. His face relaxed into the most charming smile as he caught her in his arms.

"Little Valmy — God — I am off my head wanting you," he murmured.

She clung to him, drawing a deep sigh of relief. She pulled his head down to hers.

"Oh, at last," she cried. "I think I should have died if I hadn't felt your arms around me."

"They're around you now, all right," he said a trifle hoarsely. He kissed the top of her head. "But at what a cost! Ross will never forgive me for losing my temper like that."

"You were marvellous," whispered Valmy. "At least you have the courage of your convictions. You wanted her out of the room and you got her out."

"I'm beginning to hate her, I think," he muttered. "I love you, you maddening little witch. It's playing the deuce with my nerves."

She threw back her head and closed her eyes, her lips parting a little.

"Kiss me — darling," she said.

He picked her up in his arms and carried her to the low chesterfield that stood beneath the window. Then he blew out the lamp and pushed back the curtains. The white light of the African moon poured on to the girl, bathing her in a shower of silver as she lay there on the cushions laughing up at him with her alluring eyes. He caught his breath as he looked down at her.

The Rhodesian nights are cold, but Clive was burning — suffocating with the intensity of this passion that submerged him. He opened the window, letting in a draught of cool air, drenched with perfume from the fruit-orchard. The tom-toms were silent now. There was nothing but starlight and moonshine and the mysterious beauty of the wide, boundless veldt.

Clive went down on his knees by the chesterfield.

"Valmy — little moon-maiden, little white witch — you look like a silver statue in this light — it's wonderful!"

Their lips met feverishly.

"Oh, darling," whispered Valmy. "Darling —"

"I shall never give you up," he said. "I can't live without you, Valmy. You're part of my life now."

"You're certainly all mine," she said. "But Clive, we're being a bit crazy — if Ross comes back . . ."

"She won't come back," said Clive impatiently. "And if she does, I don't care. I only want you. Let Ross go to McCrayle."

Valmy smiled — a wicked little smile.

"Yes, she'll go to him — in the end," she murmured. "And then you'll belong to me, my Clive."

"Do you love me so much?" he asked. He smoothed a wave of black, satin hair back from her forehead. He liked the marble smoothness and pallor of that forehead. "Don't you mind losing your reputation — you strange, passionate little thing?"

"I don't mind what Ross thinks or what people say," she said. "I've only been waiting for you to say you don't mind either. I'm just burnt up with love for you, Clive."

"You're burning me up, too," he whispered. "You darling — you sweet child. I don't know that I'm worth your love —" He paused, covering her small, hot hands with kisses — "I'm a brute — a rotter."

"You are not — you're my lover."

"You're mine." He put his cheek against hers, turning now and again to kiss her mouth. She lay in his arms, drowsily content, opening her eyes to gaze at the jewelled African sky. The night-wind blew upon their flushed, fevered cheeks. Out in the garden a night-jay screamed discordantly.

CHAPTER XI

IN her bedroom Ross lay face downward on the bed. She was not crying. Hers was a bitterness too deep for tears. But she was sick to the very soul. It was an intolerable cup of bitterness which Clive and Valmy had mixed for her and held to her lips tonight.

Clive's unpardonable behaviour and insults before Valmy had shown her plainly that she could never now hope for happiness with him. His love for her was dead. He was doing his best to kill hers.

Ross was a proud woman. To be humiliated before her young cousin was such a blow to her pride that it struck also at her love for Clive. Useless to have forgiven his lapse of a fortnight ago; to have done her best to forget it. He had never forgotten and neither had Valmy. And he had cast a slur on her friendship with Bill — Bill whom she had never regarded in any light save that of a friend — the oldest pal she had. It was outrageous and it was unforgivable.

The misery of a woman who sees her happiness slipping beyond her grasp submerged Ross as she lay there in the quiet bedroom.

A mosquito hummed close to her ear. She brushed it away, then sat up, pushing the heavy waves of hair back from her forehead. Her eyes were heavy, lustreless; her face livid.

Her gaze wandered to her dressing-table. There stood a small, silver-framed photograph of Clive in white flannels. The young Clive at Oxford. Handsome, smiling, the gay, charming boy who had won her heart out here in Rhodesia three years ago.

A pain stabbed Ross's heart. She sat on the edge of the bed, staring at that photograph much as she might have looked at the pictured face of a beloved person who had died. It seemed to her that Clive, the lover of her heart, the man who had worshipped her and promised to make life an unending honeymoon, had died tonight. The savage, irritable man who had stood up and insulted her just now was not the boy she had married.

Yet he was. It was Clive, her husband who had shattered her ideals, her illusions, her most sacred dreams.

She buried her face in her hands. Her whole body shook. She sat in desolate silence, suffering a pain as cruel as death itself.

A long time afterwards, Clive Derrell opened the door of the bedroom and came in. He stood in the middle of the room and looked at his wife a trifle uncertainly. He was flushed, his blue eyes were defiant. His attitude was that of a man who knows he has done wrong but intends to brazen it out.

With Valmy's kisses still hot on his lips, and the thought of Valmy whirling in his head, he was like one intoxicated, or insane — incapable of reason.

Ross slowly raised her head and looked at him. There was something terrible in the sadness, the bitterness of her expression.

"What do you want?" she asked.

"I've come to say good night to you, of course. What the hell did you get into a temper for and rush out of the room like that?"

"Did you expect me to stay — after your behaviour?"

"I don't know." He shrugged his shoulders. "If I was irritable, you were more so."

"I don't intend to be criticised by you, Clive!" she said slowly. "It's you who need criticising."

He averted his gaze.

"Well — spit it out and be done with it, Ross. What do you want to say?"

"This," she said. "I've come to the conclusion or rather, I should say, decision, that Valmy must leave this bungalow — tomorrow!"

Clive lit a cigarette carefully. Then, without looking at his wife, he said:

"Indeed? And why?"

"I needn't explain."

"I can see no reason why poor Valmy should be turned out."

"Poor Valmy!" repeated Ross. She was goaded into anger now. "How dare you say 'Poor Valmy'? It's me, me, you should pity — your wife. Oh! I've been very foolish to love and trust you. It's no use trying to deceive me any longer, Clive. My eyes have been opened tonight. It is obvious that you want Valmy. You got me out of the room by insulting me so that you could be alone with her. You're infatuated with her, and she with you. Very well. This ends things. She leaves Rhodesia tomorrow."

Clive's eyes narrowed.

"Oh, indeed? I shall have something to say about that. I'm master here, and don't forget it, Ross."

She stared at him, dumbfounded.

"You're — master? I don't — understand —"

"It's very simple," he said with a laugh. "I'm your husband, and by law your master. The ranch may belong to you, but you belong to me, and I have the right to order you about. You haven't the right to order me about. You say Valmy is to go. I say she is to stay."

Ross's heart beat so fast it was an actual physical pain. She stared at her husband through a kind of mist.

"You say she is — to stay? But I — I won't stand it, Clive. If she stays — I go. Do you hear that? I mean it. If Valmy doesn't leave this bungalow tomorrow morning, I shall walk out of it!"

"Oh, so you'll walk out of the bungalow, will you?" said Clive, in the same sneering voice which was unrecognisable to Ross. "And where will you go?"

"I don't know ... anywhere ..." she said, putting a hand to her head. "But you won't expect me to remain here with Valmy, surely, Clive!"

"You brought Valmy here. You can't turn her out."

"I brought her here believing that I was doing the right thing for my motherless and penniless cousin," said Ross. "And she's repaid me by carrying on with you. Yes, there is no other word for it—you have both just vulgarly 'carried on'."

Clive shrugged his shoulders.

"Think whatever you like—you are not going to turn Valmy out."

"You prefer me to go?"

"You won't go, either."

"Oh, yes, I will!" said Ross, swallowing hard. "No doubt you would like me to remain—to mend your socks and order your food ..." she broke into an hysterical laugh ... "and watch you make love to Valmy! My God—you're utterly lacking in common decency!"

He flushed and kicked the toe of one foot against the ground. He knew that Ross was right—that he was behaving in an abominable fashion; but he was possessed of a devil tonight—a devil instilled into him by Valmy, the temptress—Valmy, who meant more to him now than anything on earth.

"Don't preach, for heaven's sake!" he muttered. "I can't stand it."

"I'm not going to preach—I'm just going to leave you—leave this home which you, by your actions, have broken up," said Ross, fighting back the scalding tears that welled up in her eyes. "That is final, Clive. Unless Valmy goes away, tomorrow—I shall go."

"To Bill?" he queried.

The sneer, the insinuation, maddened Ross. She looked at him with eyes blazing through the tears, her body shaking.

"Oh, how dare you bring in Bill's name again? How dare you? You are vile—wicked—spiteful! I thought so much of you—I loved you so—I never dreamed you could turn into a cad like this...."

Her voice broke. Choking with sobs, blinded by tears, she turned to the bed and snatched up a scarf that hung over the rails and wound it about her throat.

"I can't bear any more," she added. "I won't stay here another moment. I'm going now—now!"

Clive caught her arm.

"Don't be a fool, Ross!" he said curtly. "It's half-past ten. Where d'you think you're going this time of the night?"

She wrenched her arm from his fingers. He had goaded her to a pitch bordering on frenzy. He had turned her from a sweet, placid woman into a distracted, passionate creature, injured, insulted beyond endurance.

"Let me go, Clive," she said. "You can stay here – with Valmy. I'm going —"

"Ross —" he said again.

But she ran past him and out of the bedroom, through the bungalow, which was in darkness, on to the moonlit veranda. Stumbling down the steps, she ran on through the flower-scented garden, ran until she reached the veldt. She paused, some distance from the bungalow, by a small, favourite kopje where often in past happy days, she used to come and read, sheltered from the sun by the green shade of a tree. She stood a moment, staring blindly up at the stars, her body trembling, violently, her breath coming in short, piteous gasps.

Here, on the veldt – the wide, open spaces, canopied by stars, full of almost unearthly beauty in the white light of the moon – she felt she could breathe more easily, think more calmly.

But she was overwrought and desperate. Clive, the husband she had adored, had taken her love and faith and trampled them in the mud tonight. He had had to choose between her and Valmy. And he had chosen Valmy! That terrible thought blacked out all others in Ross's mind for the moment. His suggestion that she would go to Bill McCrayle had been the final, shattering blow to her faith and her pride. She could bear no more.

Suddenly she crumpled up, sank on to the ground and buried her face on the crook of her arm. Great, aching sobs racked her body; great burning tears poured down her cheeks, soaking her sleeve, dripping on to the earth.

Broken love – broken faith! Can anything be worse? Can a woman suffer any pain more keen and bitter than the pain of knowing that her husband is faithless and has no love for her in his heart? Ross knew beyond doubt that Clive's affair with Valmy was no light, innocent flirtation. She had tried to believe it so – to forgive and forget it. But his conduct tonight had proved that the infatuation between Clive and Valmy was deadly serious.

Just how far things had gone she did not know, she could only guess. But it was sufficient to know that Clive refused to let Valmy leave Rhodesia. She had given him his choice . . . and he had let her, his wife, go from him.

She went on sobbing, passionately, terribly. The cold night wind caught the fringe of her silken scarf; played with it; blew about her brown, tumbled hair. But she did not feel it. She was too numbed by mental suffering to feel physical discomforts or realise that it was very cold and that she was wearing only a thin white frock.

Her world lay in ruins around her. She went down into the very depths of bitter anguish in that hour. She could not even pray. Once, she had believed in prayer. But tonight there seemed to Ross to be no God. It was no use praying. There could be no God, otherwise He would not have let this awful thing happen to her. She had been a good, loving wife to Clive. She had longed for the motherhood denied her. And her reward was — this!

In the bungalow, Clive Derrell had switched on the light in the lounge-hall. He was standing by the fireplace, smoking, his face white; his mouth a hard, straight line. When first Ross had rushed out into the garden, he had been tempted to follow. He had wondered what she meant to do; where she meant to go. For the moment he had felt anxiety — conscious that he had driven her out by his brutality, his sneers. But he had not followed. And for the simple reason that he had remembered Valmy's words, concerning Bill McCrayle: "She'll go to him — in the end . . ." Valmy had said. The subtle poison of that remark remained with Clive. Ross would go to Bill — in the end. Probably she had gone to him now — tonight.

Well — and all the better. She would have to account for her own actions, then, before she could judge her husband's. Besides, what could she prove against him and Valmy? Nothing. She had no witnesses. There was evil satisfaction in that thought for Clive. He did not want Ross to divorce him and leave him without a penny. But if the boot were on the other foot — if he could prove that Bill McCrayle was Ross's lover — he could divorce her — claim damages.

A few months ago Clive Derrell would have been horrified at the loathly meanness of this. Yet tonight he contemplated the final ruination of Ross's happiness without a pang. He had no love left for her. His whole mind was governed by Valmy, just as his body was swayed by her. To possess Valmy for his own, at any cost, was his one object in life.

So he did not follow his wife. He let her go. He was glad

this storm had broken over their heads. He could not have borne another week of unsatisfied longing for Valmy — of playing the part of dutiful husband to Ross. Altogether he felt reckless of consequences.

Valmy, who had listened to the whole scene between husband and wife, glided into the hall and suddenly confronted her lover, looking like a small, alluring child in a Japanese kimono, bare feet thrust into mules.

"Clive!" she breathed.

He started and stared at her.

"Valmy! I suppose you've heard —"

"Yes, my dear — you both talked so loudly, I could hear every word from my room. Where is she?"

"I don't know. She dashed out of the bungalow. I don't know where she's gone."

"To Bill —?" said Valmy, grimacing.

"I dare say."

Valmy shivered and walked to him, leaned her black head against his arm.

"Clive, I'm rather frightened. Bill McCrayle is such a great brute — so strong. He may take it into his head to come up here and make a row."

"Let him come!" laughed Clive. "I've got a revolver ready, my dear."

Valmy shivered again.

"I don't want any shooting. You might get hurt."

He strained her to his heart.

"Don't you worry, little sweetheart. I'll be ready for him if he does come. But he won't. Ross won't let him."

There spoke the coward — sheltering snugly behind the shreds of love and loyalty which he knew he had not wholly torn from Ross's heart.

Valmy put up a hand and caressed the man's fair hair.

"What's going to be the end of this, Clive?" she asked. "The fat's in the fire now, all right."

"It is. And so much the better. But I'm damned if I know what'll be the end of it. I dare say Ross'll come crawling back in a few minutes."

Valmy's eyes narrowed.

"I don't want her back," she muttered. "I'm sick to death of Ross. I only want you."

"Well, you've got me," said Clive, with a short laugh. He wrapped his arms around her and set his lips to her upturned mouth in a long, hot kiss. "You've got me — you're in my blood," he added. "I can't do without you now, Valmy."

"I don't want you to, Clive," she murmured. "I love you — I don't want you to stop loving me."

"You're a witch, darling. You've put a spell on me," he said. "You've made me do things I'd never have believed myself capable of doing."

"You don't regret them, do you?"

"No. But Ross ... Valmy, this is an infernally awkward position we're all in! I don't know what Ross is going to do about this."

"Wait and see," said Valmy impatiently, snuggling closer to him. "I don't believe in looking for trouble. We're alone now, Clive. Ross won't come back. She'll stay with her Bill — you'll see."

"She'll regret it if she does," said Clive, with a brutal laugh. "She won't have much chance of getting a case against me."

Valmy dragged his head down to hers.

"My lover — forget her — forget everything but me."

Pitifully weak, enslaved by this girl with her delicate beauty, her youth, her passion, he obeyed. He shut out the thought of the unfortunate wife whom he had driven out of the bungalow.

"Little witch — little witch," he whispered. "I love you, and you know it!"

CHAPTER XII

ON the veldt, in the shadow of the little tree-crowned kopje, Ross Derrell still lay face downwards on the red, sun-baked earth, blind, deaf and dumb to all around her; unconscious of anything but her overwhelming sorrow and agony.

A small, round black face peered round the kopje at the girlish, prostrate figure. Two saucer-like, rolling eyes stared with awe and interest at the 'missis' in this strange attitude of grief. Then the black, solemn face was withdrawn. A few minutes later a half-naked house-boy from the servants' compound at Swallow Dip appeared outside the pretty thatched-roofed bungalow which belonged to Bill McCrayle.

This particular house-boy, known as Twopence, instead of being curled up in his blanket asleep at this hour of night, had stolen out on to the veldt in pursuit of Ross, whom he regarded as a great and beloved 'missis'. He alone among the other boys had seen Ross rush from the bungalow out to the open spaces, and he had followed, believing it to be his duty to protect her. The Bwana Derrell had let her go alone; why, Twopence could not think. But he followed. And having seen her lie there, prostrate with sorrow, he had made up his funny little mind to acquaint Bill McCrayle with the fact. Bill was kind to him — as kind as the 'missis'. But Clive often kicked him and cursed him for being an incompetent fool.

It was natural that Twopence should turn to Bill and pour forth his anxiety concerning the 'missis'.

Bill was in bed and asleep when the house-boy's timid knock awakened him. He got up, threw a coat over his pyjamas, and looked out of the window.

"Hullo — what's up?"

"*Inkaas*," said Twopence. (*Inkaas* means 'lord and master'. In this light Twopence had always regarded Bill McCrayle). "*Inkaas* —"

"Well?" said Bill. "What's the matter? Speak up."

He was sleepy and cross at being disturbed from his rest by this young black 'imp of Satan'. But as soon as the next few words had fallen from the lips of Twopence, Bill was wide awake and intensely interested.

"The 'missis' — out on the veldt?" he said sharply. "Are you sure?"

"Yes, yes," said Twopence, rolling his eyes. "And she is wailing, *Inkaas*."

"Wailing!" repeated Bill. He drew in his breath quickly, his face flooding with colour. Ross out on the veldt, at this time of night, crying . . . was it possible?

He questioned Twopence curtly. The boy told him how he had seen 'missis' rush out of the bungalow, to the veldt, and had followed in his devotion.

"Quite right," nodded Bill. "But Bwana — Clive Derrell — didn't you see him?"

"No, *Inkaas*," said Twopence.

Bill's teeth snapped together. So there had been another

quarrel up at Swallow Dip, and this time a serious one. Ross had run away and Clive had not attempted to follow.

"Damn the man — I'll wring his neck for treating Ross like this!" he thought savagely. He drew in his head, rapidly flung on a few clothes, his boots and a coat, then appeared outside the shanty. He was no longer sleepy; his eyes were gleaming, under the thick brows. "Take me to the 'missis', Twopence," he commanded.

The house-boy grinned and nodded, and led the way to the small kopje where he had left the 'missis' a few minutes ago. She was still there. With a terrible pang of pity Bill saw the slim, prostrate figure; face hidden; lovely chestnut hair tumbled about her. She was sobbing — not passionately now, but drearily, as though in hopeless grief.

To see her thus wrenched Bill's heart in two. He had loved her for years; reverently loved her and served her — the one woman in the world. That she should have been brought low like this by Clive Derrell, driven out on to the veldt to sob in grief and loneliness, seemed to Bill a frightful thing.

His feelings toward Clive were murderous. For an instant he stood rigid, staring down at Ross, who was unconscious that he was there. Then he turned to the boy who had brought him here.

"Go back to my house, Twopence," he said. "Light a fire in the living-room. Quick. And, Twopence —"

"Yes, *Inkaas*?"

"Say nothing to the other boys of this — you understand — no say word. . . ."

"No say word, *Inkaas*," repeated Twopence fervently, the light of devotion in his rolling eyes as he looked at Bill McCrayle. He turned and began to run back to Bill's dwelling; an elfin black shadow in the white moonlight.

Bill went down on one knee beside Ross and touched her shoulder.

"Ross!" he said.

She quivered under his touch, turned her head and looked up at him. To his dying day he never forgot the pitiful sight of her face; its calm beauty marred by the tear-swollen eyes; her lips bleeding, her expression that of a creature wounded mortally.

"Oh!" she moaned, as she saw who it was who had touched her. "Oh . . . Bill . . ."

"Ross, my dear, my poor dear!" he said. He felt words inadequate. Helplessly he looked down at her, lifted his hand from her shoulder to her head and began to stroke the dishevelled hair. "My poor Ross!"

She shuddered and turned from him again, burying her face on her arm.

"Oh, I want to die – I want to die, Bill!"

"Why? What has happened? For God's sake tell me – don't try to hide things from me now, Ross."

"I – can't tell you," she said in a muffled voice.

"You can and must. I am your friend – pal, Ross. You're in trouble, and you must let me help you."

"I can't!" she sobbed.

"Ross – dear – my dear – don't cry any more," he begged her. He knew the strength of Ross's character, her fine courage. She must have been terribly hurt to be reduced to this state.

Without questioning her further, he did the thing he considered best for her sake. He lifted her from the ground up into his arms.

"Cry here, if you must – on my breast, Ross," he said, his voice shaking. "But not there on the ground."

She did not resist his embrace. Quite naturally she yielded to it, hiding her face on his shoulder, her body trembling with sobs. The anguish she had endured this last hour had broken her completely. She was like a suffering child – Bill McCrayle held her as he would have held a child, stroking her hair, murmuring words of comfort, patting her back.

"My poor dear, you're frozen with cold," he said, taking one of her icy hands between his strong warm ones. "How long have you been out here? Good God! You might get your death. . . ."

"I don't care – I don't want to live. What have I to live for?" she said in a voice of despair.

"I am not going to let you say that, Ross. Look here, I am going to take you back to my place. Twopence is lighting a fire, and you shall have a cup of coffee. No – don't argue with me. I'm going to carry you there."

She looked up at him dazedly, then round the moonlit veldt, one hand pressed to her brow.

"I – oh, I feel dazed, Bill . . . I – can't think clearly," she said.

"Don't try. Just give yourself into my hands, you poor child."

She nodded mutely. She had no desire to fight against him.

His arms, his tender voice were very consoling. She began to realise, too, for the first time, that she was half-frozen with cold.

She was tall and well-built — not easy to carry. But Bill McCrayle was six-foot-three and tremendously powerful. He lifted her up in his arms and strode with that precious burden across the veldt, towards his bungalow. As he went he lifted his face to the stars; his mouth very grim.

"As God is my witness, Clive Derrell shall pay for this night's work," he said to himself.

When he reached the bungalow he paused and looked down at the woman he had loved for so many years.

"Ross," he said, "will you trust yourself with me? Or would you rather I took you back to — the bungalow?"

He felt her shudder from head to foot.

"No, no!" she whispered. "I can't go back there — not to-night, anyhow."

"That settles it, then," he said. "You shall stay with me."

She did not answer, but let her head fall back against his shoulder with a tragic sigh. Looking down at her he saw that she was livid. The poor bitten lips tinged with blue. His heart missed a beat. Was she going to be ill? She had lain out there on the veldt in that thin white dinner-frock, unprotected against the cold night wind, for some time. The scarf about her shoulders had no warmth in it. She had caught cold . . . it might result in bad fever.

He carried her into the living-room and laid her on the small couch which was set at right-angles to the chimney-piece. He was thankful to see that Twopence had lit a good fire, which was blazing away cheerily, filling the room with warm, ruddy light. There was one oil lamp, with an ancient yellow silk shade, on the table. Bill turned this up higher. He felt that Ross needed light and warmth — anything to make her forget the depression, the misery of the night into which she had fled. What had happened between her and Clive? He did not mind now. He only knew that Ross was in extreme trouble and needed him. That was enough. To serve her was his one object in life.

Used to a solitary bachelor's life, he was not long in preparing refreshment for her. He soon had a saucepan of water on the little primus stove in the kitchenette, and within ten minutes a cup of steaming camp-coffee was ready. He carried it into the living-room and laid it on the floor by the couch.

"I want you to drink all this down, Ross," he said. "And I'm going to put a dash of brandy in it, too. That will pull you together."

"Oh no . . ." she began weakly.

"Yes, dear—please," he broke in. "You need it."

He drew a flask from a little corner cupboard, uncorked it, and poured the brandy into the coffee. Then he sat on the edge of the couch with the cup in his hand.

"Come, dear," he said, persuasively.

He treated her just as he would have treated a sister. There was an exquisite quality of tenderness in his voice, that warmed Ross more than the fire or the coffee. She made an effort to sit up and took the cup from him.

"Thank you, Bill . . . you're awfully—kind to me," she said.

Kind to her! He looked at her with eyes of worship, and for the second time that night he longed to find a horsewhip, to go up to the bungalow and thrash Clive Derrell within an inch of his life. What had he done to her? What could he have said or done to drive Ross to the very brink of despair like this? It appalled Bill, who had never seen her otherwise than a contented, cheerful girl.

Ross sipped the hot coffee and was glad of the stimulant in it. It seemed to trickle like fire through her frozen body, restoring life and sensation to her. The fire looked wondrous cheerful and comforting, too, shooting sparks up the chimney, curling vivid red tongues around the logs Twopence had piled in the grate.

Gradually the dazed feeling, the abject misery, fell from Ross just as a cloud rolls away before the sunshine. Her brain cleared; her cheeks regained some colour; her lips their natural red.

"That was—good, Bill," she whispered, handing him back the empty cup.

"I'm glad you liked it," he said.

He rose and walked to the door which led into the kitchen. Twopence was squatting on the floor, looking up at the moon, visible through the square pane of glass, with his big, saucer-like eyes. He sprang to his feet as Bill appeared.

"*Inkaas* want me?" he grinned.

"No. You can go back to the compound. You have been a good boy," said Bill kindly.

Twopence peered wistfully into the sitting-room.

"Missis, she all right?"

"Yes, Twopence, she's—all right. I shall tell her you have served her well."

Twopence beamed, rolled his eyes and then vanished through the kitchen door like a flitting black shadow. Bill went back to Ross.

He drew a chair up to the couch and sat down. Tenderly he tucked the old plaid rug he had thrown over her more securely about her body.

"Warmer now?" he murmured.

"Much," she said. "In fact, I'm — quite all right again."

And she tried to smile at him — a pitiful smile that wrung his heart. She leaned her head back in the cushions, making an attempt to pin up the dishevelled masses of chestnut hair. Bill thought what beautiful hair it was — rich brown, thick, falling below her waist. When she had pinned it into a loose coil, she let her arms drop, folded her hands before her, and looked up at him with eyes of gratitude.

"You've been very good to me, Bill," she said.

"You know that I'm only too glad to be of help to you, Ross," he said.

She twisted her fingers painfully.

"Bill, the terrible part of it all is that he — he sneered at our friendship. He — said he supposed I — would come to you."

Bill's hands clenched.

"You mean — Clive?"

"Yes. We had a frightful scene tonight, Bill; and during it, he said he supposed I would come to you — as though — as though we had been aiming for it. Oh, my God!" ... her voice broke, and she buried her face in her hands. "Oh, Bill, Bill, you don't know what I have been through!"

He had to keep his emotion under iron control to prevent himself from clasping her in his arms now and telling her how he loved her and wanted her to comfort, to protect, to adore — for evermore. But he refrained. She did not want passionate love. She was a broken-hearted child tonight, needing only friendship and tenderness.

He laid a hand on hers.

"Ross, dear, don't cry again — please," he said. "It upsets me so to see you cry."

She looked up, her lips quivering into a smile.

"I — won't, Bill. I don't think I can any more. I've cried so much already."

"You poor child! But tell me exactly what has happened — I beg of you — Ross. Don't keep anything from me."

So she told him. In a low, shamed voice she described the

humiliating, wretched scene she had had with Clive; her demand that Valmy should leave Rhodesia; his declaration that Valmy should remain; his brutal indifference to her wishes—or her suffering; his cruel jibes.

Bill listened with black rage against Clive in his heart. And when she had finished he rose from his chair, lit a pipe, and paced up and down the little room, smoking furiously.

"God! Ross, what a cad, what a swine!" he said. "I could kill him. I will kill him!"

"No, no; don't be silly, Bill," she said swiftly. "Killing him could do you no good—nor me."

"But he deserves to be shot for treating you like this—you, Ross."

"Oh, he must be mad—off his head, Bill! I am sure that Valmy has unhinged his brain in some awful way. It is so unlike Clive. He would never, never have been capable of treating me so, months ago, before Valmy came."

Bill continued to pace up and down, puffing at his pipe.

"I knew this was coming," he said. "I saw it coming—days ago."

"How, Bill?"

"I overheard Clive and Valmy in the garden, that night I dined with you. I knew then that they were infatuated with each other."

Ross bowed her head.

"Oh, it's shameful—so humiliating for me," she whispered.

"You must get rid of that bounder—divorce him, Ross."

She shivered, and closed her eyes.

"Bill, you don't know how that hurts—that word 'divorce'. I have always been so against divorce all my life. You know my views ... you know that I consider the marriage vows sacred —"

"Yes, but Clive hasn't held his vows sacred," said Bill hotly. "He's been unfaithful to you, Ross."

Another burning flush overspread Ross's face and throat.

"I'm not—positive of that."

"But I am. Good God! It's obvious."

"It seems so," said Ross, haltingly. "But oh, Bill, don't you understand their game? They've planned all this—I know it. They have driven me out tonight down here, to you. If I brought an action for divorce they—they'd take advantage of tonight's episode. Clive would bring a counter-action, try to divorce me."

"It won't come to that. I shan't ever stand by and see your name dragged through the divorce court, Ross."

"What can I do?" she asked wearily. "I—I suppose I ought to go back to the bungalow—now."

He glanced at a little clock that stood on the mantelpiece.

"D'you see the time?" he asked grimly.

She looked. It was five minutes to twelve. She was shocked to find how late it was—what a long time had elapsed since her flight from Clive, after their ghastly scene in the bedroom.

"Perhaps I had no right to bring you in here, Ross," added Bill. "But I couldn't help it. You were half dead with cold and misery, and you needed a little care, a little peace and warmth."

"You gave me all three," she said in a low tone. "And I am not sorry I came."

CHAPTER XIII

BILL put his pipe in his pocket and sat down in the chair by the couch again. Taking one of her hands, he held it gently in his huge ones.

"Ross," he said, "you know how much you mean to me, don't you? How much you have always meant—"

She averted her gaze.

"I—suppose I know, Bill."

"Well, dear, I have always felt the same and my feelings will never change. If you want my love, my protection, it is yours. I lay myself—my life at your feet."

"God bless you, Bill, dear," she said, her voice trembling, her eyes filling with tears. "But I can't take what you offer. How can I?"

"Why not?" he said breathlessly. "You aren't, surely, going back to Clive?"

"Oh, I—don't know . . ." she bit her lower lip and drew her fingers away from him. "Bill, you don't know how much I love my husband—what the marriage-tie between us means to me."

"I do know, dear. But he —"

"He's been unfaithful. Yes, perhaps so," broke in Ross. "And unbelievably cruel to me tonight. Yet I still care — just a little. You can't tear love from your heart suddenly without leaving — roots, Bill."

"God knows I understand that," he said. "On the day you married Clive I tried to tear my love for you from my heart — and the roots remained — and the love grew again. But oh, Ross, Ross! you were worth such love. But Clive is not worth it. He is a rotter. If I saw any good in him I'd admit it. But he has no good. He's a coward and a cad."

She winced and moved her head with a gesture of pain.

"He was mad tonight. Surely in the morning he will be sane — he'll see how vile he has been and be sorry for it — he'll admit that Valmy must go. Bill, Bill, don't you realise that I still — care for my husband — a little bit?"

"I do realise it," he said bitterly. "And I — I don't come into it."

"Oh, my dear!" she said, her face colouring hotly. "You are my friend — the very best friend on God's earth, but —"

"Ross, why can't I be more? Why can't I be more?" he broke in, momentarily losing his control. He slid on one knee by the couch and lifted both her hands to his lips covering them with kisses. He looked down at her and into the dark chestnut eyes under the thick brown lashes. They were dim with weeping. She looked back at him in mute appeal, as though beseeching him to be very gentle, for she could bear no more sorrow tonight. "My darling," he added, "I'd give my life to spare you from pain — to make you happy."

"I believe that, Bill," she said. "But I am Clive's wife still — whatever he has done."

"But, Ross —" began Bill.

Then he broke off abruptly. He dropped Ross's hands and rose to his feet, turning his face to the door. Ross also looked at the door. They had both heard footsteps on the porch of the bungalow; rapid steps breaking the stillness of the night. Then came the sound of a voice that made Ross blanch and Bill's heart miss a beat.

"Let me in," it said roughly. "I know Ross is in there, and I want her. Open the door — at once. D'you hear?"

Ross put a hand to her heart.

"Clive . . ." she whispered. "It's Clive!"

Bill's mouth tightened into a grim line.

"Very well, Ross," he said. "Let Clive come in. Perhaps it is just as well. I should like to speak to Mr. Clive."

He started to move towards the door, but Ross raised herself from the couch and clutched his arm. "Wait, Bill ... promise you won't — you won't lose your temper ... that you won't be ... violent with Clive! Oh, please, please, Bill —"

He looked down at her, his lips relaxing a moment.

"You dear, generous-hearted woman — don't worry," he said. "I shall do nothing to distress you. I swear that — no matter how much I feel like murdering Clive."

He gently disengaged his arm from her clinging fingers, marched to the door and opened it wide.

Clive Derrell stood on the threshold, his handsome face colourless, his eyes dark with hatred of the man who had opened the door. It was a question of 'dog-in-the-manger' with Clive. He did not want his wife himself. But he did not particularly relish watching another man take her. Valmy had sent him here on this midnight quest for Ross. With her usual cunning and utter lack of scruple, Valmy had decided that it would be a good move for Clive to go down to Bill's dwelling and demand his wife ... and then if Ross refused to return to the bungalow, he would have a case against her; make it impossible for her to divorce him.

"Well?" said Bill, sharply. "What have you come here for, Clive?"

Clive's eyes sped to the sofa, rested an instant on Ross. She was sitting up, one hand pressed against her breast, the other clenched in her lap. Her rich chestnut hair was disordered — her cheeks feverishly red. Bill knew that she was a sick woman — that those hours out on the veldt in the cold had given her a chill ... but to Clive's distorted vision, Ross looked abandoned. It was a genuine shock to him to see her there in Bill McCrayle's room, lying on his couch, at midnight.

"My God!" he said violently. "Why have I come? It's obvious. I've come for Ross. I want to know what the devil you mean by coming here, Ross?"

She looked at him with large, tragic eyes.

"You want to know that? I wonder you mind whether I have come here or not, considering you drove me here."

"Exactly," said Bill, closing the door and standing with his back to it, his arms folded across his chest. "What right have you to question Ross's actions, after your own, tonight? It's no use mincing words, Clive. I know just how things stand between you and Valmy Page. I know that you've insulted Ross and driven her out on to the veldt, half-crazy. I have no hesitation now in declaring my love for her and offering her my protection."

"Indeed!" sneered Clive. "Very romantic. Very nicely arranged, you —"

"By God, I'll choke those words down your throat, you cad!" broke in Bill. He sprang to Clive's side and for a moment towered over him, his eyes blazing, his fists clenched. "Any more of that and I won't be responsible for my actions," he added thickly. "I'll punish you as you deserve to be punished."

Ross looked from one man to the other, her heart beating with agonising speed, her whole soul sick.

"It's only because Ross has asked me not to lose my temper than I'm trying to keep it," said Bill.

Clive thrust his hands into his coat pockets and walked up to the couch. He stared down at Ross. His lips twitched nervously.

"Have you any right to criticise me, after this?"

"Every right, Clive. Bill's my friend. He may have offered me his love, but that does not say that there is anything between us except friendship. With you and Valmy — it's different."

"Anyhow, you've no right to come here."

"Never forget that you drove me here."

"Well, I've come to take you back to the bungalow."

Ross looked swiftly at Bill . . . saw mute appeal in his eyes. Her head dropped. She bit her lower lip; then raising her head again looked up at her husband, her beautiful eyes full of tears.

"You've come to — take me back. Do you mean that you've told Valmy that she must leave Swallow Dip tomorrow, Clive?" she asked in a low tone.

Clive did not answer his wife's question for a few moments. During that brief silence, she knew she must prepare herself for the worst. He did not intend that Valmy should leave Swallow Dip; otherwise he would have answered at once.

At last Clive said, in a jerky voice:

"You know I think it's unreasonable of you to expect Valmy to leave us. She's only just come out here."

"Yes," said Ross bitterly. "Just long enough to do all the harm in the world. Oh, Clive, Clive, how can you call me unreasonable? You're in love with Valmy — you can't deny it. There is — perhaps — more between you than I know. She can't stay with us. It's outrageous that you should expect me to let her do so."

Clive coloured and shuffled from one foot to the other, keeping his eyes on the ground. He was conscious of Bill McCrayle's scornful gaze. It both embarrassed and enraged him.

"Look here, Ross," he said. "I might as well say I won't allow Bill McCrayle to remain on the ranch because of the friendship between you two!"

His emphasis on the word 'friendship' wounded Ross to the depths of her loyal heart. It made Bill white with fury.

"By God, you're making it hard for me to keep my hands off you, Clive!" Bill broke out, clenching and unclenching his strong fingers. "I don't think I need remind you that Ross and I were friends for years before you came out to Rhodesia. What's more, our friendship has been absolutely decent and harmless and if you dare throw mud at your wife again, I swear I'll break every bone in your body!"

Ross shuddered and buried her face in the cushion. She felt she could not bear much more of this horrible scene. Her head was aching, throbbing with a pain that was fast growing unbearable.

Clive cast a brief glance at Bill's furious face, then shrugged his shoulders.

"Oh, well—have it your own way! But why should I believe you and you think the worst of me? How do you know that there is not a—a harmless friendship between Valmy and myself?"

"Does a man who is only a platonic friend generally visit a girl at night when his wife is away, *and* make love to her?" demanded Bill. "Bah! One can't talk to you, Clive. You're such a confounded hypocrite!"

Again Clive reddened and averted his gaze. Then he pulled out a cigarette and lit it.

"This is all a damned waste of time," he muttered.

"Agreed," said Bill. "You came here to ask Ross to return home with you. That is as it should be. But, naturally, she's not going to unless you give your word that you'll have nothing more to do with Miss Page and that she leaves Rhodesia at once."

"Charming terms," sneered Clive. "I like being dictated to by my wife's lover, I must say!"

Bill's patience snapped. With a low cry of anger, he sprang upon Clive.

He laid her on the sofa, and knelt beside her, kissing the chilled, nerveless hands.

"Ross, my darling, my darling," he murmured. "Oh, my poor dear—I am going to take care of you now—my poor love!"

He smoothed the brown hair back from her forehead. His face contracted as he felt the heat of that forehead, and of her hands. She had caught a chill, without a doubt. Unless he took the utmost care, she might die. The mere thought of losing her struck fear in Bill's heart.

He picked up the flask of brandy which lay on the table, and lifting Ross's head on his arm, poured a few drops of the fiery liquid between her teeth. She stirred and moaned. He made her drink a little more. And now she coughed and opened her eyes.

"Clive!" she moaned. "Clive!"

Bill bit his lip and muttered a fierce oath against the man who had behaved so vilely to her. She still loved him. She was delirious—calling for him. Women were like that; insulted, deserted, ill-treated, they still cry for the man who has broken them—still love him, cling to him.

"Clive, Clive," said Ross again, moving her head from side to side.

Bill set his teeth. Out of his great, selfless love for Ross, he had but one wish—to make her happy. But send for Clive Derrell he would not! Clive had chosen Valmy. Let him remain with her. He was not fit to touch the hem of Ross's dress, and he should never touch her again if he, Bill, could help it.

Bill was much too fine a man to resent the fact that Ross called for her husband in this semi-conscious condition. It hurt —hurt to think that her thoughts never turned to him, the one who loved her so devotedly. But the pitiful, repeated calling for the man who had hurt her only roused greater compassion in Bill.

He moistened her dry lips with some more brandy, then laid her back on the cushions and covered her to the chin with the rug. She flung it off at once, beating at the air with her clenched hands.

"Clive! Clive!" she moaned.

Bill took one of her hands and pressed it to his lips.

"Hush, hush, my dearest!" he said.

"Clive," she repeated. "My darling!"

"Hush," broke in Bill. "Quiet, Ross dearest."

"You'll be sorry for that," he exclaimed. "You're a swine—a bloody liar!"

He knocked the cigarette out of Clive's fingers then struck him across the sneering face. Clive staggered back.

Ross looked wildly from one man to the other; saw Bill towering over Clive, his face livid with rage, his fists clenched; her husband white, save where Bill's last blow had left a scarlet mark on his face. His lower lip was cut and bleeding.

"Bill!" gasped Ross. "Clive! Oh, my God—don't fight—don't!"

"Not in here," said Bill, panting. "Not before you—no, Ross. But outside—yes! I've listened to too many insults to you. I've kept my temper too long. But now I'm going to teach him a lesson—by God, I am!"

"Bill—no—he's mad—he doesn't realise what he's saying!" Ross cried, struggling off the couch on to her feet. "Don't fight—don't—please."

"Sorry, Ross—I must," he said.

Clive tried to ward him off, but the other man seized him by the collar and dragged him out of the sitting-room on to the moonlit veranda. With one hand he shut the door behind him, so that Ross should not see—with the other, he sent Clive hurtling down the stoep on to the grass. He was tremendously powerful, and Clive, though agile, was no match for him. He picked himself up from the ground and faced Bill, blood trickling from his swollen mouth. He lurched wildly at him, but Bill parried the blow neatly and landed a stinging blow to the jaw which sent Clive down again. Bill stood over him, his chest heaving, his eyes ablaze.

"Get up and take some more punishment, you hound!" he snarled. "Get up—come on."

Clive rose slowly and painfully and stood an instant, staggering, holding one hand to his bruised face.

"Let me alone," he said in a tone of fear. "You've got no right—"

"No right be damned!" cut in Bill. "You've said vile things to Ross, and I'm Ross's friend. Come on—fight it out! If you're the better man, you've got the chance to show it."

Clive gave a kind of sob and lunged toward him again, striking out blindly with both fists. Bill laughed—and landed a couple more smashing blows to the jaw. It gave him exquisite pleasure to punish Ross's husband; to feel the soft, shrinking flesh under his fists. Clive deserved every blow—and more than he got. He could crawl back to Valmy with those pretty purple bruises; that bleeding mouth; and one eye closed. Let Valmy see the nice mess that had been made of her good-looking lover!

The last blow sent Clive spinning down on to ground. This time he did not get up again. He lay there, dazed, sobbing, his face hidden on his arm — a shameful, craven object.

Bill bent down and shook him.

"Come along — want any more, Clive?"

"Go away, damn you!" came the hoarse, sobbing reply.

Bill laughed and picked up the coat which he had thrown down before the fight commenced. He felt full of vitality and triumph. His face was flushed — his eyes bright — his heart racing.

For days he had wanted to lay hands on Clive Derrell and mar that handsome face. He was as elated as a schoolboy who wins his first fight, now that he had done it.

As he buttoned up his coat, the door opened and Ross came out on to the veranda. He hastened to meet her, his heart smiting him as he saw the deadly pallor of her face. Two red, hectic spots burned on her cheeks. She was in a high fever. Her eyes were glazed.

"Bill!" she moaned. "Bill — what have you done?"

Then her eyes caught sight of Clive's prostrate figure in the moonlight. She swayed and would have fallen but Bill caught her in his arms.

"What have you done?" she repeated. "Clive —"

"He's had the punishment he deserved," said Bill. "Sorry, Ross, I couldn't help it. He isn't seriously hurt — don't look like that! Only a few bruises to remind him in the morning that he had better not cast any more aspersions on your character, in my hearing."

Ross leaned heavily against him, one hand to her aching forehead.

"You're ill, my dear," he said quickly. "You caught a chill out there on the veldt. You mustn't stay here in the wind. Come indoors by the fire again, Ross."

She shuddered from head to foot, and pointed at Clive.

"He — oh — we can't leave him there — I can't!"

"Don't worry about him," interrupted Bill. "Think of yourself for a change, Ross. It's time you stopped thinking of a coward who insults you because he has no defence to make for his own behaviour."

She tossed her head from side to side, her eyes bright with fever, unseeing.

"Clive," she muttered, "why don't you come to me? You love me, don't you...?" she broke off and began to sob piteously. "Clive, don't go to Valmy ... come to me ... oh, my God ... to think that you could treat me so! Oh, Clive, how could you?"

Bill's heart ached and bled for her. He realised that she was going through one of those ghastly, heart-breaking scenes with Clive. The agony of her voice nearly drove him mad. But he could do nothing — only kneel there, kissing her hand — imploring her to rest in peace.

Ross moaned and sobbed, and tossed on the couch — quiet only for short intervals. Bill rose from his kneeling position and fetched a bottle of aspirin from his corner-cupboard. He crushed two five-grain tablets into a powder and gave it to Ross; forced her to drink it down with some warmed milk. As he laid her back on the cushions again he felt that her frock was damp. She was drenched with perspiration, and her pulse was very rapid. Bill had no thermometer, but he guessed that she must have a very high temperature.

The nearest doctor was a good many miles from the ranch. Impossible to get to him at this hour of night. But Ross must be properly nursed — receive the attention of one of her own sex. That was obvious. All her clothes should be stripped from her; dry, warm garments put on.

He gave one anxious look at the beloved face which was so flushed, so pitiful; then rushed out of the bungalow to the servants' compound. He found Twopence and roused him from his sleep.

"Go up to Bwana Clive Derrell," he said. "Tell him missis ill — must have Sannie at once...." (Sannie was Ross's young Boer maid who slept at Swallow Dip.)

Twopence hastened off on his mission and Bill returned to Ross who was still sobbing and muttering — calling for Clive.

Bill sat down beside her and put a handkerchief, which he had wrung in cold water, on her burning forehead.

"Oh, my darling, my darling. God grant this is not going to kill you!" he thought.

She stretched out her arms, turning her fever-glazed eyes on him.

"Clive — come to me," she moaned.

He put an arm about her shoulders.

"Yes, yes, I'm here, Ross," he said. "Hush, darling—I'm here."

She hesitated, then gave a deep sigh and leaned her head on his breast.

"Is it you, Clive—really?"

"Yes, yes, my dearest."

"Oh, Clive," she said. "What a long time you have been coming!"

"I am here now," Bill said deliberately. "Go to sleep, sweetheart—don't worry any more."

Heaven alone knew what it cost him to impersonate Clive; to feel Ross's beloved head resting on his breast, her hands clinging about his neck.

It was the greatest sacrifice he had ever made. He made it gladly, shutting out selfish desire. He wanted only to soothe her and save her from death—or madness, which was worse than death!

He rocked her in his arms as though she were a baby.

"There, there, my darling—hush—hush!" he murmured. "Go to sleep."

"Clive," she whispered, "you do love me still—don't you?"

"I worship you, Ross."

A look of relief crossed her flushed face.

"Tell me it's all been a nightmare," she sighed. "You don't love Valmy. You love me, Clive?"

"Yes, yes, darling, I love you," said Bill.

She was still semi-conscious, but his words appeared to penetrate through the mists in her brain. She had forgotten Bill ... she clung to this man, believing him to be her husband.

"Kiss me," she whispered. "Kiss me, my dearest."

A wave of colour burnt Bill's face a dusky red. He had never kissed her ... never touched those generous lips with his through all the years that he had known and loved her. It would be bitter-sweet to kiss them now—for the first time—and know that she imagined in her delirium that he was Clive! So often in the past he had dreamed of holding Ross to his heart—of kissing her. Little had he thought that their first embrace would be such a one as this!

But obedient to her pitiful request, he bent his head and laid his lips on her fevered mouth. His strong body shook. He closed his eyes.

Ross sighed.

"How cool your lips are, darling!" she said drowsily. "Kiss

me again. It's so long since you really kissed me, Clive — *really* — like you used to —"

Bill's face burned again. He stroked her hair with trembling fingers.

"Go to sleep — try to rest, my dear," he said.

But she clung to him with her hot hands.

"Clive — show me that you love me — kiss me like you used to — like a lover!" she begged, half-sobbing.

He bit his lip till the blood came. His heart pounded and his whole body tingled with a mingling of rapture and bitterness as he felt her body straining against him.

"Ross, Ross — if only you knew!" he muttered.

"You won't kiss me — you won't be my lover again, Clive?" came the pitiful, disappointed voice.

Bill drew a short sharp breath. He could bear no more. He bent over her, holding her passionately against him. God knew he worshipped her; that more than anything on earth he wanted to kiss her — to be her lover. He had never held another woman in his arms; never unleashed the natural passion of his strong, ardent manhood, because of the love he had borne her, Ross, all these years.

His lips met hers — clung to them in a fierce kiss that seemed to unite them in one flame. Into it Bill poured all the love, all the longing of years. Closer and closer his lips pressed her mouth, and she yielded to the kiss with a responsive passion that agonised even while it thrilled him. He knew she was not responsible for her actions; and that this moment of rapture was stolen — and would, perhaps, never come again.

At last he raised his head.

"My darling, you must rest now and keep quiet."

She drew a deep sigh and her head fell back on the cushions. That kiss seemed to have satisfied her; given her a strange sense of peace, of security at last.

"Now — I know — that you — love me still, Clive," she whispered and smiled up at Bill — a divinely happy smile that wrenched his heart in two.

She closed her eyes and lay very still. She appeared to be asleep. The man who loved her so madly and had tasted such a bitter-sweet draught from her lips, stood up and wiped his wet forehead.

"My poor darling — my poor, poor Ross!" he whispered.

In the morning she would wake to sanity; to consciousness of Clive's perfidy; to the cruel realisation that he did not love her; had not kissed her. Perhaps she would not remember anything of that passionate embrace. But at least it had saved her. Her pulse was more normal; her breathing more regular. When Sannie, the little Boer maid, appeared with Twopence — carrying a bundle of her mistress's clothes, in answer to Bwana McCrayle's summons, Ross was sound asleep.

Dawn broke over the veldt — over Bill McCrayle's creeper-clad bungalow — wherein Ross still lay sleeping.

Bill had not been to bed; had not left Ross's side. All through the cold, dark hours of the early morning he had sat beside her, watching her, his arms folded on his chest, his eyes troubled and strained.

Sannie, a good little maid whom Ross had trained herself, had performed her duties as a nurse splendidly. While Bill went out to fetch more wood for the fire, Sannie had managed to take off Ross's damp clothes without waking her, and slip a warm nightgown and fur-lined dressing-gown over the beautiful body.

Now the sun was rising, and the fire went out. In an hour or two it would be much too hot in here. Sannie had taken Bill's place at the side of the couch; her big, brown eyes fixed on her beloved mistress with anxious devotion.

Bill stood in the doorway, letting the cool dawn-wind blow against his face. Quietly he contemplated the beauty of the Rhodesian dawn. The country was bathed in a soft, pearly mist — the air was fresh and invigorating. The distant kopjes were painted with exquisite colours by the first amber beams of the rising sun.

Turning from the door, he tiptoed to the couch and looked down at Ross. He sighed as he saw the contentment of her expression. It seemed a tragedy that she must awake to the pain and trouble of reality; that she could not go on peacefully sleeping.

He told Sannie to prepare breakfast. He would sit beside Ross until she awakened. The little Boer maid moved noiselessly away, and Bill sat down in the chair she had just vacated.

It was not long before Ross's eyes opened. She looked straight up into Bill's face. He saw that she was conscious now. The fever had gone. She was quite white under her tan; and her eyes were very dark.

All too soon the happy expression gave place to a bewildered one.

"Bill!" she whispered.

"Yes, Ross," he said quietly. "I'm here." She drew a breath. "What's—happened, Bill? What time is it? Where—am I?"

"You are still in my place, Ross, and it's breakfast-time. Sannie's next door, cooking. I sent Twopence up to the bungalow for her, last night. You have had fever dear—been ill."

She kept her eyes fixed on him, watching him gravely while he spoke. Then suddenly her brow contracted.

"I remember now!" she whispered.

Bill bit his lip.

"Yes, dear."

"About Clive—last night—everything. You fought, He went home. I must have fainted after that."

"You did," nodded Bill. "And I brought you in here again. Sannie and I have nursed you between us, Ross."

Two big tears gathered in her eyes, trembled on her brown lashes.

"Thank you, Bill," she said with difficulty. "It was—good of you. I—don't feel ill now—only—very weak."

"That's the fever," he said. "A day's complete rest and you'll be yourself again, my dear."

"No—I shall never be myself again, Bill."

He knit his brows.

"Don't say that, Ross. You're not to say that. You will be yourself again ... of course you will. It's only a passing weakness."

"But what's happened between Clive and me ... that won't pass," she said brokenly. "Oh, Bill, Bill, I can't forget a single thing that happened last night, and a single thing that he said. I shall never be happy again."

"Hush, dear!" said Bill. He put one of his hands over her trembling fingers. "There's no wound that time cannot heal. God's merciful in that way."

"But Clive ... is my husband ... and used to be my lover," she said, covering her face with her free hand. "A woman can't forget that."

"You'll not forget, but you'll learn to think of Clive without the pain with which you think of him now, my dear."

"I don't know—I don't know!" she cried. "I don't feel that I shall ever be able to think of him without this agony ... this awful feeling of humiliation. It *is* humiliating, Bill, to be ... deserted for a slip of a girl like my cousin Valmy."

"Poor Ross," said Bill. "Poor Ross. It's damnable. But it's got to be faced. You know you can't go back to Clive now."

She lay back on the cushions, white and exhausted. Her eyes were ringed with dark shadows.

"Don't talk any more about things. Try to rest, dear," he said. "You had a rotten night—a very nasty attack of fever and it's sapped your vitality."

"Yes," she said dully. "I know. Was ... was I delirious, Bill?"

"Yes," he said.

"What did I say or do?"

"Nothing, dear ... don't worry."

But his honest face flushed from chin to brow. He could not forget what she had said and done. The bitter-sweet memory of her kisses remained with him, filling him with longing to drink of that cup again.

"Try to rest, Ross," he repeated gently.

"How can I?" she said, swallowing a sob— "I've failed with Clive. But I haven't seen—my cousin yet."

"Valmy?" He uttered the name in a tone of contempt. "What good can you do seeing her? She's a little rotter, Ross."

"She's very young, and I brought her out here," said Ross slowly. "I mustn't forget that I introduced her to—my husband. She hasn't played the game, but he's much older and should know better. She was, apparently, mad enough to give herself to him, but oh, Bill ... it's awful to think that she can remain with him in that bungalow ... after I've gone. I must see Valmy ... make her see things from my point of view ... try to induce her to go away."

Bill bit his lip and looked from Ross out of the window at the distant kopjes on the veldt which were bathed in the hot, golden sunlight.

"Perhaps you're right, Ross. But you may only lay yourself open to—fresh insult."

"I think I can bear anything now. I have borne so much," she said. "I have no more illusions, Bill."

CHAPTER XV

IN Ross's beautiful luxurious bungalow breakfast was also in preparation. The cook, the house-boy, the smartly-uniformed servants who had been imported from Durban at the time of the Derrells' wedding, were all chattering like a crowd of women. It was common talk that 'Missis' had left the bungalow and was with Bwana Bill McCrayle; also that Miss Page was 'looking after' the Bwana here, who was sick. Nobody knew what was the matter with him, but Miss Page had told one of the boys she would take his breakfast to him on a tray.

Valmy was up early, looking fresh as a flower.

Clive had returned to her in the early hours of the morning a battered and beaten man; but that had not altered her regard for him. The sight of his disfigured face and bleeding mouth filled her with a peculiar, primitive pleasure. It was nice to think that a man had fought for her. She had been told by Clive that he had fought Bill McCrayle because Bill had insulted her. She did not know just why he had received that cut on the lip and the purple bruises on the jaw.

She entered Clive's bedroom and drew the blind a little higher, so that a shaft of sunlight spilled on to the floor and lifted some of the shadows. Turning to the bed, she sat down on the edge of it and looked with smiling, sympathetic eyes at the man who lay there.

Clive was not a lovely sight, seen thus in the early morning sunlight, with his handsome face bruised and cut; his lower lip slightly swollen; one eye ringed about with purple. He wore a sullen, bad-tempered expression, too, which did not improve him. Valmy, however, was impervious to this alteration in his appearance which she knew was only temporary. Within a few days he would be her spruce, smiling, handsome Clive again. And even now he was her lover, for he twisted his lips into a smile as he looked up at her.

"Well, darling?" he murmured.

"Are you feeling better, sweetheart?" she said. "Pluto will be bringing your tray to the door soon—a nice tempting breakfast—scrambled eggs."

"I'm not hungry," said Clive, his smile vanishing, his gloomy, sulky look returning. "I slept damn badly and my lip is infernally sore."

"Poor old boy! Never mind. Bill McCrayle is a great hulking brute. I'd like to scratch his eyes out for daring to hurt you so."

The memory of "the great hulking brute" made Clive flush darkly. He sucked in his breath with a whistling sound.

"Next time I meet that fellow I'll brain him. He took me unawares last night, Valmy."

"Of course," murmured the girl in a sympathetic voice. "He's a great coward. I always loathed him, and I can't see what Ross finds to like in him."

"Come and kiss me, little witch," he muttered. "Tell me you love me still."

She leaned toward him.

"You know I do, Clive."

"Even with a black eye and a split lip?" he said with a short laugh. "That's a test for your love."

"Nonsense!" she laughed. "You'll soon look yourself again."

She lay against him quietly and he held her close, shutting his eyes.

There came a tap on the door.

Valmy called to the servant:

"Is that the Bwana's breakfast, Pluto?"

"No, Miss. Him not ready yet. But Missis, she on veranda and asking for you," the man called back.

"Missis!" repeated Valmy sharply. "Ross . . ."

"Ross here?" muttered Clive. "Good lord! What has she come for? She might have had the decency to keep away after last night!"

"I wonder why she's come," whispered Valmy. "She's asking for me, Clive. Shall I go – or not?"

"What's the use of your going, my dear?" protested Clive.

"No use. But still —"

Valmy bit her lips and walked to the window. She peered cautiously out; saw Ross standing on the veranda. There was something tragic in Ross's figure; shoulders drooping, as though with fatigue. She was leaning against one of the posts, and her face was hidden. Poor Ross, who had been so proud – so devoted to her husband and her home. Today, she came here in anguish and humiliation; the discarded wife, to plead with her husband's lover!

Valmy walked out of the room through the hall and on to the sunlit veranda. Boldly she approached the cousin whose goodness and generosity she had repaid with base treachery.

"Well, Ross!" she said.

At the sound of the girl's defiant voice, Ross raised her head — looked at her.

"I scarcely know what to say to you, Valmy," she began.

Valmy dropped her lashes. She could not stand the gaze of those clear, accusing eyes. She thought Ross looked desperately ill — changed — in one short night. Hers was the face of a woman who has received a great shock — suffered agony.

Bill had not wanted Ross to come to the bungalow. To begin with, he had not thought her well enough. But she had insisted upon getting up and coming. Valmy noticed that she had on the flimsy dinner-frock she had worn when she had run away from the bungalow; and a silk scarf around her shoulders. In spite of the hot morning sun, she was shivering.

"You're ill, Ross," Valmy said, stammering. "Would — would you like to sit down?"

"No, thank you," said Ross. "And I'm not going to stay here — unless you decide to leave."

"I suppose that's what you've come to say?"

"Yes," said Ross. "I've come to ask you to go away from my home — from Rhodesia — at once."

Valmy sucked in her lips. Her face grew crimson.

"Oh!" was all she said in reply.

Ross gripped the post against which she leaned.

"Valmy you must realise that it's your duty to go!" she said with sudden passion. "You have no right to remain here, just because Clive has lost his head and wants you to. Have you no decent feeling — no honour? Do you wish to be responsible for the ruination of my home and happiness! Do you realise that you're not only stealing my husband from me, but driving me from my home?"

"What's the use —" began Valmy.

"One moment," said Ross. "There is something more I want to say. You imagine I've come to plead with you because I want Clive back, don't you?"

"I dare say," muttered the girl.

"You're wrong," said Ross, closing her tired eyes. "I'm thinking of you, Valmy. You're my cousin. You're motherless, fatherless; you've been very spoiled — allowed to grow up without good counsel. Wicked as you've been over this affair, I'm sorry for you, because I think that one day you'll wake up and regret this terribly."

"I shall not. Clive loves me as much as I love him!" declared Valmy.

"He does now . . ." Ross winced. "But supposing he gets tired? He loved me once . . . he grew sick of me. I know him better than you do, Valmy. What will you do if he treats you as he has treated me—deserts you for another woman?"

Valmy tilted her head.

"He won't do that. I'm not afraid."

"Oh, my God!" said Ross, covering her face with her hands. "What madness! How can you think that a man who has treated his wife so badly will be faithful to his —" she broke off. "It's all too terrible. But I beg you to think well before you decide to remain with Clive."

Valmy was breathing very quickly. Her eyes were hard. She had been touched by Ross's appearance and first words of pleading; but this intimation that Clive would grow sick of her in time infuriated her. She took it in the light of a challenge.

"You only talk like this because you're piqued!" she flung at Ross.

The insult made Ross wince. A feeling of futility came over her.

"Very well, Valmy," she said. "We'll say no more. I've failed. Bill was right. I ought never to have come and laid myself open to—fresh insult. Remember always that I warned you . . . not from pique"—she shook her head, her lips twisted into a smile —"but from the desire to save you."

"I don't want to be saved!" muttered Valmy. "And, anyhow, what about you and Bill McCrayle?"

"Ah!" said Ross, in a gentle, terrible voice. "If you have anything to say about that—say it to—Bill McCrayle. Goodbye."

She turned and walked down the steps of the veranda into the garden. She was shaking from head to foot, but she held her head erect. She was not going to show Valmy how mortally she was wounded.

Valmy stared after her, conscious of a queer, frightened feeling.

"Ross!" she called. "Ross! . . . what—what about your . . . your clothes . . . if you're going away . . . ?"

Ross halted as she heard the stammering voice. She looked back at Valmy.

"I shall be obliged if you'll see that my belongings are packed and ready for me—when I send for them," she said.

Valmy set her teeth. Turning, she walked into the bungalow to find Clive up and dressed, in the drawing-room. His handsome face was still bruised and distorted from last night's affair, but he looked fresher, more attractive than he had looked in bed.

"Well, darling?" he said. "What's happened? What did she say?"

To his surprise, Valmy flung herself into his arms and burst into tears. He held her tightly, stroking her dark, close-cropped head.

"Why, Valmy, sweetheart, what's the matter? Don't cry. What's Ross said to upset you so? I wish I hadn't let you go to her!"

"I hate her—I hate her! I'm not sorry for her now!" said Valmy, sobbing passionately.

"What did she say?"

"That I'd regret this all my life ... that you'd grow as sick of me as you have grown of her. You won't, will you, Clive? Say you won't!"

He pressed her against him, his cheeks reddening slowly.

"Of course I won't. What rot! She only said it from pique."

"I told her that. But she tried to make out she wanted to save me," said Valmy, in a sobbing voice. "She said I couldn't expect you to be faithful to me."

"How rotten of her! Of course it was pique—she needn't have insulted you!" muttered Clive.

"She said she didn't want you back, anyhow," said Valmy. "She only came because she wanted to save me ... but that's what she said. I believe she only came to insult me."

"Don't think about it," he said.

"You won't grow sick of me, will you?" she asked, twining her arms around his neck.

"Never. You're so different from Ross."

"And am I going to stay here with you always?"

"Yes. There's no reason why you shouldn't. Ross won't dare try to turn me out of here and take the ranch ... she knows I'll bring her into court with Bill McCrayle, if she does."

Valmy's tears had dried like magic.

"You and I—alone—together. Oh, Clive!"

Their lips clung in a mad, breathless kiss.

Ross reached the bottom of the garden. For a moment she stood motionless—one hand to her throbbing head—one to her heart. Then she nodded to herself once or twice as though making up her mind about something.

"I can't stay here—I mustn't stay with Bill," she said, half aloud. "I must go away—right away—from them all!"

She felt ill, broken, sick of struggling. She would get away—to peace—somewhere over the sunlit veldt there, where the blue ridge of hills lay so lovely, so misty in the distance; where the tall kopjes sparkled in the hot Rhodesian sunlight with a hundred varying colours.

"I must run away—right away," she repeated to herself.

One of the 'boys' from the servants' compound came past her, leading a horse by the bridle. Ross looked at him dazedly—then detained him.

"Where are you taking that horse, Chita?"

"Bwana, missis," the 'boy' grinned in reply.

"Don't do that. Keep here—for me," she said. "No—wait. I will hold the horse. You go to the bungalow—ask Miss—Miss Page to give you a bag with my riding clothes and boots—my brush and comb—and things for the night. Then come back with it to me, here. You understand?"

"Yes, missis," he nodded, still grinning.

About an hour later, Bill McCrayle walked into the Derrells' garden, his lips grimly set. He had come to find Ross—Ross had not returned to the bungalow, and he feared some harm might have come to her.

He chanced to meet the same 'boy' who had handed over the horse to Ross. Bill detained him.

'Chita, have you seen Missis?"

"Yes, Bwana . . . she gone out over veldt . . ." the boy pointed to the distance, showing his white, gleaming teeth.

"Gone out there!" said Bill sharply. "Who with?"

"Alone. She make me get her horse and clo's—I bring him in bag," grinned Chita. "Missis take him and ride away all alone. She say she not coming back."

Bill uttered an exclamation. He stared at the sunlit veldt. He could guess what had happened.

"My God!" he said to himself. "I understand. She's failed with Valmy and she's run away."

Run away—alone—ill—in a desperate state of mind. Bill turned and began to hurry back to his bungalow. He was going to get his own horse. If Ross was riding away, out there into the wilds – he would ride and follow. He would protect her. Nothing on earth would prevent him from following and making sure that no harm came to her. He only prayed as he ran that he was not too late.

By midday Ross had ridden deep into the heart of the wilderness, away from the ranch; from the Assistant-Administrator's bungalow – from all the old familiar scenes and the people who had known her.

The heat was intense – Ross was far from strong. But she seemed unconscious of physical discomforts. Her mount carried her splendidly – not flagging until she had ridden many miles. She had attached the canvas bag containing her 'kit' to the saddle. She rode astride, having changed her frock for her riding-suit, once she had reached the solitary spaces where she knew she would find privacy.

Her face was white under its tan – her lips set. She stared before her at the distant ridge of mountains that were veiled in a haze of hot sunshine. A curious, blank expression lay in those warm, brown eyes. There was a dogged tilt to the brown head under the soft, felt hat. Ross had made up her mind to leave everything and everybody, and she was determined to carry on – no matter what happened.

She had asked Pluto to get her rifle and some ammunition for her. She had been cool and collected enough to appreciate the fact that it was necessary for her to go forth into the wilderness armed. But just where she was going and what she meant to do she did not know. Her brain was fogged. She was so dazed by suffering, by the misery that Clive had heaped upon her, she could not look clearly into the future. She did not even know where she meant to sleep tonight. It might be rolled up in a blanket in the shadow of a kopje, with a fire beside her. Or she might run across some Colonist's bungalow. She neither knew nor cared. She only wanted peace – and forgetfulness.

She rode on grimly; heedless of the fact that she was drenched in perspiration and that her whole body ached. Now and then she put up a hand to brush away the flies, or paused by some delightful, sparkling stream, to let her horse drink. Then she went on again. The sun grew hotter; the trees scarcer. There was a little shade now. The path which Ross rode became tortuous and covered with pieces of granite.

At last she took pity on her horse. His flanks were quivering and streaming with moisture. Ross slid from the saddle. She sat down on a huge boulder by a wonderful kopje covered with brilliant, vari-coloured lichen. Taking off her hat, she fanned her face with it and closed her tired eyes a moment.

All round her was vast silence and solitude. Not a living being or human dwelling or even a native kraal, in sight. Opening her eyes, she saw a bright green lizard on the ground near her. She put out a hand and touched it. The little thing scuttled away and disappeared into a stunted shrub. Ross sighed and let her head fall on her hands in a weary way.

She had come out here into the wilderness on the spur of the moment — a wild, desperate impulse. But where was this journey to end? She had rushed away so hurriedly, she had forgotten to bring food. It was not the first time she had trekked over the veldt. Years ago, before she had married Clive, she had trekked with her beloved father right down as far as Karonga. But they had had proper camping kit with them, half a dozen 'boys', and mules.

"I suppose I've been a fool to come like this," Ross whispered to herself. "I shall lose myself — without food — and perhaps I shall die."

She laughed to herself; a queer, broken little laugh that was lost in the vast silence. The memory of Clive and Valmy was blotted out. Suddenly she thought of Bill. How worried, how frantic he would be when he found that she had run away.

"Poor Bill," she thought, "Poor, faithful Bill!"

She rose and mounted her horse again. It was no use sitting here and brooding. She had better go on . . . go on . . . until she could go no farther.

Another hour of hard riding, and Ross reached a stage of exhaustion. It was the hottest time of the day. The sun beat mercilessly from an intensely blue sky. She managed to lead the tired, sweating horse to a few trees; tied him to one of them, then sank down on the ground.

She was half blind and sick with fatigue.

The veldt seemed to spin round her; become black. She shut her eyes and drifted into unconsciousness. She had come to the end of her tether now.

So Bill McCrayle found her.

It had been hard riding for him in the heat of the noontide, and the most distractingly anxious journey of his life. He was agonised by the fear that he might miss Ross and never find her. But fortunately he took the same track that she had taken. And he was not alone. Twopence — the faithful and devoted 'boy' — came with him, walking stolidly along, leading a mule laden with packages. Bill had come out into the wilderness in a hurry, but not without the camp-kit which he thought necessary. He guessed that poor Ross had rushed off with inadequate kit, and that she would need food and attention. He had brought plentiful rations and cooking utensils. If Ross had made up her mind to trek into the wilderness, he would trek with her. She must have somebody to look after her.

He had just begun to despair of tracing her, when he came upon that clump of trees, and the horse tied up to one of them. And then he saw Ross, lying on the ground, with her eyes closed, her head resting on her arm.

For one awful moment he feared she was dead.

He slid from his saddle and rushed up to the still figure and knelt beside it. He gathered her into his arms and pressed her to his breast.

"Ross," he said. "Oh, Ross, Ross, my dear!"

She stirred and her brown lashes lifted. Her eyes looked up into his. His heart gave a great leap of gladness.

"Oh, Ross!" he said. "I thought you were dead! My dear, my poor dear, you have ridden so far — it has been enough to kill you, in your condition. You were ill when you left Swallow Dip."

She put a hand up to her head. She had come out of that long faint, but she was still dazed and ill.

"Bill," she said. "You — you've followed me —"

"Yes, and thank God I've found you," he said. "You would surely have come to harm if you had been left alone, my poor darling."

She gave a long sigh and shut her eyes again.

"Why did you come?" she whispered. "Why didn't you let me die? I'm so — tired of fighting."

"You shan't fight any more," he said, his eyes fierce; his arms holding her closely, strongly. "I am going to fight for you, Ross."

She did not answer him but lay limp and still in his arms. He laid her gently back on the ground, then beckoned to Twopence who stood at a respectful distance.

"Up with the tent — quickly," he commanded.

"Yes, *Inkaas*," said the boy.

The tent was erected in the shade of the trees. The camp-bed was put up and within a few minutes Ross was lying on it, covered with a light rug, and Bill was sitting beside her, fanning the flies away from her face ... such a pinched, weary face ... it made his heart ache to look at it.

Twopence lit a fire and soon had some milk warmed and ready for the beloved 'missis'. Bill added a dash of brandy to the milk and supporting Ross in his arms, made her drink it all. She revived quickly after this drink, and lay on the bed quite conscious. She even managed to smile her gratitude. Bill sat beside her. He held one of her hands.

"You're better now, dear?"

"Much better, Bill, thank you."

"It was terribly wrong of you to run away like that from me, Ross."

She moved her head restlessly on the pillow.

"What could I do, Bill? I failed—with Valmy. My heart is absolutely broken—I felt I couldn't bear it any more. I just ran away."

"And if anything had happened to you, Ross, it would have broken my heart," he said, unsteadily.

Her brows contracted. Her fingers pressed his weakly.

"Dear old Bill!"

"Oh, Ross, you don't know how I worship you!" he broke out. "The thought of you alone, unprotected on the veldt, was frightful to me."

"I'm glad you found me," she said.

The tears trickled down her cheeks. It distressed him to see how weak she was; how unlike the brave, spirited Ross he had known in former days. Tenderly he drew the rug over her shoulders.

"Go to sleep, my dear," he said. "I'm not going to let you talk now. Later—when the sun goes down—you will feel better."

"Dear Bill," she said again.

She fell asleep, her hand fast clasped in his.

CHAPTER XVI

When Ross woke from that long, health-giving sleep, she felt a different woman. A little more milk and brandy and by sundown she was almost herself again; there was more colour in her cheeks; more light in her eyes.

She sat up in bed, watching the gorgeous sunset sky. Bill had fixed back the flap in the tent. The air was cooler. He, himself, had slept and felt refreshed. He sat on the floor, by the bed and looked out at the veldt.

"Now," he said, "now we must talk this out, Ross."

"Talk — what out?"

"This," he said, waving a hand round the tent. "You've come out here, trekking into the wilderness, Ross, and I've followed. We're together, alone. You have got to decide, Ross, whether I am to take you back to the ranch — or whether you'll stay out here in the wilderness — with me!"

A warm wave of colour spread over Ross's cheeks. She gripped the rug that lay lightly across her knees and held it convulsively.

"Oh, Bill — my dear!"

"You ran away — you intended staying away, I know," he went on. "You didn't want one of these hateful divorce cases — to have your name dragged through the mud just because Clive chose to bring a counter-action — so you ran away — meaning to find — what? Death, probably, if I hadn't followed you."

"Yes — that is true, Bill," she admitted.

"But now I have found you, I don't want to let you go, dearest," he said. He turned to her and took both her hands in his. "I love you — I've loved you for years. Let me look after you and help you to find happiness. Let's make a new home together — a little farm. We both love Rhodesia; we both love the lonely, beautiful places on the veldt. Listen, dearest — I'll take care of you, but ask only for your friendship, not your love — now. In time you may be able to forget Clive completely and turn to me. I am content to wait — to ask you just to come with me as a friend — until you can give me your love."

Ross's pale face flushed a deeper pink. She put out a hand and laid it on his shoulder, looked deeply into his earnest eyes.

"My dear, how wonderful you are!" she said. "Not many men would be content — with friendship. Besides, is it possible? If we go trekking together, alone and —"

"It's quite possible if a man makes up his mind to keep his emotions under control," broke in Bill. "You know me, Ross. You know if I give you my word to be only your friend until you give me permission to be — your lover —" his voice shook a little. "I'll keep it."

"I would trust you. But it isn't fair to you, and I can't — *can't* love you — like that, Bill, old boy."

"No, dearest — I know. I understand. Love and passion must be repulsive to you."

"I am so broken, so lost without my husband, my faith, my ideals," she said pitifully. "Everything has been taken from me except your loyal friendship."

"A poor substitute for the rest, perhaps," said Bill. "But all I have to offer. Still I believe if you come with me you'll find peace eventually, Ross."

She looked past him at the distant mountains. They were exquisite — scarlet, gold, sapphire in the African sunset. Her heart ached. She was still quivering from the sharpness of the blow that Clive had dealt her. Yet she found it difficult to turn down this wonderful friendship which Bill offered. She knew so well that she could trust him. It would be an ideal existence — to trek with him until they found some perfect spot where they would make a home; a little ranch; work together; bury the past utterly — and begin life again.

Who knew but one day she might grow to care for Bill in the way he cared for her? Who could tell? Love begets love — and this love of his for her was fine, beautiful beyond compare.

She turned to him suddenly — tears magnifying her eyes.

"I'll stay with you, Bill," she said. "I can't go back — to my home. It isn't my home any more. Make a new one — for me, Bill. I'll stay with you, trust you, work with you. And if you'll be content with friendship for awhile, one day I may be able to offer you more."

His face flushed, his eyes grew bright. He held both her hands in a grip that made her wince.

"Oh, Ross!" he said huskily. "Ross!"

She tried to smile through the tears.

"I think it'll be rather lovely—building up a little home somewhere in the wilderness," she whispered. "But it'll be hard work. And Bill, think of all the labours of years you've spent on our old ranch. Won't you resent giving that up—having to start again?"

"I shall resent and regret nothing," he said in a passionate voice. "While your father was alive I loved working on that ranch, Ross, but honestly once Clive became the head, I hated it. I only stuck it because you were there, too."

"Poor old Bill!"

"I'm not to be pitied," he said, throwing back his head. "I'm the happiest man on God's earth this moment. To have you to take care of, and work for, has always been the ambition of my life, Ross. Beginning again is nothing. I shall glory in it."

She caught her breath. Such love as this was too overwhelming. She could not check the tears that poured down her cheeks. And she could not check that bitter, inner regret that Clive, her husband had not loved her like this. But the mere thought of Clive seemed disloyalty to Bill, now. She had burnt her boats. She had decided to leave her old home and her husband ... to link her fate with Bill's. She must think only of him.

"My dear," she said, drawing one of her hands from his so that she might brush away her tears. "It all sounds ideally peaceful. And it's all rather astonishing, too. Who'd have dreamed that I should ever come to such a decision?"

"Not I," he said. "I never dared hope you'd throw in your lot with mine, my dear. And don't let the right or wrong of it worry your sweet head. You've been driven to it. You've not deserted Clive. He has deserted you."

"Yes," she said in a low tone. "I don't think I have much to reproach myself for, Bill. I gave Clive his chance."

A moment's silence. Then Bill said:

"We'll stay here tonight, Ross. I want you to rest thoroughly. Then tomorrow, while it is still cool, let's ride on. We have Twopence to look after us. He's a good little cuss."

"I'm glad he came," said Ross.

"We'll move on north," said Bill. "There are some settlers farther on, farming. I have come across them before. We may find a small cattle ranch no longer wanted—take it between us."

"I still have my banking account left to me," said Ross, with a ghost of a smile. "I can send to Durban for some money, Bill. We can have it wired to Livingstone and fetch it there."

"Shall we trek towards the Zambesi?" suggested Bill. "Settle near the river, Ross?"

"It would be lovely," she said. "I do love the old Falls."

"Then we'll go that way—north-west," said Bill.

He spoke excitedly. He was elated. At last Ross was going to make his dreams come true. She was going to trek beside him; she would be his to protect, to work for through the golden days ... the starlit evenings and one day ... his pulses thrilled and leaped as he looked at her; one day, perhaps, she would turn wholly to him and give him her love as well as her friendship.

He could never forget that one, exquisite, stolen moment when she had rested in his arms and her lips had clung to his. Then, she had been delirious. She did not know she had ever kissed him. But one day she would know ... and she would kiss him again.

He slid on one knee by the bed and bent his lips to her hand.

"Ross," he said huskily. "You realise, don't you, dear, that there'll be no turning back, once we go on?"

"Yes, I realise that, Bill," she said steadily.

"You may—never be free—never be able to marry me," he said with difficulty. "But—will you mind that?"

"No," she said. "I don't think I shall mind. Once upon a time it would have all seemed terrible and unmoral. But now I've changed—curiously. I don't think I shall be doing wrong to come with you—it seems perfectly natural to do so."

"Thank you," he said. Again his lips touched her hand. "God forgive me if ever I let you regret the step you've taken, my dear."

The glorious lights of sunset, playing over the hills and kopjes, faded gradually into a deep blue mist of night. Darkness came ... and the moon rose round and shining, flooding the veldt with silver light.

In the little tent, Bill still sat beside Ross, smoking his pipe, talking, planning for the future. Outside Twopence had lit a fire, for it was swiftly growing cold.

Ross had been silent for a long while. Through the aperture in the tent she watched the stars appearing one after the other in the sky, gleaming down at her like little winking eyes. She felt curiously serene. She had passed through a terrible storm, but she felt as though Bill had steered her ship into harbour — the harbour of his wonderful love.

She drew a long sigh and looked at him. The strong profile; the fine, massive head gave her a great sensation of power, of security.

"Bill," she said. "You've been marvellous to me."

He looked at her with a smile, removing his pipe from his mouth.

"Oh, rubbish."

Her hand stole out and sought his. His strong fingers closed warmly about it.

For a moment silence reigned again. Then Bill rose to his feet and put his pipe in his pocket.

"You must go to sleep now, Ross," he said. "Don't forget that you've got to get quite well and strong before you start out on this long trek with me."

"I shall be perfectly well in the morning," she said, smiling up at him. "Good night, dear Bill, and — God bless you."

"Bless you, my dear," he said huskily.

"Bill, wait — where are you going to — to sleep?"

"That's all right, dear," he said, smiling. "I've got two jolly good blankets to roll up in, by the fire."

"I've taken the tent," she said, distressed.

"I brought it for you, my dear. Don't worry two seconds about me. I shall be warm as toast by the fire. Sleep well. I'll bring you some coffee at dawn, and then if you're feeling absolutely fit, we'll move on."

He walked out of the tent and fastened the flap, shutting out the cold night-wind. Ross turned over on the camp-bed and closed her eyes. She did not sleep for a long while. Her brain was a jumble of thought. But she tried not to let her mind dwell on the husband who had treated her so abominably, or on Valmy, her cousin, who had stolen him from her. She tried hard to think only of Bill who had been so good to her, and who was content to stand beside her, patiently, loyally, and wait until she chose to give him the love for which he longed.

Finally — worn out with thinking — she slept.

Previously, that afternoon, Clive Derrell had walked down to Bill McCrayle's bungalow meaning to find out definitely what his wife intended to do.

"We can't go on playing the fool — me rushing down there

and she rushing up here—every day," he had said to Valmy, during luncheon. "We'd better thresh the thing out properly."

To his surprise he found Bill's shanty deserted, except for Sannie, Ross's little Boer maid who was sitting on the stoep, nursing her head on her knees, weeping bitterly.

"What are you crying for?" Clive asked her in a sharp voice. "Where's Missis—where's Mr. Bill?"

"Gone," said Sannie, timidly, lifting her brown, tear-streaked face. "Mr. Bill, he fetch his horse and mule and pack up tent and food and go out on to the veldt."

"With Missis?" Clive's heart began to beat very hard and jerkily.

"Yes, to follow Missis. She went first."

Clive's lips twisted into an ugly line. He stood there in the hot sunlight, staring down at Sannie's miserable little face, with narrowed eyes. So Ross and Bill had gone—out on to the veldt. In other words, they had 'bolted'—together. Valmy's prognostication had been correct. She had said in the beginning that if Ross were driven hard enough, she'd run away with Bill.

And now that Ross had done it, Clive was not so certain that he liked it. He took it for granted that Ross and Bill were lovers; that as lovers they had gone away together. They had taken one tent; two horses; a mule; Twopence the house-boy, and rations. Obviously they meant to travel far; never to come back.

Clive left Sannie weeping there alone, and walked back to the bungalow, his handsome face distorted. Valmy met him in the hall. Her beautiful face was pale; her eyes shadowed. She looked languid, as though the intense heat of the midday affected her.

"Well?" she greeted Clive.

"They've bolted," he said.

"Bolted?" she echoed.

"Yes, done a bunk out on to the veldt," he said, with a short laugh. He flung himself into a chair, tapped his boots with the riding-crop he carried. "I can't say I expected to find that."

Valmy's cheeks coloured. She bit her lower lip, then looked out of the window at the distant kopjes, and smiled.

"Ah! Well—I'm not surprised," she said. "And I'm jolly pleased."

"H'm," said Clive.

Her green eyes widened as they turned to him.

"Aren't you pleased?" she asked in an astonished voice.

"Why should I be? Is a man usually pleased when his wife runs away with some fellow?"

Valmy's expression was now one of almost ludicrous amazement. The inconsistency of Clive's remark following upon his recent behaviour to Ross, was beyond her comprehension.

"Well!" at length she gasped. "Men say women are contrary creatures, but you're pretty contrary, Clive, if that's how you feel! You said you didn't want Ross any more – that you only wanted me, and now you've got me, and Ross has gone, you – you don't like it!"

He flushed and averted his eyes.

"Oh, rot! I don't say I don't like having you. You know I do. But I'm not particularly pleased at the thought of Ross eloping with that damned brute, McCrayle."

"Are you afraid he won't be good to her?" sneered Valmy.

Clive rose and began to pace up and down the hall.

"I dare say he'll be good to her," he said. "But I'd rather Ross had gone away alone – to Durban or somewhere. What does she want to trek out on the the veldt with McCrayle for?"

"Oh, my dear Clive, you're really a dog-in-the-manger," said Valmy, angrily. "You don't want Ross yourself, but you don't want anyone else to have her."

"Maybe you're right," said Clive, with a short laugh. "Men are like that."

Valmy tapped one small foot on the floor. Her red lips were set; her eyes mutinous.

"Well, and what are you going to do? Follow your dear wife and save her from Bill McCrayle's clutches?"

"Damn it all, no!" said Clive, pausing before the window. He stared out with moody eyes. "I can't do that. They have gone. Let them go."

Valmy swallowed hard. Relief surged through her. For one desperate moment she had feared that Clive meant to rush after Ross and bring her back. Men were "like that", he had said. Well, men were funny creatures, she reflected, not knowing whether to laugh or cry. Clive apparently wanted what he couldn't get, and then when he'd got it, wanted more. That thought made Valmy blanch and quiver. Were Ross's words going to come true? Would she live to regret having given herself so completely to Clive?

She walked across the room to him – put an arm around his shoulders.

"Clive," she said, "what are you so upset for? This was only to be expected."

"Oh, yes," he mumbled, without moving.

"You—you can't, surely, mind that Ross has bolted with Bill McCrayle—so long as you have me . . . ?" She licked her dry lips as she spoke.

He did not answer for a moment. His restless eyes were staring out at the sunlit veldt. Somewhere out there, beyond the kopjes that were visible from this bungalow, Bill and Ross were riding together. Clive could not grow accustomed to the thought. For so many years he had regarded Ross as a loving, strictly virtuous wife. He had behaved like a brute and a beast and driven her from her home. He had tired of her caresses and turned to her cousin for passion, for sensation. Yet he could not resign himself to the idea of that virtuous young wife running away with another man. His face still smarted from the blows that Bill McCrayle had dealt him. He hated Bill with a deadlier hatred than he had thought it possible to conceive for any fellow creature. And it was with Bill that Ross was now trekking, farther and farther away from this ranch.

He would not have minded if Ross had decided to go away by herself, or to Elinor Feltham; any woman friend. But he did mind Ross going away with Bill. That was undeniable. Whether he was tired of her or not, he felt an insane desire to rush after her and fetch her back; lock her up somewhere; prevent Bill from getting her. The idea that Bill would have a right to all the intimacies that he, Clive had had; would hold Ross in his arms as a lover; affected him in an extraordinary way.

He turned away from the window, smothering an ugly word. He was at war with himself and the world in this moment. Even Valmy had no power to soothe him. Having behaved in a mad, brutal fashion he now began to wonder, at his leisure, why he had done it; at any rate, why he had allowed Ross to elope with Bill McCrayle. He had driven her to it; he knew in his heart of hearts he could not blame her. What was more, he had played for it, at Valmy's instigation. But now he had gained his ends he was dissatisfied and angry.

Dead Sea fruit! Yes, that was it. He had turned his wife out of her home and eaten of forbidden fruit. And he found the taste ashes in his mouth.

He flung himself back in the chair and put his head in his hands.

"My God!" he said savagely. "Ross—with McCrayle! I can't seem to get over that!"

Valmy felt suddenly cold in the heat of the day. Every drop of colour had left her cheeks. Her eyes blazed resentfully at her lover.

"You feel pretty badly about it, don't you?" she said in a trembling voice. "And you told me last night that you wanted nothing on earth but my love!"

He moved his head impatiently, without looking up at her.

"That's still true," he muttered. "But now Ross has gone with McCrayle, I'm not so sure I care about it—that's all. I tell you I'd rather she'd gone alone."

"Well, she's gone with Bill and there's an end to it," said Valmy in a loud, hysterical voice.

Clive hunched his shoulders and said nothing. After a moment Valmy came to his side—touched his head with her hand.

"Clive," she said, with a sob, "how can you be so beastly to me?"

Somehow her touch, her voice, irritated the man at this moment. He sprang up, shaking her off.

"Oh, let me alone," he said brutally. "A man isn't always ready for love and kisses, if a woman is. You've got to learn that if you don't want to make a fellow sick of you, Valmy!"

She fell back, scarlet, terrified by his sudden change of mood. Where was the adoring lover of last night? Had Ross's elopement made such a difference that he no longer wanted her?

He gave her no further chance to question him or plead with him then.

"Excuse me, if I leave you," he said shortly. "Now McCrayle's bolted, I shall have to manage the ranch myself. There'll be a lot of work to do. I'll be in later."

"Clive —" she began.

But he walked out of the hall. Valmy rushed to the window and saw him mount his horse and ride away towards the fields wherein the Kaffirs were at work.

Valmy's heart beat fast. Her eyes smarted with hot tears. She felt sick and frightened by Clive's treatment of her. Turning away from the window, she dropped into a chair and began to sob hysterically.

Deep down in her wayward, wicked heart, she realised that whatever happened in the future she had brought calamity upon herself. She had stolen Clive from Ross. She had been unscrupulous and immoral. It was only to be expected that since she had allowed Clive to make her his mistress, he would treat her as such. But it was a terrifying, humiliating thought, and she shrank from it.

"I won't let him make a light o' love of me," she sobbed to herself furiously. "I won't let him —"

But later, when she was calmer, she told herself that tears and reproaches would not be likely to win Clive back. He had got into a horrible mood because Ross had run away with McCrayle. Well – it was only natural. Now it was up to her to make him forget Ross and Bill and rest content with her.

Darkness had fallen when Clive Derrell returned to the bungalow. He remained out in the fields the whole afternoon, venting his spite on the unfortunate natives who were tilling the ground, and looking after the cattle. By the time he had finished swearing at them and having two of them thrashed for some trivial offence, his temper had improved. He waited until sundown – then rode home to Valmy.

The girl had been sitting on the veranda for hours, anxiously awaiting him. Through all her life she had never suffered such anxiety as she suffered that afternoon — alternating between the hope that he would come and the fear that he would not.

When she saw his familiar figure on his horse, her heart gave a great leap of gladness. She wanted to burst into tears, but dared not show him hysteria for she knew he had no patience with it. She set her lips in a smile and rose to meet him, trembling slightly. She had put on her prettiest afternoon dress; black lace with long light sleeves. It made her skin look milk-white.

"Hullo, Clive," she said. "Done some good work?"

"Oh, yes," he said. He mopped his hot face with a silk handkerchief. "Making the darned niggers work — curse them, they're lazy devils."

"Sit down, dear," she said. "I'll fetch you a whisky and soda."

Clive's hand suddenly clenched. Not so very long ago, when he had come home like this, Ross had been on the veranda to greet him – had smiled in her gentle, sweet way and suggested bringing him a drink. Comparisons are odious, and he did not particularly care about comparing Ross with Valmy. Better to cut out the thought of Ross. He had been trying all the afternoon not to think of her or Bill McCrayle.

He looked up at Valmy. She smiled, narrowing her wonderful eyes – a habit, when she looked at him. His pulses began to race. She was deuced attractive in that black frock, he thought, and she was his ... she belonged to him now ... they were quite alone.

"Come here, baby," he said in a husky voice.

It was the old lover's tone; the old pet-name. She thrilled and came to him swiftly, holding out her hands. He pulled her down on his knee.

"Sorry I was so rottenly bad-tempered at lunch-time," he said. "But it kind of made me sick to think of Ross going off with McCrayle. But let's forget it. Kiss me, sweetheart."

She raised eager lips to his.

"I love you, Clive," she said. "I do love you. Tell me you love me, too—that nothing matters so long as we've got each other."

He did not tell her that, but he set his lips to hers in a kiss that was satisfying to them both. Later that night—while Ross lay serenely sleeping in her tent, far away in the wilderness, and Bill McCrayle curled up in his blankets, by the fire—Clive sat in the drawing-room on the sofa, with Valmy in his arms.

The black lace dress had been discarded for a silk wrapper that left her throat and arms bare. Her dark hair was tumbled over her head. Her eyes looked drowsy, content. Her arms were locked about his neck.

"So you still love me?" she whispered.

"Yes," said Clive. "You're the most distracting little temptress ever put on earth."

She gave a low laugh.

"I like tempting you, my Clive."

"Seems to me I'm fond of yielding to temptation," he said dryly. He was temporarily lulled to forgetfulness of Ross and Bill in the arms of this girl for whom he had forsaken Ross, his wife.

The warmth of the fire; the charm of the lovely Rhodesian night drove the evil mood and ugly thoughts away from him. He was once more Valmy's lover. She nestled against him quite contentedly; feeling positive that she held him in the hollow of her hand. Languidly she stroked his smooth fair head with her right hand. She looked up into the vivid blue of his eyes.

"Clive, isn't it wonderful—being alone and so happy? It was awful when we had to steal every kiss and be scared of discovery."

"Yes," he said in a slightly absent-minded way.

Half the charm of an 'affair' for Clive Derrell was the danger and uncertainty and difficulty of it. But he did not tell Valmy so. He ran his fingers through her hair.

"Darling child," he whispered.

"Darling Clive," she whispered back.

"I adore you," he said (and meant it for the moment). "You're as sweet as honey, and as intoxicating as wine."

"You told me on the boat that I was champagne," she said dreamily, smiling.

"So you are. And I'm tight," he laughed. "We might as well forget everything but the fact that we're crazy about each other, Valmy."

She gave a long sigh and drew his lips down to her mouth.

Valmy, like most women, could never understand that a man may be brimming with love and passion at night — and be sick of her in the morning. When Clive came to breakfast that next day in a somewhat snappy, touchy mood, Valmy did not like it.

She failed to realise that Clive — satiated with love for the moment — was thinking of his wife and Bill McCrayle again. Had she been sensible she would have kept quiet and left him alone when he showed a disinclination to talk to her or kiss her. But she was foolish. She resented his swift changes of mood.

"You needn't snap at me like that, Clive," she said, after he had flung a short answer to one of her many questions about 'their future'.

"I didn't snap so far as I know," he said coldly.

"Yes, you did," she said.

He got up from the table, wiping his lips with his napkin.

"I'm going out to the ranch," he said shortly.

Valmy also rose.

"Am I to be left all alone again for hours?"

"You'll be all right, my dear child. There are plenty of books about."

"I'm sick of reading. I want to come with you."

"You can't," he said. "A man doesn't want to be bothered with a girl when he's at work."

"Ross used to go round the farm with you!" Valmy flung at him very foolishly.

Clive turned a furious face to her.

"I don't want Ross's name brought up every five minutes, thanks," he rapped out. "In any case, Ross knew everything there is to know about a South African farm, and you don't!"

Valmy flung back her head.

"Perhaps you're sorry I'm not as clever as Ross!" she sneered.

"Perhaps you'll make me sorry," he snarled. "And perhaps you'll make me so sorry, before you've done, that I shall get my horse and ride out after Ross and fetch her back here — see?"

Clive's speech made Valmy shrink from him just as though he had hit her. She sat down in a chair heavily. She trembled a little. She no longer sneered. Her long, greeny eyes filled with tears and her red mouth drooped at the corners. Her whole face took on a childish, woebegone expression.

"Oh — Clive!" she whispered.

He hunched his shoulders. Bad temper always made a cad of him, and Valmy had thoroughly annoyed him.

"It's your own fault if I'm nasty," he snapped. "You should be more tactful. If you'd had a husband you wouldn't have wished me to keep on bringing up his name."

Valmy lowered her head. Her cheeks were crimson. She would have liked to have snapped back at him, but she dared not. She was beginning to know this lover of hers too well. In a pleasant mood he was charming; in this kind of mood he was a perfect brute, she reflected. Yet she still loved him and wanted his love. She was by no means sick of him. She could not afford to be, either. She had forsaken everything for his sake. She had only had him here alone for a couple of days. She was not going to let it all end — so soon.

Clive marched up and down, passed her chair, his handsome face irritable, his hands in his pockets.

"Now for lord's sake, Valmy, don't speak to me of Ross again," he said, after a pause. "And don't demand every minute of my time because I can't give it to you. The daytime is meant for work. Leave love-making until the night."

Her head shot up swiftly; her tear-filled eyes flashed resentment at him.

"You used not to feel like that, Clive. You used to want to kiss me and be with me any time of the day."

"You didn't belong to me then, my dear, and now I've got you altogether, haven't I? We can't be eternally kissing and slopping over each other."

She bit her lip fiercely.

"I see," she said, catching her breath. "Well, you've changed pretty quickly. I suppose it's just because I *belong* to you that you treat me anyhow."

He stopped in front of her, his face as resentful as hers.

"That's a beastly thing to say to me, Valmy."

"Well, isn't it true?" She was sobbing now.

"No—it's not."

"Then why be so unkind to me and—and threaten to get sick of me and—and follow Ross?"

With a gesture of impatience he turned from her, and stared out of the window. The sun shone brilliantly over the veldt. The fresh glory of the Rhodesian summer was vanishing. Everything was beginning to look dry and brown and parched. To Clive it seemed symbolic. The first flush of passion—of an intrigue with a girl like Valmy Page—appeared colourful, enchanting. Yet so soon the bright colours faded—everything looked seared and grey.

His silence, the sullen look on his face made Valmy's heart sink. She wiped away her tears with a shaking hand, then rose and crossed to his side.

"Clive," she said huskily. "Don't let's quarrel. We've thrown in our lot together. Can't we be happy—as happy this morning as we were last night?"

Clive put his tongue in his cheek and did not break his alarming silence for a moment. Then he turned to the girl and put his hands on her shoulders. Her tear-stained face and the piteous look of entreaty in her eyes roused a spark of tenderness in him. But there was very little tenderness or decent feeling left in him. He was rapidly becoming hardened and more selfish than ever—the result of self-indulgence—and he knew even as he looked down at Valmy that his feelings toward her were only passionate ones; that she would not be able to hold him for long.

"Don't look so tragic, old thing," he said curtly. "Sorry if I was nasty. Now let's drop the row."

Her heart beat swiftly, and she still felt resentful and alarmed by his attitude. But she tried to smile.

"Right-ho, Clive," she said. "I'm sorry, too."

He bent down and kissed her on the lips. It consoled her in some measure. But she felt the kiss to be devoid of warmth and passion. Long after he had gone down to the farm, she sat staring before her with anxious eyes, wondering what the end of this would be. While she had had Clive at her feet an adoring, passionate lover, she had felt lighthearted and satisfied.

But it was very different in moments like these when he showed plainly that there was no real depth in his passion for her and that he would as readily cast her off as he had taken her on. The whole business assumed an aspect that was both terrifying and humiliating to Valmy.

"How easily a man gets tired," she thought, as she tried to amuse herself in the bungalow through many lonely, depressing hours, that morning.

Yes, she had to acknowledge that.

A man does tire easily — where there is no real love. Passion never lasts. It is a fire that burns itself out. Only where it is combined with love and respect and self-sacrifice does it ever endure. Valmy had yet to learn that bitter lesson. She was to drink of a cup far more galling and distasteful than the one she had so lightly helped to raise to her cousin Ross's lips.

Clive had not entirely sickened of Valmy or of the affair, however. He was always in a better humour towards sundown. He began to drink heavily, in order to drown the memory of Ross and Bill McCrayle; to drown his own conscience which more than once this day had given him a nasty twinge.

The sin he had committed was not likely to elevate him. It dragged him down. He had been a moderate drinker up till now, but this evening he took far too many whiskies and sodas. He grew noisy and excitable.

Valmy, who had spent a wretched day alone, was thankful to find him in a good temper. She shut her eyes to the drinks. He sat on the veranda, with an arm around her, and kissed her until she deceived herself into the belief that he loved her as much as he had ever done.

"I'm sick of Swallow Dip. It's too much like hard work without McCrayle, and it's damned dull," he said. "Supposing we clear out, Valmy mine?"

Her greeny eyes sparkled at him.

"Oh, Clive — what a lovely idea. Where shall we go?"

"Durban," he suggested. "We'll put up at an hotel. I'll buy you a wedding-ring and you can pretend to be my newly-made wife and we'll have a rattling good time. I know a top-hole place there where we can dance every night."

Valmy's pulses leaped. She put her arms around his neck and hugged him.

"Clive, you darling. I'll just adore it."

"Better than staying in this God-forsaken place and staring

at mountains and kopjes all day," he grunted. He tossed down his sixth whisky.

Valmy, suddenly very pleased with life, nodded her head.

"Rather, I should say so! Durban sounds marvellous."

"You can wear your pretty frocks and the other fellows'll envy me," said Clive, lazily.

A remark of that kind would have offended Ross. But Valmy took it as a compliment. She was a foolish, blind moth, circling round the flame, scorching her wings, but going on, desperately, to the death.

"I love you to be so proud of me, Clive," she said.

"I'll get Vandecken to look after this place," added Clive, pouring out a fresh drink.

"What's going to happen, Clive?"

"What I've said."

"But I mean — in the future," she said breathlessly.

"Oh, I don't know and I don't care," he said, shrugging his shoulders. "I'm not going to worry my head over things any more."

Some of Valmy's high spirits were dashed to the ground by the remark. She did not wish to irritate him, destroy this cheerful mood of his, so she dared not question him further. But she would have given much to know exactly what he intended to do — with her. She would have liked him to get a divorce — to marry her. Her present position was much too precarious.

Clive, however, was in a state of mind when nothing mattered, so long as he had a 'good time'. He had had a joint-account at the bank in Durban with Ross, ever since they married. He fully expected to find plenty of money to his credit. He did not for a moment suppose that she would now put a check on him and prevent him from drawing any cash that he needed. He knew that there was no spite, no meanness in her character. He intended to take full advantage of the fact.

"When shall we go, Clive?" Valmy asked.

"Soon as I can arrange it," said Clive. "But I've changed my mind about Durban. Several people know me there. We'll go to Johannesburg."

"I've heard that called one of the wickedest cities in the world," murmured Valmy.

"It'll suit us, then." said Clive. "We're both wicked enough."

The girl shivered, despite the warmth of the late afternoon. The laughter sped from her eyes. Somehow she no longer felt able to laugh with Clive or joke with him about their 'wickedness'. She did not share in this dare-devil inconsequent mood of his, tonight. She lay so quiet in his arms that he grew surprised and stopped his flow of careless 'chaff'. He looked down at her flushed face.

"Hullo – what's the matter with you? My champagne's a bit flat tonight. Ha! ha!" he laughed at his own wit.

She shivered again.

"Little stupid – what are you depressed about now! We'll have a good time in Johannesburg, won't we?"

"Yes," she faltered, her dark brows fiercely knit. "But, Clive —"

"Well?"

"You – you won't leave me there or do anything dreadful like that, will you?"

He roared with laughter.

"Silly little ass – why should I? No, my dear, we'll dance and do a theatre if there's anything amusin' going, and forget the world."

His temper was improving every moment. In a semi-intoxicated state he saw life through a rosy haze.

Valmy was sweet and quite in favour again. Ross and Bill McCrayle could go away and stay away – he didn't care. He was going to enjoy life with Valmy now . . . in Johannesburg.

For a long while Valmy let him ramble on, telling her of the 'good time' they would have. They would spend at least a fortnight there – have a suite of rooms in the best hotel – forget Swallow Dip and everybody connected with it.

"And damn the consequences and the future. Live and let live!" Clive finished magnificently.

The girl did not move or speak. She was haunted by strange fears. Perhaps for the first time in her life something akin to remorse was attacking her. She had expected to have everything her own way once she had ousted Ross. But now she was not so sure. Clive was a moody, unstable creature and if he were going to start drinking, there was no knowing what might happen in the near future.

The mists of night crept over the veldt. The stars twinkled out, pale at first, but later as it grew darker they were marvellously big and bright. The kopjes rose like mysterious shadow-shapes against the moonlit sky.

Clive continued to hold Valmy in his arms, and caress her. He had reached a sentimental, maudlin state. She clung to him and kissed him back with almost desperate passion; seeking to forget her fears and doubts.

But for Valmy it was the beginning of the end and, deep down in her heart of hearts, she knew it.

CHAPTER XVII

ALL that golden Rhodesian day, Ross and Bill had been trekking across the veldt.

Ross had risen at dawn and put on her neat, cool holland riding coat and breeches, and felt — as she put it to Bill — 'as fit as a fiddle'.

"You're sure you think you ought to do a day's hard riding, Ross?" he had asked anxiously before they started.

Ross assured him that she felt herself again. The weakness and exhaustion following her attack of fever had quite passed.

Indeed, Ross felt more at peace during that day than she had felt for weeks. She had 'burnt her boats'; left Clive and Valmy and Swallow Dip behind her. She had agreed to go forth into the wilderness with Bill McCrayle — and knew him to be a veritable tower of strength. Now, all she must do was to keep fit and be a suitable companion for him; help him build that new home which he was so keen to make for her.

At midday, when the sun grew very hot and the earth seemed baking and cracking with heat beneath the horse's hoofs, they rested — Twopence prepared their lunch, which consisted of bully-beef, bread and treacle, and a pot of tea which Ross found most refreshing. Twopence was invaluable. He discovered a kraal close to the resting place and brought back a jug of new milk to the '*Inkaas*' and the beloved Missis; and there also came with him a black moon-faced lad who tremblingly approached Ross and Bill, bowed to the earth and offered his services.

"He bad boy — father beat him. He want to come with us," Twopence said, proudly pointing to his shivering, but grinning protégé.

Ross and Bill exchanged amused glances.

"It's not a bad idea to let him come with us and help Twopence," said Ross.

"A very excellent idea," said Bill. "We'll keep him."

"And call him Fourpence," added Ross.

So 'Fourpence', enchanted with his new name and his new employers, became one of the little party so cheerfully struggling forth to a new and unknown life in the wilderness.

Bully-beef and bread and treacle does not sound tempting. Nevertheless to hungry trekkers of the veldt it is manna. Bill was delighted to see Ross eat a large meal.

"You're really better, dear," he said. They had lunch, and sat, side by side, on a big iron-stone in the shadow of a small kopje. "You look it, too."

"Good!" smiled Ross. "That being so, Bill, I'm going to smoke one of your cigarettes."

He handed her a box, and lit a match for her.

"There you are."

"I shall have the old friend," he said and drew his pipe from his pocket.

"You — and your pipe!" she laughed.

He watched her in silence a moment. Deep thankfulness for the amazing gift of her comradeship out here on the veldt, filled his heart. He thought how beautiful she was. There was colour in the sun-browned face. The brown eyes were clear and bright, and she was ready now with that wide, boyish grin of hers. Ross had suffered badly through Clive's treatment of her. She had been through the hell that only a proud, good woman can suffer over such humiliation. Such suffering was not going to crush Ross. She was going to rise above it. She was no longer broken and despairing. She was the old, courageous, cheerful person. The shadow of grief which lay behind the brave eyes made her even dearer — if possible — to Bill than she had been before. Whatever she felt now about Clive she was not going to show it. Bill knew that. In her veins ran the fighting blood of the early Colonists who had come out to Rhodesia to battle their way into her heart and till her soil and make her what she was today. Ross was a fighter, and Bill adored her for the fearless way in which she rode at his side and put the bitterness of the past resolutely behind her.

What a woman to love! What a woman to bear fine, brave sons to a man — for Rhodesia!

Bill's rugged face burned as he thought of this. He turned

his eyes from her and stared before him at the sunlit veldt, smoking fiercely at his pipe. Every fibre of his being yearned to Ross – his hands ached to hold her. But he was not the man to forget the compact he had made with her. They were to journey together as comrades – until the memory of the past had been wiped out. He must wait for the day when she would turn to him willingly and take him for her lover.

They rested until five o'clock that afternoon, when the worst heat of the day was passed. Later, they moved on – Twopence and Fourpence following with the mule and the luggage; a strange, rather pathetic little band on the 'trek'.

By the time darkness had fallen, and the cold night-wind blew across the veldt, Ross was tired out – healthily tired, this time. They found a pleasant clump of trees and there pitched the one and only tent. For supper, there was a treat. During the afternoon, Bill had shot a couple of quail. Twopence roasted these over his fire.

Ross and Bill ate their quail with relish, sitting inside the tent on either side a Tate sugar box, with a newspaper for a table-cloth. It was primitive and not particularly comfortable. But they enjoyed it; Ross said that she had not eaten a meal with such relish for days.

"This sort of life is going to do me a world of good, Bill!" she said, after they finished their supper, and settled down for a smoke, outside the tent, by the fire that burned warmly under the starlit sky. "I was getting too fat and comfortable in my luxurious bungalow back at Swallow Dip."

He smiled at her.

"My dear, I feel you're roughing it terribly, but I love it."

"So do I," she said. "I've enjoyed the day's trek and I'm feeling very pleasantly tired and ready for sleep."

She leaned her charming brown head against the canvas of the tent and looked up at the sky a moment. How wonderful the stars were – the blazing white stars of a South African night. A cool night-breeze blew across her face, bringing the scent of the sun-baked earth – sweet and alluring. All about them was silence, starlight; infinite space; vast solitude. They were in the wilderness indeed. There was peace and beauty unmarred by the machinations of civilisation or the fret and turmoil of existence they had left behind.

Suddenly her eyes filled with tears. She turned to Bill. He was not looking at her. He was staring ahead of him, smoking his beloved pipe. She was filled with deep gratitude to him for bringing her away from sorrow and despair, to this healing wilderness. She put out a hand and touched his arm.

"Bill," she said.

At once he turned his head and looked down at her. He was immediately concerned by the tears that gleamed on her lashes.

"Why, Ross, you're crying!" he exclaimed.

"For happiness, tonight, instead of for sorrow, Bill," she said. "I can't quite explain it, but I feel as I sit here, looking at the stars and at the veldt, that one has no right to grieve or worry so long as there is some sort of existence left to one. I feel so happy – in a queer way. Do you understand?"

"I do and I'm glad you feel like that, Ross," he said with emotion. "I was so afraid you'd find it unbearable. I'm a dull fellow, Ross – not an amusing companion."

"You're the best pal a woman can have and I'm intensely grateful," said Ross. "I don't say I can forget Clive – Valmy —" she winced. "Not yet, anyhow. It's like dying and beginning life all over again. But I am going to learn how to forget out here with you."

He put his pipe in his pocket. His heart began to beat with swift, hard throbs. The sweetness of her filled him with intense longing for her . . . a longing hard to fight against.

"That is all that I want you to do, Ross," he said. "Forget everything – begin again."

"Clive seems thousands of miles away from me now," she said in a low tone. "It's hard to believe I was ever his wife – how much he meant to me – and I honestly think something died in me when I left Swallow Dip for good, Bill."

Bill did not speak, but he nodded his head. She gave him an almost apologetic look.

"My dear, forgive me – for speaking of Clive, but I just wanted to tell you how I feel."

"Why, Ross, there is nothing to forgive," he said. "I want you always to tell me what you feel. I can't possibly expect you never to mention Clive or think of him just because you've come away with me."

"I don't want to think often of him," said Ross. "It's much better to bury it all completely. But of course, as you can understand, it's difficult to put him entirely out of my mind. I was so terribly fond of him, Bill. He was everything to me after Daddy died."

"Yes, I know, dear," Bill answered very gently.

"Once I would have thought it impossible to put him out

of my life, but one never knows what one can do, does one? As I said—the past seems like another life altogether."

He turned to her suddenly and gripped her hands with a strength that made her wince.

"Ross, if only this new life would grow to be as wonderful as the other used to be, to you," he said in a husky voice. "I love you so! I've loved you for so long. I want you to be happy with me—happier than you were—with *him*."

Her face flooded with colour and she looked away from him, as though what he said and implied distressed her.

"Bill, I am going to try—you know. But it's too soon and —"

"Oh, I know," he broke in. "I know that passion must be the last thing you want now. You've had such a rotten experience with Clive. I can't expect you to turn to me at once. I know!"

"Give me time, Bill. I need your friendship more than anything."

He raised her hands to his lips.

"I must seem a selfish brute to you. You'll soon loathe all men, Ross."

"What nonsense," she said, trying to laugh at him, although she felt nearer tears than laughter. "I don't hate anybody—not even Clive."

"You're a saint, my Ross."

"Heaven forbid. What a frightful character to have!' she laughed. Then added seriously: "But I don't hate Clive or even Valmy. I just don't feel I ever want to see either of them again. I'm certainly not in love with Clive any more. He has killed that!"

McCrayle did not say how glad he was. He kept silent, secretly rejoicing.

"But I'm sorry for him," went on Ross. "He has a pitifully weak nature. I'm sorry for Valmy too. It's awful Bill—my own flesh and blood—Aunt Jenny's daughter. It's dreadful. She's bound to suffer for what she's done. But don't let's talk of them. Let's talk of ourselves. As for you dear old Bill—far from being a selfish brute—you're an angel to me."

The tears were dripping from her eyes now. Her voice broke. Bill bit fiercely at his lip. He put his head between his hands.

"You're the angel, Ross. You're too good for me, anyhow— for any man."

"I won't have you say that! I don't want you to feel that. I'm as weak and stupid as I can be. And I know what human nature is ... My God, Bill—there's a passionate side to my nature, too, you know."

He did know. Hadn't she lain in his arms that night in his bungalow? He had felt that heart of hers throbbing under his—felt her lips cling and burn against his. She had believed him to be Clive. Well—the day must come when she would kiss him, Bill McCrayle, like that of her own free will. And he was going to wait for that day to come.

Alone with her here on the deserted veldt, under the stars, the witchery of the Rhodesian night stirred him to a very natural longing for her.

And Ross understood. She was beginning to understand men and human nature so much better now than she had done in the past. She had suffered through her love for a husband who had denied her his. She could fully comprehend Bill's suffering. Hadn't he cared for her and had to suppress that affection for years.

Her heart ached for him. She watched him through a mist of her tears. She hated Bill to be miserable. He was so awfully good to her. Yet she did not know what to say. How could she offer him love? Her heart felt emptied of passion. All sex-emotion had died within her when she had left her husband and cut the tie that bound them. Oh, if only there were no passion, no love of that kind between men and women! If only they could be friends—what a lot of trouble would be avoided!

She put out a hand and laid it on Bill's curly head. He was really like a boy who needed to be mothered. The maternal instinct in Ross was by no means dead.

"Dear old boy," she said. "Don't be depressed. What can I say to cheer you up?"

He turned to her. His face was puckered, his eyes ashamed.

"Sorry, Ross—I'm a great fool. Forgive me but I love you too much."

"I know, dear. And I'm terribly fond of you, but I—I can't give you passion just yet. Wait, Bill—be patient—give me time my dear!"

"I'm a damn fool," he said. "I'm off for a walk—by myself."

The fineness of the man's nature made her respect him deeply. So easily he might have forced her into his arms, alone with her here in the wilderness. She did not want him to go off alone—uncomforted. She suddenly put her arms about his shoulders and drew his head down on to her breast. He gave a great sigh and yielded to the divine consolation of that embrace.

"Oh, my darling," he whispered.

He wound his arms around her and stayed like that, motionless, silent. She looked over his curly head at the moonlit veldt. Her eyes were full of sympathy and understanding. She too neither moved nor spoke. She could feel the hard throbbing of his heart; the shaking of his great body. She held him as a mother might have held a child and he clung to her. Her breast was a soft pillow; her sun-browned neck was smooth and warm. Her thick chestnut hair, falling in a rope to her waist, brushed across his eyelids.

Once or twice he stirred, lifted his head and with eyes still shut, kissed her warm throat.

Ross did not begrudge him those kisses, neither did she object to the clasp of his arms. He was a dear and she would have given anything on earth to have cared for him as he wanted. Once she leaned over him and pressed a kiss on his forehead.

"Great baby!" she whispered. "You haven't ever really grown up, old Bill."

He smiled — said something inarticulate. Gradually the frantic beating of his heart slowed down. He gave Ross one little convulsive hug, then let his arms fall away from her and rose from his knees. Standing up, he lit a cigarette. The flame, illuminating his face in the darkness, showed Ross that his eyes and lips were calm and strong.

She too stood up, looking at him with great tenderness.

"Bless you, my dear," she said. "With all my heart I admire and respect you. And now, good night."

He turned and looked down at her, his grey eyes wistful.

"Are you sure you don't despise me?"

"Don't be an old idiot, Bill!"

"How many women on earth would understand a chap so well. You're too sweet!" he said.

"Oh rot," she murmured smiling. "Don't think about it. One of these fine days you and I are going to have a jolly nice ranch — be happier than we deserve to be."

The glorious promise of those words made McCrayle thrill.

"Oh, Ross!" he said. "You deserve the greatest happiness in the world."

"Good night, dear," she said.

"God bless you, darling," he said.

He held the flap of the tent open for her. She passed through and he followed her with eyes full of worship — and of hope.

CHAPTER XVIII

FOR a week Ross and Bill continued to trek across the veldt with their two black boys, their horses, mule and luggage. They advanced in the cool of early morning and late afternoon; rested in the hottest hours of the day; slept soundly under the stars at night.

Neither of them knew what was happening in the ranch they had left behind, and neither seemed to care. They had both found peace and beauty in this Rhodesian wilderness and both of them found some new quality to admire, to respect in each other, day by day.

Ross grew brown with the sun and stronger than she had ever been, during that week of hard riding, simple diet and wonderful, health-giving sleep. The discomforts of the journey; the mosquitoes; the difficult trek through forest and over river and plain did not deter her or spoil her pleasure in it.

She had become so accustomed to spoiling Clive, putting up with his moody, temperamental nature, she found it a relief and a delight to be with Bill, who made no demands upon her and refused to be waited upon. He was always amiable and eager to serve her – to make sure she had what she wanted. She was learning the joys of being spoiled in her turn.

Their comradeship was a wonderful thing. They shared the difficulties, the pleasures of that trek in perfect concord and sympathy. They had many things in common beside this love of Rhodesia. Bill was a wonderful shot and Ross was keen. When they came upon buck they saw to it that there was a change from the usual repast of tinned bully-beef.

Since that one night of weakness, Bill had not wavered from his compact with Ross. He had not broken through his reserve and asked one kiss, one embrace from her. She rejoiced in the fine, clean strength of him.

At the end of a wonderful week, she found more than ever that the memory of Clive and her disastrous marriage was fading; becoming a ghost of long ago, a ghost too tired to follow all the long, long miles that she rode across the veldt with Bill; until it was too remote to hurt her.

Then, one golden, shimmering morning, they reached the end of their journey. Quite by accident they came across the little ranch in which they were to eventually settle down. When they first came in sight of it, they reined in their horses and gazed at it, with eyes bright with admiration and hearts overflowing with delight in this beautiful country to which they belonged.

First they saw a kopje, shady with trees; then the little creeper-clad bungalow built upon it, commanding an exquisite view of the sweeping country; the blue mountains in the distance. To one side of the bungalow, a stream of water poured, crystal-clear over great granite boulders, down to a gleaming pool below. It was like an oasis in the desert; a tiny park, a space of shade and cool, of flowers, of fresh green things, in the midst of the dusty, burning, glaring South African veldt.

"What a picture," said Ross. "Oh, Bill, I wonder who owns it? Somebody who loves Rhodesia, I know. What a time it must have taken to build that darling little bridge over the river, and grow all those lovely flowers. Just look at that banana, by the veranda — and the gum trees!"

"And just look at the rice-fields and the mealies!" said McCrayle, the practical man who appreciated useful fertilisation before beauty.

"We must stop here and plead with the owner to let us stay," smiled Ross.

They rode on to the little ranch — two tired, dusty travellers with the glow of health on their faces, and undimmed light of adventure in their eyes.

They dismounted and handed their horses over to Twopence, who passed the care of the mule on to his new companion. Fourpence was 'fagging' for his mentor.

Ross and Bill could not see any signs of human life around the bungalow, but beyond, in the cattle-kraal, figures were moving amongst the herd.

Ross and Bill climbed up to the little bungalow and reached the porch. Brilliant-coloured creeper hung over it enchantingly. It made a bright splash of crimson and green and gold against the brown thatched roof.

"I wonder if anybody's in?" murmured Ross.

The door opened and a tall man with grey hair and a sun-bitten face stepped out on to the veranda. He paused as he saw the strangers and then greeted them with evident pleasure.

"Good day," he said. "This is an unexpected visit. We are

the only settlers for miles about here, and rarely see a white man or woman from one day to another. Have you come far?"

"From the south," said Bill, taking off his hat and fanning his hot face with it. "We've been trekking with two 'boys' for over a week."

"Making for any particular part?"

"No," said Bill, with a smile at Ross, who was wiping her own flushed face with a handkerchief. "We've just come on a wild adventure—to find a little ranch. We thought of going towards Livingstone."

"Why not stay here?" asked the owner of the ranch. "This ranch happens to be going cheap."

"Do you mean it?" Ross and Bill said together, with bated breath.

"Why, we simply love this place. We've been thinking how adorable it is," added Ross.

"Won't you step inside and have something to eat and drink?" said the man, smiling at her. Like all Colonists, he was hospitable to strangers. "My name's Trensham. I'm really from Jo'burg, but I came out to this part with my wife a year ago."

Ross and Bill sank gratefully into the chairs offered them in Mr. Trensham's cool, charming living-room. Here the green matting blinds shut out the fierce sun. It was not luxuriously furnished like the beautiful bungalow Ross had left behind her, but it was comfortable and clean. A few minutes later they were drinking coffee and eating delightful rice-cakes, made by Trensham's well-trained cook-boy. After the many days of tinned food the fresh coffee and cakes seemed delicious.

"So you're going back to Jo'burg, are you?" said Bill, offering his host a cigarette.

Trensham took the cigarette and lit it.

"Yes," he said shortly. "I've finished with this place."

"But it's so charming—how can you leave it?" murmured Ross.

"For many reasons," he said. "It is a decent little ranch— might pay well in time, but it's a long way out in the wilderness —too far from civilisation for most people, and that's why I'm going to sell it cheap. I haven't had a soul after it; if you decide to take it, it will be a bit of luck for me."

"It seems just what we want," said Bill.

"I may as well tell you," said Trensham. "the main reason why I'm selling up is because I've lost my wife."

Ross's eyes rested pityingly upon him. She had been studying him and saw that he was young to be grey-haired, and that in spite of the healthy bronze he looked haggard and drawn. Obviously he had been through some great trouble.

"I'm terribly sorry," she said. "You mean she —"

"She didn't die," he broke in. "She ran away from me."

Ross's face burned. She dared not look at Bill. But Trensham relieved the tension of the moment by blurting out his tragic little story, as though relieved to be able to tell somebody.

A year ago he had brought his bride here. She was a Johannesburg girl — pretty and captivating. He had feared she might find life on the veldt too lonely and dull but then she had been in love with him and had laughed at his fears. She had not been on the ranch many months before she grew bored and irritable. Then — a month ago — a wealthy South African diamond-merchant passed this way *en route* for Livingstone, and stayed with them for a week or two.

"He was a low hound," Trensham said in a bitter voice. "He took advantage of the fact that Milly, my wife, was discontented and sick of fighting with me to make a living. When he went away — she went with him. That's all. It's an ugly story and not an uncommon one. I can't bear to stay here now so I'm going back to Jo'burg to my own people."

McCrayle did not look at him. He thought: 'Poor devil!' This affair seemed to have broken him up. He had obviously adored his young wife — and they had only been married eleven months. It was very hard on him.

"I'm so sorry, Mr. Trensham," said Ross. "I'm afraid you'll think hardly of women after this."

"Oh, I don't know," said Trensham with a short laugh. "Some women are all right, I suppose. I dare say you'll settle down here and be quite happy. Perhaps you'd like to stay the night, anyhow and look round, and then if you want the ranch, I'll sell it gladly and clear out. I haven't got much in the way of sleeping accommodation, but I can give you the double room my wife and I used to have, and turn into a little single one myself."

Much later Trensham showed Ross and Bill into the double-bedroom that adjoined the living-room.

He had set a small oil-lamp down on the dressing-table, and smiled at them — a weary, cynical smile of a disillusioned man. And then:

"Good night, my friends," he had said." Sleep well and pleasant dreams. You can regard this as your future room and your future home, now you've decided to buy it. Good night! May you be happier here than I have been."

Ross said: "Thank you, Mr. Trensham" — her face one burning flush, her lashes curving on her hot cheeks. Bill muttered: "Good night, old chap."

And now Trensham had gone and they were quite alone. They had heard another door shut and knew that Trensham was in the little slip-room which he had prepared for himself.

In silence they stood staring round them, both too embarrassed to speak; shy of each other; uncertain what to say or do under the awkward circumstances.

The bedroom was decently furnished with a fumed-oak suite and double bedstead in a green mosquito-netting. One or two cheerful prints hung on the white-papered walls. There were clean, white-frilled curtains framing the casement windows, which were open, admitting all the scents and sounds of the African night.

The room was partially in shadow, for the small oil-lamp threw a very indifferent light upon things. One rather pathetic reminder of the girl-wife who had grown tired of life on this lonely ranch and run away, stood in a corner — a wicker work-basket on legs. It was the feminine touch, and Ross, looking at it, felt a queer contraction of the heart as she remembered all the dozen-and-one little treasured possessions that she had left behind her at Swallow Dip.

Through the open window came the sound of tom-toms and chanting from the servants' compound. The room seemed full of the rich perfume of sun-warmed earth and flowers.

Ross put a hand to her throat. The little pulse in it was throbbing.

"Bill," she said, "this — this is rather dreadful, isn't it?"

Bill gave her a sudden humorous smile.

"You're right, Ross. It is a bit difficult."

"But what could we do?" she said, with a gesture of her hands. "Mr. Trensham took us for husband and wife, and I — I didn't see how we could deny it."

"Under the circumstances, no," said Bill, lighting a cigarette with a hand that shook very slightly. "His own wife having just run away from him, he would scarcely have received us very genially had he thought that we were — an eloping couple."

Ross's brown eyes rested on Bill's rugged face a moment, full of trouble.

"Oh, Bill," she suddenly broke out, with tears in her voice,

"I haven't been very — very bad to come away with you, like this, have I?"

"Good God, no!" he answered quickly. "You haven't done wrong at all. You mustn't compare yourself with Trensham's wife. She had a good, devoted husband whom she had no right to leave. Your husband was a rotter and drove you away by his unspeakable conduct with Valmy, under your own roof. You can't compare the affairs at all. My dear — my dearest" — he came close to her, took one of her hands and held it tightly, his heart full of pity and dismay as he saw the tears gather in her eyes and roll down her cheeks — "don't be so upset. You haven't been bad. Ross, you're the best little woman on earth. You and I have come away as pals — not lovers — you know that."

She tried to smile, but her lips quivered.

"I know. But it's rather upset me, Bill, coming in contact with this poor man whose wife has just deserted him."

"You're too tender-hearted, Ross," said Bill, gently squeezing the hand in his. "But although Trensham is to be pitied, Clive is not. He is not a deserted, stricken bridegroom, you know. He has that girl with him."

Ross shivered. Her face suddenly flamed. She flung back her head.

"Yes, you're quite right, Bill. I've done nothing to be ashamed of, and Clive is not — like Joe Trensham. I ought not really to be so upset."

"Of course not," he said. "You must never reproach yourself, or compare yourself with an ordinary runaway wife, for a single moment. As for Trensham mistaking us for a honeymoon couple why, my dear, that was inevitable, and it would only have upset him if we had denied the fact."

"Yes. Possibly he wouldn't have sold us the ranch, either."

"More than possible. He wouldn't have known the circumstances under which we left Clive and wouldn't have believed us if we had explained, so far better to let him go on thinking us married."

He spoke lightly, but inwardly his heart was aflame, and his pulses throbbed as he stood there in the quiet little bedroom holding Ross's warm hand in his own. To be here tonight, like this, with her . . . God! it was wonderful after all the years of despair through which he had passed since her marriage with Clive Derrell. At the same time, it was a cruel whim of Fate — for he knew he must not stay here with her. Joe Trensham could think what he would, but facts remained. He, Bill, was not Ross's husband—not yet had he the right to take her in his arms. He was her 'pal'; he had sworn to take care of her and make her happy. To overstep the bounds just because Joe Trensham's mistake gave him a loophole was the last thing in the world he would do.

"And now we must think what best to do, for tonight," he added after a pause.

"Yes," said Ross. "What can we do, Bill?"

"You must have this room, of course," he said, dropping her hand and moving quietly across to the window. He felt it would be easier to discuss things, farther away from her. The mere contact of her hand roused such a passion of longing within him. It was a longing that must be suppressed, so deliberately he turned his back on her and stared out at the veldt which was shimmering in the gorgeous moonlight. "You sleep here, dear," he went on, steadily smoking, "and I'll creep into the next room and lie on the sofa."

Ross bit her lip.

"You can't do that," she said nervously. "Mr. Trensham might find you there—might come out for something during the night, or catch you early in the morning before you were awake, and then the fat would be in the fire. He wouldn't understand why we—we slept apart."

Bill bit his lip.

"Yes, that is so," he admitted. "But what else can I do? Have you any suggestion to make, Ross?"

She hesitated; looked round the room; then at Bill. Her heart gave a curious little leap. For the first time she felt something deeper, more thrilling than mere friendship and esteem for this man who had taken her away from sorrow into the healing beauty and solitude of the wilderness. His face was turned from her, but she knew from the rigid stiffness of the fine figure, and the incessant smoking, that he was fighting another battle with himself tonight—a fiercer battle than the one he had fought out on the veldt when they had first set forth on their journey.

His tremendous strength and self-control gave her a feeling of intense pride in him—because he was hers. Yes, she admitted this to herself with a kind of exultation. This strong, splendid male creature was hers ... her devoted friend and—her lover. He adored her and wanted her. He adored her in silence, because she willed it so. So easily he might have taken advantage of this peculiar position in which they were placed; might at least have broken down the barrier by pleading with her — reminding her that she had come with him of her own free will. But he had not done so. He had remained her friend and she felt a sudden rush of tenderness — tenderness akin to love for him.

Her heart beat very fast as she stood there in the little shadowy bedroom, looking at Bill. She asked herself what it meant—that strange stirring of her pulses tonight at the sight and thought of Bill McCrayle. Was she really 'bad'? Could she be changing — she who had always thought hardly of people who changed their affections lightly and frequently? Had she not — only a few weeks ago — loved her husband with all her heart, soul and body, and thought there could be nobody in the world to equal him, to come between them and their love? Yet now the memory of Clive was abhorrent, and she, who had imagined her heart broken and her passions forever dead, thrilled for another man!

She felt ashamed and bewildered.

"I'm not quite sure what we can do, Bill," she said. "Unless we both sit up all night and talk."

"That's impossible. You've had a lot of trekking and hardship, and you need complete rest in a good soft bed, Ross. I'll sit up."

"Oh, no — you need rest, too," she protested. "You've got to settle up a lot of business with Mr. Trensham tomorrow."

"Nothing to worry about," he said, turning to her now with a smile. "I've only got to go round the ranch with him again and see that everything in the inventory is correct and sign the deeds that transfer the place to us."

"It's all rather wonderful," said Ross, softly. "Fancy our having a little ranch together, Bill!"

His grey eyes glowed at her.

"It's a marvellous thought to me, Ross. But I wish I could have bought the whole place myself, for you."

"Nonsense!" she smiled. "I like sharing in it. By the way, Bill, I mustn't forget to write that note to my bank — about — Clive —" Her straight brows contracted — "and I'll get Mr. Trensham to post it in Jo'burg, as he's going off tomorrow."

"I'll remind you," nodded Bill.

"Meanwhile, what about sleep tonight?" she asked. "We've got off that most important topic."

Bill pursed his lips.

"I'll get out of the window and sleep on the veranda," he suggested.

"No—much too cold," said Ross, shaking her pretty brown head. "You might get a severe chill after the heat of the day."

Suddenly she walked to the bed and pulled back the clothes. Then she turned to Bill, her eyes twinkling.

"I've got a brilliant idea, Bill," she said. "There are two mattresses on this bed. You shall have one of them and sleep—in a corner of this room."

He walked slowly towards her, his strong face red under its bronze.

"My dear—do you think —?"

"I think I can trust you," she said, with an adorable blush that made his heart jerk. She looked so young tonight—so much happier and better than he had seen her look for weeks, with that bright colour on her cheeks and that sparkle in her eyes.

"Yes, you can trust me all right," he said. "But—do you mind me in here?"

"I shan't mind. I shall go fast to sleep and forget about it," she said.

"But I shan't," he thought. "My God ... I shan't forget you're there so near to me, my dear, my lovely one!" ... Aloud he said: "Well, perhaps you're right, Ross, and it will be wise for us not to make Trensham suspicious. I'll help you haul off that top mattress, and perhaps I can sneak one blanket."

"And the eiderdown," she said, beginning to pull off the bedclothes. "You mustn't get cold."

"I shan't be that, I shan't undress tonight," he said.

"You'll certainly be warmer if you don't," she agreed.

"I'll sleep over there in the corner, near the door," he said. "Like a large dog, my dear."

"My dear, faithful Newfoundland," she laughed.

But there was a queer, shy note of happiness in her voice that Bill had never heard before.

He helped her arrange the mattress on the floor, then insisted upon lending a hand to tidy her own disarranged bed again. Finally they both faced each other, flushed, awkward, treating the whole thing as a huge joke.

"I'll say good night, Ross," Bill said.

"I'm going into the next room for a last cigarette, and it'll give you a chance to go to sleep, too. Then I'll creep in to my mattress without disturbing you."

"All right," she smiled and nodded. "Good night, Bill."

His breath began to come quickly. He looked down at her. In the shadowy, lamp-lit room she looked intensely sweet with her brown hair, disordered by her exertions of bed-making, tumbling about her face. He had never seen her look more attractive. She was like a girl of seventeen tonight. The hot blood coursed through his veins. If only he might kiss her — hold her once in his arms — ease a little of that aching longing for hands and lips that gave him no rest, day or night.

He did not speak, only held out his hand. Ross read the longing in his eyes. Her heart overflowed with compassion for him. Impulsively she raised her face to his.

"Good night, Bill," she said.

He trembled and caught at her hands.

"Dear — may I?" he asked.

"Yes," she whispered.

Gently he put an arm about her shoulders and drew her towards him, then laid his lips on hers. Just for an instant he clung to that cool, sweet mouth, then he let her go and turned away.

"Oh, Ross!" he thought. "It never seems to me you've ever been a married woman. And I've got to take care of you. I've got to — and I will, by God! I'll never shake your confidence in me."

He went quickly out of the room and shut the door. Ross turned to the bed and began to take off her riding-skirt and blouse. When she had slipped into bed — she lay awake for some time, staring at the little circle the oil-lamp cast on the whitewashed ceiling. Her heart beat very swiftly and her eyes were large and bright.

"Bill," she whispered to herself. "Dear old Bill —"

Her lips throbbed from the imprint of his lips. She trembled a little as she thought of that good night kiss. It had been very brief — but how closely his mouth had clung!

Ross could not blind herself to the fact that Bill loved her with all the strength and passion of his manhood. Neither could she deny that his love seemed very good to her and made her feel very grateful and tender toward him. One day it would do more. She would be able to return it. Yes, she felt that now. She would be able to love him as he loved her.

"Not yet ... but one day, Bill ... who knows?" she whispered to herself.

Her passion for Clive was dust and ashes; out of the ashes — like the Phœnix — a new love was arising — a new-born love, still so young, so delicate, it must needs be cherished very tenderly and carefully until it reached maturity.

And so Ross fell asleep, dreaming of that love, wondering at it; thanking God that it had come like a wonderful, white star into the darkness of life for her.

Later, Bill McCrayle crept into that bedroom and found that the lamp had burnt out and that Ross was fast asleep. He struck a match and stood by her bed, gazing down at her. How lovely she was to him. Her beautiful hair in one thick, satiny rope, was lying over the blanket that was pulled up to her chin. Her brown lashes lay darkly on the curve of her cheeks; her lips were parted lightly and her breath came evenly.

A long, long time, Bill stood watching her. Then he stooped down and very gently pressed a kiss on her head.

"God bless you, my darling," he whispered.

She did not wake. He turned to the mattress in the corner of the room. The room was flooded with moonlight. The white curtains bulged gently inward, caught by the cool night-wind. There was silence save for Ross's gentle breathing. The tomtoms in the compound had ceased. Bill McCrayle slept.

The next day, Joe Trensham completed the signing over of the ranch to "Mr. and Mrs. William McCrayle," and left the place for ever, to return to Johannesburg.

Then Ross and Bill were able to arrange the sleeping accommodation as they chose; and, of course, Bill insisted upon Ross keeping the big bedroom, while he took possession of the little one.

So they started on their joint ownership of Trensham's ranch —a new, perfect, partnership. At least they told each other it was a perfect partnership; revelled in the beauty of the bungalow on the kopje, with its sparkling stream and shady wood; its fertile mealie-land and excellent herd of cattle. But each knew in their hearts that it needed something else to make it quite perfect. And for that—the divine rapture of love between man and woman—between wedded lovers—they knew they must wait.

Bill's love for Ross was infinitely patient and unselfish, and hers for him was yet so young and shy it scarce had voice to speak. Apart from any romantic feeling, Ross was still Ross— and although she was Mrs. Bill McCrayle in the eyes of the 'boys' on this ranch, she felt that she was in reality still Clive Derrell's wife. She could not forget that. She felt bound to work with Bill on a purely platonic basis until she knew definitely what the future held; what Clive and Valmy meant to do.

Meanwhile she was happy and he was happy. There was much to be done on the little ranch to improve it. The very best antidote for an aching heart is hard work, and nobody knew that better than Bill McCrayle.

CHAPTER XIX

WHILST Ross and Bill were spending the days quietly and peacefully on their little ranch, tucked away in the heart of the veldt, Clive Derrell and Valmy were fast nearing the end of a reckless, riotous month in Johannesburg.

As soon as Clive had reached the town, he had wired to his wife's bank in Durban for cash amounting to several hundred pounds, and as he had always had the right to draw upon Ross's money as well as his own (of which there was little left) and the bank had not yet received Ross's order to cancel Clive's credit, he was sent the cash.

Thence onwards he lived in a fool's paradise. He deliberately put the memory of Ross, and the home he had ruined, away from him. With Valmy as his wife, he stayed in the most expensive hotel in Johannesburg, occupying a suite of rooms with a lovely view of distant mountains, over the dump-heaps of powdered quartz; the chimney-stacks of factories, and the business houses of a very busy South African town.

In these days he found Valmy an alluring and satisfying companion. She was in her element. Clive bought her new clothes, took her to every dance that was going, introduced her to the men whose casual acquaintance he made in hotel bars, as "my little wife," and behaved as though he were perfectly happy to be with her and never intended that the charming state of connubial bliss should end.

She tactfully refrained from bringing up the name of Ross Derrell; or from mentioning Ross's sudden and dramatic exit into the wilderness with Bill McCrayle. She accepted Clive's presents and accompanied him to places of amusement with the same ardour that she accepted his kisses and caresses. She lived a little too wildly and recklessly; blinding herself to the inevitable end ... for a wild fire of this sort must burn itself out, and she knew it ... but she danced on ... the poor, foolish moth around the flame that will finally consume it!

In Johannesburg the days were blazing hot. Valmy wore the thinnest of thin garments. Her bedroom was always full of flowers. It was all very much gayer than it had been at Swallow Dip, and she found plenty to smile at; plunged madly into every gaiety that Clive suggested. He was still drinking heavily and persistently, but he was never actually drunk, so Valmy shut her eyes to it. He had not much time to show any ill-humour. He had been too busy amusing himself and helping her to be amused. He had never been more lover-like, either, and Valmy could not complain of any lack of kisses or caresses.

It was a bubble—certain to burst. And when it did burst, Valmy got the worst of it. The woman always does.

One night, Clive and Valmy went downstairs to a big dance which was being held in their hotel in aid of some Johannesburg charity. They were both in fancy-dress, and each in their way attractive, Clive as a toreador—a disguise that suited him, with his sleek hair and slim figure; Valmy as 'Bacchante'—her white shoulders nude, her graceful little body very thinly clad in chiffon draperies which only reached her dimpled knees; a cluster of wild grapes dangling over each ear. But they had both changed considerably since they had left the ranch. Late nights, dissipation both of body and mind, had set a mark on those two faces. Clive had become coarsened; slightly bloated, with the eyes a little bloodshot and mouth loose. Valmy was thinner, more haggard; violet shadows under her green eyes; too much salve on her lips and rouge on her cheeks.

They had dined well tonight and they joined the dancers in the ballroom in high spirits. For the first half of the evening, Clive danced with the girl who was thought in this hotel to be his wife. Then he made some excuse and slipped off to the bar. Valmy watched him go, the corners of her red mouth drooping. He was going to drink more than was good for him tonight; already he had taken a great deal. She felt worried and rather annoyed.

In the bar, Clive Derrell met a tall, bronzed Colonist who was not in fancy dress like the others, but in an old khaki suit. Clive—feeling 'merry'—hailed him cheerfully and asked him to have a drink.

The Colonist gravely accepted. A few minutes later the two men were chatting freely. Clive informed the stranger that he was 'on his honeymoon' in Jo'burg; and the man responded by telling him, bitterly, that the idea of a honeymoon no longer appealed to him.

"My wife ran away from me," he confided in Clive. "I've just sold my ranch to some fellow and his wife, and come back here to my people."

Clive, interested, questioned him. It did not take long for him to make the very thrilling discovery that the deserted Colonist had sold his ranch to Bill McCrayle.

"Bill McCrayle, by gad!" he said incredulously. "You mean a great, big feller, with curly hair."

"That's the one," said Joe Trensham. "And a very charming wife he had, too."

Clive set down his drink. His fingers shook so that he could scarcely hold the glass. His face changed from red to white.

"Describe her," he said hoarsely.

Trensham gave a fairly accurate description of the woman with brown eyes and lovely brown hair who had accompanied Bill McCrayle.

"Nice, sensible woman she looked," added Trensham. "And seemed so fond of him. He worships her, too. When he said 'Ross' you could hear the love in his voice. But I'm right off love. You never can tell. My missus seemed to care for me at first. You never know what a woman'll do."

"No – by God, you're right," said Clive.

He leaned against the bar, staring at Trensham with unseeing eyes. He was shaken by this unexpected news; this description of the woman – who had once been his adored wife, and Bill McCrayle – in the wilderness. Trensham made out that they were fond of each other. And they were living there together ... Ross and Bill ... *Ross and Bill*! ... the thought bit like acid into Clive Derrell's very soul. He had deserted his wife, left her for Valmy Page, driven her from her home. He had only himself to blame. Yet now, somehow, when he heard of her living with Bill McCrayle, in peace and happiness, he was possessed with insensate jealousy. Every spark of feeling he had ever had for Valmy seemed to die out as he stood there listening to Trensham enlarge on his story of the sale of his ranch to 'The McCrayles'. The McCrayles. Ross and Bill ... living there as husband and wife ... Bill McCrayle usurping the position that had once been his, Clive's! Ross's lips thrilling to Bill's kisses, as once they had thrilled to his! Strange how the idea rankled—how it filled him with the almost fiendish desire to kill Bill McCrayle!

It was a jealousy as primitive and fierce and cruel as the passion that had first led him to forsake his wife for the arms of her cousin. Now he had had Valmy, he was satiated—sick of her. He became suddenly conscious of the rotten waste of this life he led with her; of the exquisite thing he had lost when he had lost Ross's love.

Too late for such thoughts. Too late for jealousy or anger or remorse. Yes, he knew it. He poured out another drink and tossed it down his dry throat. His eyes, his hands, were burning hot. At least he could prevent Bill McCrayle from marrying Ross, he told himself with devilish glee. He would not divorce her, and she could not divorce him now that she had taken the plunge herself.

He went on drinking until his brain seemed on fire. But he remained sober enough to ask Joe Trensham just where to find his ranch on the veldt .... *in case* ... in case he ever thought of going there ... of paying a visit to Ross and Bill. He laughed a trifle wildly at the thought; bade good night to Trensham, who had labelled him 'a drunken swine', and went back to the ballroom.

Valmy, who had been waiting for him, held out a hand.

"Come on, old thing. I'm aching to dance!"

But her smile died and her arms dropped to her sides as she saw his face; flushed, sullen; his vivid blue eyes full of hatred.

"What on earth's the matter, Clive?"

"I'm fed up with this dance," he said roughly. "I'm going up to bed."

"Oh, Clive—it's such fun, and —"

"You stay if you want to—I'm going to bed," he cut in. "You can do what you want—go to blazes if you want, in fact!"

Valmy stared at him, utterly dismayed.

"Clive!"

"Don't start whining, or I'll go back to the bar and get drunk," he threatened.

She gave a short, nervous little laugh.

"Seems to me you're drunk already, Clive."

"Maybe I am," he said, narrowing his eyes. "But if I am, it's with fury as well as whisky."

"What on earth are you so angry for?"

"I've just met a man who has sold his ranch to *Mr. and Mrs. Bill McCrayle*."

The scarlet on Valmy's cheeks deepened.

"To Bill and Ross? Well, what of it?"

"It's not very pleasant for me to hear of my wife settling down to a honeymoon with Bill McCrayle, is it?"

Valmy's heart gave a jerk.

So that was what was the matter! ... Clive was jealous ... jealous of Bill McCrayle's possession of Ross. It was not a pleasant thought for Valmy. She clenched her hands.

"My dear Clive," she said, her voice shaking, "you seem to forget that I—I am your wife now. Ross shouldn't matter. She didn't matter—at Swallow Dip."

"I know that. Perhaps I was a fool," he said, with a brutal laugh. "At any rate, you are not my wife, my dear Valmy, and Ross still is."

She went white under her rouge at that. He saw the expression on her face.

"If you're going to make a row, come upstairs and make it," he said.

CHAPTER XX

IN dead silence she followed him from the ballroom up to their room. In the big bedroom, full of the scent of dying flowers, she faced him; a white-faced, pinched-looking Bacchante, with two lurid dabs of rouge on her cheek-bones and a trembling, scarlet mouth.

"Clive," she said, "I'm not making the row; and, after all, I do think you needn't speak to me quite as you do, sometimes."

He threw himself into a chair and flung his toreador's hat into a corner. Lighting a cigarette, he glanced at Valmy out of the corners of his eyes in a sullen, vindictive fashion. She did not appear in the least beautiful or alluring to him tonight. He thought her ugly with that rouge on her face and that frightened, sagging mouth of hers. He was already blaming her for his downfall. He was a coward, resentful because she had been instrumental in separating him from Ross.

"You've nothing to complain of, my dear," he said shortly, pitching a burnt match into the fireplace. "You've had a damned good time."

"Clive!" she cried, staring at him with terrified eyes. "Why are you talking like this? What has come over you?"

"Oh, I don't know," he muttered. "But somehow the description that chap gave me of Ross and McCrayle drives me mad."

"You're mad," said Valmy. "Mad for what you can't get ... and then when you've got it, you don't want it any more. You wanted me at first, because I was unobtainable; and because Ross has gone with Bill, you want her back."

"*You* say so. I haven't said it," he flung at her, his eyes sly. "But now you come to mention it, how well you know me, Valmy! Perhaps you are right."

She licked her lips and drew nearer him. Her rouged, haggard little face was piteous now.

"Clive, you're only joking," she panted. "You can't mean you — you've grown sick of me?"

"I'm not so sure," he said. "I've had a good deal of you — never had you out of my sight for a month now."

"A month. My God! is that the limit of your powers of fidelity?" she asked hoarsely. "Are you so sick of me that you're going to throw me over, now?"

"Oh, I don't know, Valmy. You're making all the fuss — leave me alone."

"To brood over what you've heard about Ross! Oh, yes, I know! Well, I shan't let you do it. It isn't fair. Clive, Clive, I love you — I've given up everything for you!"

She flung herself on her knees before him, holding out her arms, the tears pouring down her cheeks.

"Clive, don't get sick of me — don't! Forget about Ross. *Clive...!*"

He regarded her coldly. He was unmoved by her supplication, by the sight of her tears. She was right. He was sick of her. His was that nature ... changeable, fickle, the type to have passionate intrigues and then tire of them. And the sweet woman he had once had as wife, had become once more a woman to be desired — because she was unattainable; because she had given her love to Bill McCrayle — Bill whom Clive loathed.

"Clive, put your arm round me. Be kind to me. Don't torture me like this. Tell me you're only fooling."

"There's no question of fooling. I'm simply mad because

Ross is out there on the veldt, living with McCrayle," said Clive. "Get up, for heaven's sake, Valmy, and don't make a scene."

She caught his hand and pressed it to her throat. The tears ran down her cheeks, smearing the rouge. The bunches of grapes on either side of her head looked ludicrous, lop-sided, altogether unattractive. But she fought wildly for the man she still loved, although she knew him to be a cad and a brute.

"Clive, be kind to me. I love you so. Last night you were sweet to me. Oh, why —"

"Go to hell, Valmy," he said thickly.

She rose from her knees and flung herself into his arms, twining her arms about his neck. She covered his face with kisses.

"Clive, I love you! Be kind to me!"

He took her delicate arm in a cruel grip and pushed her away from him.

"I can't stand this sort of thing tonight, Valmy," he said in a savage voice. "Leave me alone, I say."

She crouched on the floor in her crushed chiffon draperies; shivering, miserable, scared, her eyes distended and burning in her haggard little face. She stared at Clive as though at a ghost.

He did not look at her, but got up and began to pace the room, obviously brooding over all that the Colonist down in the bar had told him about 'the McCrayles'. Suddenly his eye lit on a white envelope that lay on the table in the centre of the room. He picked it up.

"A letter for me. Who from?" he muttered.

Turning it over, he saw that it was from the bank in Durban. He ripped open the envelope. That reminded him he was getting very short of cash. He must send to Durban for some more.

He read the letter from Ross's bank manager. His face became almost ludicrously astonished and dismayed.

When he had finished reading it, he flung it on the floor, uttering an oath that made Valmy shudder.

"My God!" he said, violently. "So that's what she's done. Now we're in a nice mess, you and I, my dear Valmy!"

"Now what's the matter?" Valmy asked in a voice of despair.

"Read that," he said, tossing the note across to her.

She read it in silence. It was to inform Mr. Clive Derrell that his wife had stopped his credit . . . that he no longer had the power to draw upon her money and that his own savings were rapidly dwindling. In fact, he had only ten pounds left in the world. In addition to that, the beautiful bungalow and ranch he had so recklessly left, with Valmy, was no longer his to return to. It was up for sale.

In other words, Clive was a ruined man. He saw now what a fool he had been. He had forsaken Ross and incidentally lost Ross's money and Swallow Dip. He stood tonight a penniless man without prospects – entirely through his own fault.

But although he admitted his folly, now, more than ever, hatred flamed within him – for Valmy who had so gaily and blithely assisted him to dance down the road to ruin.

"You see," he said between his teeth. "You understand what that means? Bill McCrayle – damn him! – has persuaded Ross to close my account. I have only ten pounds left of my own. I've spent every penny of my savings here, in this infernal hotel – on you."

Valmy sat there, crouching on the floor, shivering from head to foot, her face ghastly.

"I suppose it's only to be expected that Ross would not let you draw on her account any longer," at length she said in a low, dreary voice.

"You thought that – yet you let me squander money right and left here, eh?"

"I – didn't think much about it, Clive."

"Nor did I. But we've got to think about it now, my dear, haven't we?" he said, with a brutal laugh.

She stared up at the face that had been so handsome and that was now so vicious. Where was the charming, debonair Clive with whom she had fallen so wildly in love? This man was a howling cad. And for him she had given up everything.

A curious bluish tint crept about her mouth.

"What are you – going to do?" she whispered.

"Leave here at once," he said. He began to take off his toreador's costume, tearing at it with impatient fingers. "Get away while they're all at the ball."

"Get away?" repeated Valmy through parched lips. "But why?"

"Before they can hand in the bill, you little fool!" he said. "I can't pay it and I'm not going to languish in a Johannesburg prison for your sake."

Fear – naked and terrible – sprang to Valmy's eyes. She stumbled on to her feet across the room to Clive and caught at his arm with shaking fingers.

"But you aren't going to — leave me, are you?" she stammered.

"I'm afraid I must," he said curtly, pushing her away. "I'm very sorry this has all ended so unpleasantly, but there you are! You've had a good time and now you'll have to fend for yourself, Valmy."

"Oh, my God!" she said wildly. "You can't mean to leave me? Clive, Clive. . . ."

"They can't do anything to you," he said. "You can tell them you aren't my wife. They can't prosecute you."

"But what am I to do? Where am I to go? I'm a stranger in South Africa. Clive, you brought me here. I've sacrificed everything for you. Clive. . . . You mustn't leave me! I shall die. . . ."

"Don't start blaming me. You led me away from Ross in the first place," he said, as he rapidly changed from the fancy dress into a riding-suit. "It's all been your fault, my dear Valmy. Blame yourself."

She clung to him.

"Oh, Clive, how can you be so heartless? Where are you going?"

He clenched his teeth.

"I'm going to Ross," he said. "I'm going to get her back — and get the money back, too. I'm not going to let Bill McCrayle have her and all that's behind her. I know where to find them. Trensham told me. I'll interrupt their perfect idyll, my dear Valmy; and if I know Ross, she'll soon consider it her duty to come back to me by the time I've finished playing the returned penitent!"

Valmy's hands fell away from Clive's arm. She stood staring at him, rigid, white-faced, eyes distended in a face that seemed suddenly to have grown pinched and small.

Then as she saw him put on his coat and reach for his hat, the colour rushed to her cheeks. She stumbled towards him and caught his arm again.

"No! Clive, no! You can't go back to Ross now . . . you can't leave me . . . you mustn't!"

He shook her off.

"I shall do what I choose. Don't try to stop me, because you're wasting your time, Valmy."

"But why do you want to go back to Ross?" she gasped, catching at her throat. "Clive, you must be crazy. You left Ross

—ran away with me—now you want to return to her just because you've heard she's living with Bill McCrayle."

"Quite so," said Clive, with an ugly smile. "It doesn't please me, somehow, to picture Ross living with that hulking brute."

Valmy began to laugh—hysterical laughter—the tears pouring down her ghastly cheeks.

"Oh, it's too funny!" she gasped. "You are mad . . . mad! This solicitude for Ross when you left her . . . for *me* . . . oh, my God, it's funny!"

"Glad you find it so," said Clive. He walked quite coolly to the dressing-table, took a handkerchief from the drawer and put it in his pocket, then pulled his case out and lit a cigarette.

Valmy watched him, her slim body in a crouching attitude, her hand still catching convulsively at her throat. She was shaking with that terrible laughter—in the grip of hysteria. She felt bemused at the thought that this man, for whom she had given up everything, was about to abandon her.

"I'm hanged if I'm going to let McCrayle have Ross and all her money," said Clive. "No—not quite. And I'll wager a good deal that she is only living with him because she was piqued by my conduct. She doesn't love him. It's me she's always cared for. She'll be quite ready to come back to me if I swear I'm sorry and that I'll be good to her!"

Valmy did not speak, but she stopped laughing. She felt suddenly sick and dizzy. Much as she had loved Clive, she could not help but see in this hour what an utter scoundrel he was; what a blackguard he had been from the very beginning—thinking only of himself. Still—she had loved him madly, and she still loved him, after the fashion of women who cling to men who ill-treat them.

"If you take my advice, Valmy, you'll slip out of this hotel without being seen and let the bill go to blazes," Clive told her curtly. "I'll leave you a few pounds, and if you feel you'd better go back to England, you can call at the G.P.O. here in a few days' time, and I'll send you the necessary for your passage home. It's not much use you remaining in South Africa."

She found speech then, her voice dry and hoarse.

"So you've really done with me, have you, Clive?"

He avoided her eyes.

"I'm sorry, my dear, if it's all ended very abruptly, but you must see for yourself that one can't live on love and kisses. I'm badly in need of money, and I've got to go where I can get some. I can't stay here with you, now can I? Be reasonable!"

"Reasonable!" she repeated, with a tremulous laugh. "Oh, heavens!"

"Cut out the dramatic stuff, Valmy!" he said. "Why can't you look at things from a sensible point of view? That's the worst of you women—you never can end an affair in a sporting way. There must be a howling scene and reproaches and all the rest of it. We've had a topping time together. Now it's got to end—for financial reasons."

"It sounds very simple," said Valmy. "But it's a bit different for the woman, Clive, and that's what men like you don't understand. I—I've given you everything, and you're deserting me."

She broke into wild weeping, covering her face with her hands "I shall kill myself if you leave me!" she added.

"Oh, no, you won't!" he said. "You haven't the courage. Besides, don't be a little idiot, Valmy. Go back to England and pretend all this has never happened."

She raised her face. It was streaming with tears; blotched; a mask of the pretty face that had fired Clive's senses in the past. Yet it was infinitely more sincere. This was the real Valmy ... a woman awake at last to the realisation of her folly.

"How can I pretend it has never happened?" she asked pitifully. "You seem to forget—I loved you, Clive."

Cad though he was, he was touched now. He put an arm around her and awkwardly patted her shoulders.

"There, there, old thing. I'm frightfully sorry about it all. I wouldn't have left you, honestly, if this beastly business about the money hadn't turned up."

She clung to him, sobbing.

"Clive, don't leave me—don't go back to Ross! If you've ever loved me, don't leave me now!"

"I must," he said. "I've got to go and find Ross and get her and the money back. Then I might be able to see something of you again—you never know, and —"

"Oh, don't!" interrupted Valmy. "Don't!" She drew away from him, shuddering. Even she, bad though she had been, could not sink to such depths as those insinuated by Clive.

"You can't go back to Ross—get her back—then see me again," she said, hoarsely. "That would be horrible!"

Clive reddened. Then he marched to the door, jamming his hat down on his head. He was 'sick of the scene'. He'd had enough, he told himself.

"Well, I'm going, Valmy," he muttered. "Take care of yourself, my dear girl — that's all I've got to say. You've plenty of money to get on with, and if you call at the G.P.O., as I said before, in a few days' time, you'll find some money waiting for you. Then you can get back to England. Good-bye!"

She gave a great cry — stumbled across the room and caught his hand.

"Clive — no — don't go!" she implored. "I can't stand being left all alone! Clive, Clive, what will become of me?"

"What I've said. Let go, and don't be a fool!" he said, roughly.

She looked wildly around her.

"But the luggage — everything — Clive!"

"Leave it here — send for it later. If I get hold of some money within the next day or two, I'll settle up the bill by post, then they'll let you have your trunk. Good-bye! I must go now. I've got a long way to travel before I find Ross and McCrayle. Good-bye, Valmy!"

He pushed her none too gently from him. She lost her balance and fell, in a crumpled little heap, to the floor. He took advantage of this to get away quickly and closed the door after him.

She lay where she had fallen, her chiffon frock crumpled, her hair dishevelled; her face hidden on her bare arm. "Bacchante!" was the goddess of wine and fun and song no longer. She was a tragedy ... that most pitiful of all things — a woman deserted by her lover — left to reap the harvest of sin, in tears and anguish — alone.

Her breath was caught by terrible, hoarse sobs. She was fully alive to the fact that Clive had abandoned her — that she would never see him again. She had had her little hour of love and passion and gaiety ... it had burnt itself out .... too fierce a flame to last ... and there was nothing left but the ashes of bitterness and remorse.

In this hour of her agony, Valmy Page remembered the words that Ross had spoken to her on that morning at Swallow Dip, when she had come, not to win Clive back, but to try to save her cousin from her folly.

"One day you'll wake up and regret this terribly," Ross had said. "What will you do if he treats you as he treated me — deserts you ...?"

Yes, Valmy remembered those words in this hour ... and she knew that Ross had not spoken without knowledge of Clive's character. What she had prophesied had come to pass. Clive had deserted her, Valmy — as he had deserted his wife. And she did regret it — terribly. For what had she left? Nothing! Where was she to go? What was she to do? How could she be certain that Clive would get the money from Ross, for her passage home? The only possible thing was for her to slink back to England, whence she had come. But even then, the thing she had done could never be wiped out. She had ruined Ross's happiness and stolen Clive Derrell. That could never be wiped out.

A bitter cry broke from Valmy's lips.

"My God! My God! What have I done ... and what am I to do now?"

But there came no answer save the hollow echo of her own voice. Valmy was alone — utterly alone. Her punishment had commenced.

"As ye have sown — so shall ye reap."

Valmy Page learned the terrible significance of those words during the next few days.

She slunk about the hotel, looking like a little ghost ... white-faced, haggard, eyes no longer brilliant and beautiful, but dim with crying and full of abject misery and fear. The manager made polite inquiries about "Madam's husband" and Valmy stammered something to the effect that "her husband had had to go to Bulawayo on business."

"He will no doubt be returning shortly, to settle up the bill," the manager added, pleasantly.

"Yes, of course," Valmy muttered.

But her throat felt dry and hot as she moved away from the man. She sensed the curiosity and suspicion behind his amiable smiles and inquiries. No doubt he guessed that Clive was not her husband at all, and had deserted her. And if Clive failed to put in an appearance — which was inevitable, she told herself wretchedly — she would be turned out of the hotel and her luggage confiscated.

She dreaded any such humiliation. Day after day she crept about the place, scarcely daring to raise her eyes; eating nothing ... for she was too sick with misery to eat. And day after day she called at the G.P.O. hoping to find a letter from Clive with the promised money. She had but one desire; that was to get back to London. She was a stranger in Johannesburg. The big South African town frightened her, now that she no longer had Clive to protect her. Several men in the streets stopped her and spoke to her. But she fled from them all, terrified and ashamed. She began to pray for the first time in her life; to pray passionately to the God whose laws she had so recklessly broken – that she might receive the money for her passage home and get out of this devastating country.

No word came from Clive. He seemed to have vanished out of her life.

She began to fear that he never meant to send her money. Soon she would find herself stranded in Johannesburg; homeless and penniless. She knew that no decent English family would receive her or help her if they knew her history. She had behaved disgracefully to Ross – run away with Ross's husband. What hope had she of sympathy or aid from any clean-living woman?

Days and hours of torturing anxiety, coupled with remorse, racked Valmy into a state bordering on insanity. Finally her overwrought brain communicated its grief and fears to her body. She did not get up, one morning. The chambermaid found her tossing and moaning in the grip of a high fever.

It did not take long for the manager of the hotel to decide what to do. 'Mrs. Derrell,' as she called herself, had obviously been abandoned by the man who had brought her there; a long bill was unpaid, and hotel managers are by no means philanthropists. An ambulance was sent for. Valmy was ignominiously carted off to the free hospital in Johannesburg ... and her possessions remained with the hotel in lieu of the settlement of her bill

It was the crowning humiliation to Valmy to come to her senses and find herself in the narrow bed of a hospital ward, with all the flotsam and jetsam of Johannesburg. And when an English nurse approached her bed and asked if she wished to send for any relative or friend, Valmy merely shook her head and hid her burning face on the pillow. She had no relatives; no friends to send for. She could not send for Ross or for Clive, even had she wished to. She did not know in the least where they were. Besides, she was not seriously ill. The nurse said she had a "bad attack of fever and nervous prostration." She would get better. Then she would have to face what lay before her ... if Clive did not send the money for the passage home.

She lay in the narrow bed, her head aching and buzzing, her heart sick within her, conscious that she was only paying the just penalty for her sins.

CHAPTER XXI

ONE afternoon in the middle of January, Ross and Bill sat in the little sitting-room of their ranch, staring out of the window somewhat ruefully.

Rain! rain! rain! For three consecutive days and nights it had been pouring with rain. At first it had been lovely and refreshing; the parched earth had sucked in the moisture; the stream had bubbled and become swollen and more radiant than ever; the green things had looked really fresh and green at last. Of course, Bill and Ross had expected the rains to set in, and the mealies were harvested and everything was as it should be. But the rainy months are very trying in Rhodesia. Wagons and cars taking forage to the towns get stuck; there are impassable swamps; terrific thunderstorms, a pest of house-flies and fleas, and it becomes difficult to keep milk fresh or meat untainted.

"It's sure to clear up soon, Ross," said Bill, filling a pipe as he spoke. "It doesn't very often rain all day and all night in Rhodesia, does it?"

"No—this is most unusual," she smiled. "We generally get rain all day and fine all night, or vice-versa."

"If only it'd clear up a bit, I could get out and do something," said Bill. "I'd rather like a nice fat wild-pig."

"So would I!" said Ross.

Their eyes met. They smiled at each other. There was frank camaraderie and happiness in the eyes of both the man and the woman. They were wonderfully happy together on their little ranch. They agreed over everything. They spent long, happy days, long happy evenings firm friends, co-workers; both putting the sordid, unhappy memories of the past behind them — both rejoicing in the peace and plenty and delight of the new, sweet life in the wilderness.

And there was something more in Ross's eyes now; more than mere respect and affection for Bill. Lately she had been discovering a much deeper feeling, a much more thrilling emotion at the sight of his rugged face, which was ever alight with worship for her; at the sound of his deep, cheery voice; the touch of his strong, capable hands.

He had grown to mean so much more than she had ever dreamed he could mean. The love she had borne the husband who had behaved so badly, had died. The wounds he had dealt her were no longer aching. They were just scars. Bill had no thought in life beyond her; no desire save to win her love. What wonder that Ross turned to him — felt love blossom and burst into flower in her heart, as the days went by?

He did not know that love had come. He believed she was still just a friend who depended on him; a pal who was working with him, living with him as a sister might have done.

But beneath his steady comradeship, burned that vital fire of passionate love which was as pure and strong as it was deathless. Ross knew it — gloried in it. No longer did she fear it, or look upon him with compassion, feeling it impossible ever to make him as happy as he deserved to be for his loyalty and courage. She thrilled at the thought of it; waited in secret for the hour, the day, when she could tell him that she had grown to care ... that if only she could gain her freedom, she would surrender to him — everything that a tender, loving woman longs to give to the man of her choice.

Towards the end of the afternoon the rain ceased. But the sun remained hidden behind a great bank of heavy cloud. It was one of those sodden, grey days of Rhodesia when the veldt was hidden in a weeping mist and the kopjes and mountains rose like ghosts through the wet grey clouds of vapour.

It was terribly hot and sultry. Every door and window of the little bungalow was open, and Ross went about gasping and looking pale and drawn. Bill had gone out to inspect the cattle-kraals.

He came back in time for a late tea.

"Phew!" he said, mopping his forehead. "What an atmosphere, Ross!"

"There's going to be a terrific storm," said Ross, fanning herself with a paper.

"You look white, my dear," he said, concerned. "You're not going to get fever, are you?"

"Oh, no!" she laughed. "I'm all right. Only this sort of heat knocks one over."

"Well, take care of yourself, dear," he said, tenderly. "I don't like to see you looking so pale."

She gave him her wide, boyish grin. His solicitude for her never failed to please her. It was so wonderful to be loved as Bill McCrayle loved her; to be looked after in this sweet gentle way. She had grown so used to looking after Clive ... it was rather a change to be taken care of, instead. And she could not help looking back, remembering, with a swift stab of pain, what Clive had been like in the rainy season; irritable, short-tempered, grumbling; making the worst of everything.

Bill was different; patient and cheery. She scarcely remembered a day when he groused for longer than a few moments —and then only because his patience was sorely tried by the very trying Kaffirs who worked on the farm.

Suddenly she said:

"Bill, I can't help wondering what's happened to Clive, and Valmy."

Bill felt for his pipe. In moments of stress that pipe was a refuge.

"I—don't know, dear," he said.

"I hate talking of them—I know it hurts you—and I hurt myself, in a way," she went on. "But it doesn't really matter any more."

"Thank God for that," said Bill.

"I can't help wondering what has happened," she repeated. "You know, Bill, we just—cleared out, left everything. What can be taking place back there on the ranch?"

"You instructed your lawyers to put the place up for sale," said Bill. "No doubt we'll be hearing that someone has bought it, soon."

"Yes," she nodded, biting her lower lip. "And Twopence will be back with the wagon—and my various things."

Two weeks ago, the faithful and trusty 'boy' had been sent with a wagon to trek back to the ranch whence he had come, and fetch the things the beloved 'Missis' required.

"In a way I feel mean and spiteful for preventing Clive from drawing on my account, and taking the farm away from him," said Ross, with knit brows. "Yet what could I do?"

"You did the only thing possible, dear," said Bill. "For you to support Clive—after all that happened—would be to countenance the wrong he is doing—in living with Valmy."

The blood rushed to Ross's face.

"God knows what the end will be for those two," she said, with a deep sigh. "But Clive had a few hundreds of his own and I dare say he'll take Valmy to some town—get some work and look after her."

Bill made no reply. His lips closed rather grimly. He could not imagine a man of Clive Derrell's temperament taking to

162

hard work and looking after the girl with whom he was but temporarily infatuated. But he said nothing to Ross. He had no wish to make her anxious on behalf of the two who had never had one decent, single thought for her.

Ross spoke no more of Clive and Valmy. But later that evening, after supper, Bill put an arm about Ross's shoulders and looked deeply into her eyes.

"Dear," he said. "Tell me — frankly — you never regret coming out here with me — do you?"

She answered without hesitation:

"Never, Bill — never for a single second. I have been perfectly happy here with you."

The tone of her voice, the tranquillity in her eyes drove any lingering doubts from his mind. His arm dropped away from her. His heart was at peace. She was 'perfectly happy'. That was all that mattered to Bill McCrayle.

They parted at bedtime — as usual — with a friendly handclasp. But they met again in the living-room within an hour. A violent thunderstorm had broken over the veldt; a veritable demon of storm chasing across the rain-soaked plains. The lightning flashed from one part of the heavens to another; dancing from kopje to kopje with a kind of demoniacal glee. Ross was used to these terrific Rhodesian thunderstorms but, tonight, the storm seemed unusually fierce and prolonged. She did not even undress. She had flung herself down on the bed, knowing that sleep was impossible. Then she got up and went into the living-room.

Bill too was unable to sleep. The deafening peals of thunder crashed and rolled from the distant hills. He heard Ross pacing up and down the room, and so he opened his door.

"You, too!" he said.

She turned and looked at him, echoing his laughter.

"Oh, so you're up, Bill! What an awful storm it is! I can't sleep."

He lit a cigarette and stood smoking for a moment. A brilliant flash of lightning lit up the room, followed by a crash of thunder that seemed to shake the whole bungalow. Ross shivered and drew nearer Bill.

"I don't like this at all, tonight," she said. "I hope the roof won't be struck and cave in!"

"I sincerely hope not. We should get horribly wet if it did."

She gave a nervous little laugh.

Silence for a moment. More lightning, another clap of terrific thunder. Bill saw that Ross was trembling, and that she was quite pale. He crossed to her and put an arm about her shoulders.

"Poor little woman! You scared?"

She turned to him, quite naturally. She stood there in the shelter of his strong arms, feeling the hard throbs of his heart, indescribable emotion shot through her; a kind of ecstasy she had experienced only once in her life before ... that was when Clive had first wooed and won her. But this emotion was different, in some vague way. It was deeper, finer; delicate, yet aflame.

Before she knew what she was doing, she had put her arms up about his throat. Bill stood still, his face flushed, his eyes very bright. His other arm went about Ross, drawing her closer to him. He sensed what she was feeling. A thrill of almost terrible rapture went through him. Ross loved him — Ross whom he had worshipped for years seemed to care for him — that way — at last.

Closer, closer he drew her. And then suddenly he bent his head and kissed the brown head.

"Ross," he said. "Ross — dear — dearest Ross!"

She did not speak. She raised her face to his. It was pale, emotional, ecstatic. Her eyes closed; her head tilted back in an attitude of surrender.

His lips found hers; clung to them. They clasped each other and their kiss seemed to last an eternity. The storm rolled on, magnificently. Neither Bill nor Ross heard the thunder or saw the lightning now. Locked in that embrace, they were lost to time, to place, to everything but the fact that they loved each other.

Bill's hour had come. The thing he had waited for, prayed for, had come to pass. Ross loved him; Ross's lips clung to his, giving him kiss for kiss. The deep emotions he had known lay beneath that quiet, placid exterior, had wakened to life, to force — for him. He kept his arms wrapped about her, kissing her with deep kisses that made her breathless against his heart.

At last he raised his head. He sighed and looked down at her eyes. They opened and were looking up at him with all the exquisite shyness of a young girl who has yielded to the kiss of her first lover.

He hugged her to him, bent his head and kissed her beautiful hair reverently.

"Oh, you darling — you darling thing!" he cried in a shaken voice. "Oh, Ross, you beautiful darling soul!"

She laughed shakenly and her hands were locked about his neck.

"Bill—my dear, my dear!" she whispered.

"You love me—you love me at last, Ross?"

"Yes, I love you," she said. "I love you more than I ever thought it possible."

He thought of Clive. He held her jealously to him, covering her cheeks, her eyes, her lips with kisses.

"You mean that? Ross, my darling, tell me it's true and not a dream! So often I've dreamed of holding you in my arms and hearing you say you love me. Is it true—after all these rotten years?"

"It's true," said Ross. "I love you with all my heart and soul, Bill. I didn't think I'd ever love another man—after Clive—but I do!"

He gave a low laugh.

"Oh, Ross, Ross—to think of hearing you say that!"

"You've been so patient, so sweet and good to me—so understanding," she said. "How can I repay you? I've wasted all these years. I ought to have married you when you first asked me, Bill, darling. I know that now."

"Dear Ross, this moment repays me for everything," he said. "I want nothing more on earth. To have you here with me—as a comrade—has been happiness. To have you here as my wife . . . will be divine."

"Your wife . . ." she repeated. Her cheeks lost their flush and her eyes grew troubled. "Bill . . . if only I can be your wife," she added. "But can I?"

"Of course. You and Clive must be divorced. I must marry you, Ross."

"Yes. I want to marry you, Bill," she whispered. "I love you so, my dear, I only want to stay here with you for the rest of my life."

"My darling!" He buried his face on her soft, warm neck. "I adore you. But you know it. I needn't tell you. When did you begin to care for me?"

"I don't know," she said almost shyly. "I can't tell. It just —came, Bill, gradually."

"Thank God," said Bill.

He looked back on that night in his old shanty when she had called for Clive, and he, Bill, had taken her in his arms; felt the sweetness of her arms and lips for the first time. But he would not tell her of that. Her arms, her lips were his a thousand times more tonight. She was the real Ross, knowing what she said and did. And she said she loved him; she gave him her kisses gladly and freely. It seemed to him like a miracle.

Later Bill said:

"Ross, I shall never rest now until you're free to marry me."

"What shall we do?" she asked, looking at him with her warm brown eyes.

"I don't know yet," he said. "We must think. We'll get into touch with Clive, somehow."

"Yes," she said, in a low tone. "We must."

Bill held her more closely to him.

"My love," he said. "I love you so! I don't know how I'm going to wait."

She smoothed back the thick, curly hair with a tender hand.

"Dearest, I know . . . but we've got to wait. It wouldn't seem right if —"

"You can trust me, sweetheart," he broke in. "I'll not do anything to make you think less of me."

"I know so well how much you can be trusted," she said. "You are the most wonderful man in the world, Bill . . . to me!"

Their lips met. For a long moment there was silence. Then Bill gently released her. His breath was coming very quickly, and his heart beat so fast it nearly suffocated him. He loved her so . . . and she loved him . . . it was hard to let her go; to know that he must wait until she had gained her freedom . . . long weary months before he might claim her as his wife! But it never for a moment occurred to him to suggest any other course. Honour, to Bill McCrayle, was stronger than love.

"You'll be getting a chill, my dear," he said. "Go back to bed. The storm's dying down. You feeling all right?"

She nodded — her face rosy from his kisses her eyes bright with happiness. Bill walked to the window and pulled back the curtains. The rain was falling very gently and the lightning played fitfully over the veldt. From the distance, now and then, came a low, sullen roar of thunder but the storm had abated. Clouds chased each other across the dark heavens — a crescent moon suddenly appeared in between the heavy clouds.

Bill opened the window a little. The night wind brought with it a rich perfume of wet earth and crushed flowers. Bill drew a deep breath of it, then turned to Ross.

"Peace after the storm, Ross, my heart," he said.

"In more ways than one," she nodded. "Oh, Bill, Bill, how happy I am!"

"We shall be marvellously happy, once we belong to each other — for ever," he said.

"But whatever happens, nothing can ever really separate us — can it, Bill?"

He came to her quickly, folded her in his arms, buried his face in her lovely hair.

"Nothing, my darling. You're mine, and I'm yours. And now, good night, and God bless you!"

"God bless you, Bill, dear," she whispered.

Morning came.

Bill and Ross met in the living-room for breakfast. The memory of last night was with them both. They looked at each other shyly — gladly.

Ross seemed to McCrayle like a young girl in her fresh white frock.

His face flushed and his eyes glowed as he looked at her. He caught her in his arms, kissed her ardently.

"Ross, you darling!" he cried, with his lips against her hair.

"Good morning, Bill," she said demurely. "You must behave, you know! Fourpence will be in with the breakfast in a moment!"

"What do I care?" he asked, with a boyish laugh. "I don't mind if the whole world sees . . . I'm so happy."

And then the most unexpected thing in the world happened. Fourpence, the new house-boy, came rushing into the room — not with the breakfast — but with an exciting piece of news.

"White man coming up road, Missis!" he announced, grinning. "Him all alone — on horse."

"I wonder who it can be," said Ross.

"Let's go and see," said Bill.

With their arms about each other, they walked on to the veranda. There was no sign of last night's storm. It was a calm, lovely morning.

But the moment Ross and Bill saw the figure of the man who had dismounted and was walking slowly up to the bungalow, their world was plunged in darkness. They exchanged astounded, dismayed glances.

"My God!" said Bill. "Clive!"

"Clive!" echoed Ross.

She stood motionless on the veranda, both hands pressed to her heart. It beat with swift, painful jerks. Clive ... here ... it was incredible! Yet she knew they had not made a mistake. He was coming nearer every second. The slim figure, the rather arrogant poise of the head, the swinging walk were all terribly familiar.

She watched him and shrank from all the bitter, agonising memories he revived for her.

She had hoped never to set eyes on her husband's face again. She had said good-bye to him for ever; thought of him as dead. She had given her love to Bill McCrayle, and it seemed almost a sacrilege that Clive should come now to disturb that peace and happiness which she and Bill had found.

Bill's feelings were indescribable. He only knew that he loathed this man who was coming towards them. Loathed him for the brute, the cad he had been to this sweet woman at his side. He felt passionate resentment against him for coming. How dared he come? What right had he? Where was Valmy? What had happened to make Clive show his lying, deceitful face here?

He put out a hand and swiftly laid it on Ross's shoulder. She could feel it shaking.

"Ross —" he said under his breath.

"All right, darling," she answered, steadily. "Don't worry. Whatever he says ... it will make no difference to us ..."

Her words were a relief. For an instant Bill had faced the possibility that Clive's coming might make a very great difference. He knew Ross's gentle nature. He was terribly afraid she might deal kindly with the husband she had once loved. For he was positive — as soon as he looked upon Clive Derrell's face — that he had come to whine for pardon.

What Clive, himself, was feeling can well be imagined. He looked at the man and the woman who stood side by side on the sunlit veranda, and cursed himself for the day he had ever thrown Ross aside — driven her into Bill McCrayle's arms. How happy they both looked! He had never seen Ross look so well — so attractive. She had a glorious colour — golden tan. Her eyes were bright; her whole bearing was that of a buoyant, healthy, happy woman, glad to be alive.

And he had left this glorious creature; left her for a slip of a girl — Valmy, whom he had last seen in Johannesburg with rouge on her cheeks and mascara on her lashes — a haggard, dissipated little idiot who had wept and moaned at his feet!

"I must have been mad," he told himself savagely as he came up the step towards Ross and Bill. "Ross is worth ten of Valmy ... and Bill McCrayle has won her—damn him!"

He had the grace to look and to feel ashamed when at length he stood before the wife he had so terribly wronged. He took off his hat and fingered it nervously.

She looked at him without flinching. But inwardly she was far from calm. The sight of her husband had no power to rouse her to anguish or bitterness, now. But it embarrassed her. She felt uneasy. He was a stranger to her—bloated, coarsened. Yet the handsome features were still there; the sleek, fair head; the well-shaped hands. A good deal to remind her of the old Clive—whom she had loved and for whom she had suffered the greatest agony and humiliation. She felt sick at soul to look at him and remember all that had been between them.

Clive was the first to speak.

"Well, Ross," he said awkwardly.

"Why have you come here?" she asked.

He chewed at his lower lip and glanced furtively at Bill whose rugged face was impassive.

"I—want to see you, Ross," said Clive.

"What about?"

"Oh—lots of things! I—I've been thinking a lot about you lately, Ross, and I—"

"Pardon me," she interrupted, her heart beating very fast, her beautiful colour all gone, "I think it is a bit late for you to have begun to think about me. You had no right to come. You went your way. I have gone mine."

"Quite so," he said, fumbling with his hat. "But that's what I want to see you about. Won't you grant me a few minutes' talk, Ross—alone?"

CHAPTER XXII

For a moment Ross did not speak. Then she said in a low voice, without looking at him:

"I'm sorry. I have nothing to say to you, Clive. I'd much rather not enter into any discussion — it would only be — beastly — for us all."

"Oh, but you must —" began Clive, angrily.

"Pardon me — Ross shall do exactly as she wishes," broke in Bill McCrayle. "I quite agree with her — it is far better to avoid a painful scene."

"What do you want to interfere for?" muttered Clive. "Ross is my wife and —"

But once again he was interrupted — by Ross.

"I was your wife. But I don't admit that you have any claim on me now — at all," she said in a clear, hard voice. "If you have anything to say — please say it to Bill."

Then turning, she walked quickly into the bungalow and closed the door after her.

Clive smothered an oath. He made a movement as though to follow her. But Bill stepped in front of him.

"You heard what she said — kindly respect her wishes," he rapped out.

Clive clenched his hands.

"Damn it, man, why shouldn't I speak to her? I've come a pretty long way in order to do so."

"That's your affair. If I were you I'd go back where I came from — without much delay."

"Oh, indeed!" sneered Clive. "Well, I'm not so sure I'm going to do that. After all, what right have you got to prevent me from seeing my wife?"

"Try to remember that you deserted your wife and have no claim on her," said Bill, in a quiet, level voice. He did not want to lose his temper. "You heard what she said: if you have anything to say — I'm here to listen to you."

Clive dropped into a chair and wiped his face with his handkerchief. There were beads of moisture on his brow and upperlip and he was deadly pale. Inwardly he seethed with rage —

hatred of Bill McCrayle. He realised without much doubt that this big, muscular figure stood between him and Ross. He had expected to come back and play the 'prodigal'—make tender, repentant speeches to Ross; work on her sympathy, her gentle nature, until he had secured her pardon. Instead, he found her cold, immovable, refusing to discuss things with him; in fact, deliberately turning her back on him. It was not so easy to make repentant speeches to Bill McCrayle.

He tapped his foot nervously on the ground. Then, without raising his eyes to Bill, he said:

"You're pretending to be the injured party, McCrayle, but, hang it all—you ran away with my wife—eloped with her—didn't you?"

Bill crossed his arms on his chest, a grim smile playing about his fine lips.

"Elope is scarcely the word."

"It comes to the same thing—you went off together."

"After you had driven Ross from her home by your conduct."

"Well, you've done just as much wrong as I have, anyhow. You've been living here with Ross —"

"One moment," interrupted Bill, his face flushing. "You'd better just get into your mind this one, plain truth. Ross and I have not lived together in the sense you mean. She has never been unfaithful to you—although she owes you no fidelity. She and I have lived here together as friends—as brother and sister might have done."

Clive gave him a swift, incredulous look, then gave a short laugh.

"That's hard for me to swallow, McCrayle."

"It may be," said Bill. "But it's the truth."

Instinctively Clive knew that Bill was not lying. He realised —not for the first time—that this man to whom Ross had given her trust and love was infinitely more worthy of it than he, Clive, had ever been. But that knowledge did not help to improve his temper.

"What I want to arrange with you, Clive," said Bill, "is that you give Ross her freedom."

"Why should I?" snapped Clive.

"Well, you can't want to remain tied to Ross," said Bill, uneasily. "You, yourself, want to be free, don't you?"

"Why?"

"To marry Valmy Page."

171

Clive pitched away his half-smoked cigarette with a violent movement.

"No," he said. "I don't want to marry Valmy."

"But good heavens, Clive—you must!"

"My dear McCrayle, I'm not a quixotic ass," he said in the old, irritable voice Bill knew so well. "I don't see that I must marry Valmy—just because we've been lovers."

"What a damned swine you are!"

"Call me what you like, I'm not going to marry Valmy."

"Where is she?"

"In Jo'burg."

"Jo'burg!" exclaimed Bill, staring. "You went there?"

"Yes."

"And you've left her there—alone?"

"Yes," said Clive in the same sullen voice.

Bill looked at him much as he would have looked at a reptile.

"God—I can hardly keep my hands off you!"

"Why should it concern you?"

"It doesn't—but it will upset Ross terribly. She's very tender-hearted and generous. She'll be horrified to think that her cousin has been deserted and left alone in Johannesburg."

"Valmy's all right—I'll send her some money," said Clive.

"Where is she?"

"I don't know—unless at the hotel where I left her, but I told her to go for letters to the G.P.O."

"I'll see, myself, that she gets some money," said Bill. "She may be in terrible trouble. However wicked she's been, she's a young girl—and a kinswoman of Ross's. One can't let her starve—in Jo'burg. It's damnable!"

"Apart from all that—I came here to tell Ross I'm sorry for what I did," muttered Clive.

"And what's made you sorry?" said Bill, with a scornful look at him.

Clive got up and turned his face from Bill. He drummed his fingers on the rail of the veranda.

"See here, McCrayle," he said. "Am I going to be allowed to talk to Ross—or not?"

"She doesn't want to see you," said Bill.

"Very well," said Clive. "You two can stay here and I wish you joy of it. I shan't set Ross free, so you won't be able to marry her. That's a cert."

Bill's eyes blazed.

"I see. You mean to be spiteful—to hurt Ross a bit further."

"And you, yes," said Clive, harshly.

"You're rotten — through and through," said Bill, clenching his fingers. "You'd better quit soon — get out right now!"

Clive thrust out his jaw aggressively.

"That's all you've got to say, is it?"

"Yes — except that I ask you again — to give Ross her freedom so that she can marry me."

"I'll never do that. And she can't divorce me, otherwise I'll bring a counter-action. Nobody'd believe you two had lived here for weeks alone — as friends."

"You have that advantage," said Bill between his teeth, "and it's only to be expected that you'd make use of it after the other unspeakable things you've done."

Clive gave him one angry, resentful look, then jammed his hat down on his head and began to walk slowly away.

Bill's hands clenched at his sides. He watched Clive walk down the veranda steps. He wanted to go after him — thrash him until he begged for mercy. If he persisted in this mean, revengeful spirit, it meant that he, Bill, could never have Ross for his wife. It was cruel — and terribly unjust.

When Clive was out of sight, Bill slowly turned and walked into the bungalow.

He found Ross in the sitting-room, restlessly pacing up and down. Her face was white, and her warm brown eyes wet with tears. She looked swiftly at Bill as he entered. She walked up to him, clasping her hands.

"Oh, my dear — what has he been saying?"

"Good many things," muttered Bill. He took the sun-browned hands in his — kissed them both — then drew her to the sofa and sat down beside her. "My poor darling," he added, "this has upset you."

"It was rather a shock — seeing him," she said in a low voice. "But I simply couldn't face him, Bill. It was altogether too painful."

"Of course," nodded Bill.

"Why did he come at all?"

"To ask your pardon, apparently."

"And did you — tell him we want to marry — that I want my freedom?"

"Yes, and he refuses to give it to you, I'm afraid," said Bill, shrugging his shoulders with a hopeless gesture. "He's beyond my understanding, Ross. I felt certain he'd be only too pleased to arrange a divorce so that he could marry Valmy."

"But has he deserted her?"

"Yes—left her in Jo'burg. The poor, wretched girl! That reminds me. We must wire her some money at once. I can't bear to think of any young girl starving in a town like that."

Ross's eyes filled with tears. She touched Bill's head with tender fingers.

"That's typical of you," she said. "You're right. It would be criminal of us to leave her stranded. I'll send her enough money to pay her passage back to England, and write a note, telling her to go back. She must try to wipe out what she has done by leading a decent life in the old country."

Bill drew a sharp sigh.

"I can only think about ourselves at the moment, Ross. What are we going to do?"

"God knows," she said in a low voice. "If Clive really means to be so spiteful, it'll just wreck all the happiness we thought we'd found."

McCrayle set his teeth and suddenly drew her into his arms, holding her in a fierce, possessive way.

"Ross, Ross," he said, "you can't mean that if Clive refuses to set you free, you'll leave me!"

She put her arms about his neck and drew his head down to hers.

"Bill, old boy, what can I do? I love you—you know it—I love you with all my heart and soul. But how can I marry you—if Clive won't set me free?"

He covered her face with kisses—lingering, passionate kisses on her eyes and cheeks and lips.

"Darling, Ross, darling, I can't give you up!" he said. "All these years I've worshipped you and waited for you—hungered for your love. I thought I'd won you at last. Ross darling, don't leave me now!"

"I want to stay with you, Bill," she said. She hid her face against his coat-sleeve. "There's nothing in life for me now—but you. But what can I do?"

"Stay with me, Ross. Stay with me, dearest. I can't let you go. It'll break my heart!"

"And mine," she said, with a sob.

He covered her hand with kisses, held her hungrily to his heart. Inwardly he cursed Clive Derrell . . . cursed him for all the sorrow he had brought on Ross in the past—for the pain he was going to bring upon her now.

"Clive must free you, Ross," he said. "My God, I feel as

though I could ride after him and kill him — choke the life out of him!"

"Do you know where he's gone?"

"No — but I presume back to Jo'burg. We'll get into touch with him somehow and put the thing to him again — appeal to him."

"I'm afraid appeals won't touch him," said Ross bitterly. "He's changed terribly. He is a hard, selfish man, Bill."

"And he had the nerve to think he could get you back," muttered Bill, hugging her to him.

"He was very much mistaken, Bill."

"Thank heaven!"

"No — appeals won't soften Clive," went on Ross. "But money —" Her sensitive face flushed. "It seems a horrible, sordid business, but somehow I think it's money he wants, Bill."

"You think he might give you the chance to divorce him if he — were given money?"

"Yes, but it sounds so disgraceful, Bill."

"It is," he nodded. "The man's a disgrace in himself. But we can't afford to let any opportunity escape us, Ross. We want to marry — and if the only way of gaining freedom for you, is to buy it — then for heaven's sake let us do it that way. Write to Clive — tell him that I'll settle money on him if he'll go through with the divorce immediately."

A glimmer of hope brightened Ross's eyes.

"Yes, that might work. But I'll settle the money —"

"No!" interrupted Bill. "I won't have you give him a farthing of your money. I've saved a tidy bit, as you know. Let me be the one to settle Mr. Clive."

She drew his head down to her and kissed him passionately.

"How good you are to me, Bill — how dear! I don't know what I'd do without you — how I'd face life alone!"

"You won't have to — I swear it," he said. "You shall face it with me, my dear — one day — you'll see."

"And meanwhile —"

"Meanwhile, we shall go on in our little ranch as we've been doing," he said, without a hesitation. "Just — pals."

She said nothing, but she held him to her with arms that were eloquent of her love and her deep gratitude for his great patience and understanding.

About one mile away from the little ranch, Clive Derrell slid from his saddle and sat down for a rest under the shade of a tree. It was midday—and too hot to ride any farther until sundown. He had received no hospitality at the bungalow he had just left, and considered himself an injured party. He was not only hot, but hungry. He decided to camp here for the day and make definite plans for the future.

He gave a sharp order to the Kaffir who had accompanied him on this trek; followed him with a luggage-laden mule. The black-faced, grinning boy proceeded to put up Clive's tent, light a fire and prepare a meal of stewed bully-beef and potatoes.

Clive leaned against the trunk of the tree, watching—his brows drawn together in a heavy scowl. Now and then he put up a hand to brush the perspiration from his forehead or irritably fan away the flies. He was in a furious temper. His reception from Ross had been altogether different from the one he had hoped for. Now, what was he to do? he asked himself savagely. Ross refused to see him, and obviously wanted to remain with Bill McCrayle. Well—he'd see to it that she did not get her freedom. His lips curled spitefully at that thought.

"She shan't marry him," he muttered. "That's a dead cert. But now, what am I going to do?"

He had no money. He had hoped to get some out of Ross, but under the circumstances the question of money had not arisen at all. Where could he go? If he went to Bulawayo or some other near town—Livingstone—any of them—how could he get work? He knew no trade save that of farming and it was not easy to get a job on a ranch. Besides, after being joint-owner of a large, flourishing ranch, it would be pretty humiliating for him, Clive Derrell, to have to be subordinate to some rotten little Colonial farmer.

He drew a bottle from his luggage, uncorked it, and took a long draught of raw, Cape spirit. Then he sat back and began to brood again. At intervals he took sips of the stimulant. The strong spirit on top of an empty stomach had the natural effect of going to his head. He grew muddled and at the same time his thoughts were bitter—angry—revengeful.

Ross was still his wife. By gad, he'd like to show her who was the master ... he'd like to take her in his arms and force her to kiss him as she had kissed him in the old days. He'd like to break that proud, haughty spirit she had shown him today! As for Bill McCrayle—his feelings towards Bill were murderous. He blamed Bill for everything. Bill had wormed himself into Ross's affections; no doubt was after her money as well as her love. Bill had done everything possible to influence Ross against him, Clive. Yes, Bill McCrayle was to blame. He'd like to shoot him down like a dog.

The 'boy' brought Clive a plate of beef and potatoes, but Clive refused the food—swore at his servant savagely and sent the plate with the food flying into the air. The 'boy' slunk away, rolling his eyes.

"De Bwana got de seben debils in him," he muttered.

Clive stared before him with bloodshot eyes. He continued to take nips of the raw brandy. The longer he sat there, drinking, brooding, the darker grew his thoughts.

Why should Ross refuse to see him? What right had she to shut the door on him? She was his wife. He would go back—force her to see him—force her into his arms—punish her until she begged at his feet for mercy.

It was her duty to return to her husband. He'd break down that cool dignity—have his revenge on her for her refusal to see him this morning.

Crazy thoughts continued to filter through his sodden mind. His desire for revenge assumed dangerous proportions. To bend Ross to his will—force her back into his arms—that desire grew and grew until it obsessed him.

He began to form plans—cunning plans for carrying out his intentions. They were making a mistake, he thought, that pretty pair back at the ranch, if they imagined he had just slunk off and left them free to love each other. He'd show them! He was quite justified in what he meant to do. Ross was his wife—Bill McCrayle had alienated her affections. He had every right to go back and insist upon Ross listening to what he had to say.

He knew that it was the custom for Colonists to sleep between the hours of two and five—the hottest part of the day. By the time he got back to the ranch, it would be two o'clock—Ross would be in her room, preparing to retire. He would creep in through the window, without being seen by Bill McCrayle and threaten to shoot her—to shoot them both down like dogs unless she listened to him.

He lurched on to his feet, shaking with mad laughter. He called to the 'boy' who kept at a distance, eyeing him furtively, terrified by the wild expression on the Bwana's face.

"Here—clear up this mess and take down the tent," said Clive thickly. "We're going back to the farm."

"Going back," echoed the boy.

"Yes, damn you — don't stand there gaping at me! I want to get back by two o'clock."

The 'boy' muttered a reply and hastened to obey the order. But Clive yelled after him:

"No — I've changed my mind. I shall go alone. You can wait here until I come back."

"Yes, Bwana," said the boy.

Clive swayed a little on his feet. His hair was rough, his eyes strained and red, his jaw thrust out in a stubborn, brutal way. He was mad with drink.

He took his gun and made sure that it was loaded. Then he swallowed another mouthful of brandy and climbed into the saddle. . . .

A moment later he was riding over the sun-baked veldt, heedless of the burning heat — of the sweating, panting animal into which he dug his heels.

CHAPTER XXIII

In the little bungalow, hidden away by the trees on the crest of the kopje, Ross and Bill had retired to their rooms for their 'siesta' after lunch.

Just before Ross entered her bedroom, she had yielded to Bill's tender arms — responded with wistful lips to his kisses.

"It can't be wrong for me to kiss you, can it, darling?' she said. "It's so — so comforting."

"Of course it's not wrong, darling." he answered tenderly. "You've never done a wrong thing in your life."

"Oh yes I have," she leaned her brown head on his shoulder. "But I just can't help loving you, Bill."

He held her tightly to him for a moment, his lips pressed against her mouth for a long, silent moment. Then he let her go, and walked into his own room.

He took off his coat and flung himself down on his bed. He had drawn the green blinds so that his room was protected from the fierce rays of the noontide sun. It was suffocatingly hot. He wondered if there would be another thunderstorm later.

He closed his eyes and tried to sleep.

In her darkened room, Ross, too, was trying to sleep. But she tossed and turned on her bed.

"How close it is!" she thought.

She had put on a wrapper and loosened her beautiful brown hair. But she could not sleep. Her mind was too active. She kept on thinking of Clive . . . shivering at the memory of his changed, bloated face.

Forgive him — that was difficult enough! But to take him back, live with him again — never, never!

With all her heart she longed to be Bill McCrayle's wife. She loved him intensely — with all the power and passion of her being.

She lay still, trying to doze. But she found it impossible and at last she rose and began to walk up and down the little room — plaiting her beautiful flowing hair into a long, lovely braid. Finally she slipped back into bed again.

The blind at her window flapped suddenly. She lay still. The colour drained from her cheeks. She stared at the window. A man was climbing noiselessly over the low sill and had vaulted into her room. She stared at him, stupefied — and afraid. The man was her husband. Clive with a strange wild look in his eyes and a gun in his hand.

Before she could move or cry out, he sprang to her side and gripped her arm.

"Don't scream, Ross!" he said in a hoarse voice. "If you do — if you let Bill McCrayle know I've come back, I — I'll kill you!"

She looked at him with dilating eyes. She trembled from head to foot. She wanted to cry out for Bill — disregard Clive's threat — but no sound would come. For the moment she was startled into speechlessness.

"You understand," said Clive. "If you don't give me a hearing, Ross — I'll shoot you! I'm a desperate man."

The colour rushed back to her face in a burning flush.

"Clive!" she panted. "Are you mad? What have you come for? How dare you come into my room like this?"

"I'm your husband," he said roughly. "I have every right to come."

"You have no right! But I refuse to talk to you," she said,

trying to wrench her arm from his fingers. "I shall let Bill deal with you."

"Be careful, Ross!" he said, in a menacing voice. "If you drive me too far, I swear I'll shoot you."

Her terrified eyes sped from his distorted face to the gun in his hand. Her heart pounded so fast that she could scarcely breathe. She realised that Clive was not responsible for what he said and did. She knew from his wild eyes, his tainted breath that he had been drinking heavily. She shuddered as she lay there. She wondered whether to call Bill or to try to pacify Clive herself. She was really afraid of sending for Bill. There might be a ghastly scene — a fight — terrible consequences.

"Look here, Clive," she said. "What have you come to say to me?"

"Ah! You mean to listen to me?"

"Yes. I will hear what you have to say — but you must say it quickly — then go."

He gave a rasping laugh; still keeping her arm in one hand, the gun in the other.

"You fool — you would have done well to listen to me this morning, Ross."

"Don't waste time," she said. "What do you want to say?"

His mood changed. Anger and desire for revenge evaporated. He became maudlin. She was so deuced good-looking, this wife of his ... a wonderful woman .... he had been a fool ever to leave her for Valmy.

"Ross," he said in a whining voice, "you don't think I'm very happy, do you?"

"You don't deserve to be, after all your wickedness, Clive."

"But Ross — I came here to say how sorry I am — how much I regret all that's happened."

She did not speak for a moment. She felt sick and wretched as she looked at him — this travesty of the handsome charming boy she had loved and married. His face was terribly altered his half-drunken speech nauseated her. She wondered how he had the audacity to come back and steal into her bedroom like this.

"Ross," he said. "I know you're thinking vile things about me and I suppose I deserve them in a way. But I swear I'm sorry. I swear I want to put things right again."

"There's only one possible way of doing that, Clive."

"What?"

"Set me free — and marry Valmy."

"No," he said, with a laugh. "I'm not going to do that."

"Then what do you intend to do? Why have you come all this way to see me?"

"Isn't it obvious, Ross . . .?"

"No," she said very coldly.

"I want your forgiveness."

She stared at him, genuine amazement in her eyes.

"My forgiveness?" she repeated.

"Yes . . . Ross, you loved me once — you're still my wife — for God's sake don't turn me down — forgive me."

She could not speak. She was too astounded. This unexpected plea for pardon worried her. She was a kind, generous woman without a grain of malice in her composition. She considered it wrong to refuse pardon to any living creature who asked it; no matter how much she had been hurt or wronged. Yet Clive's penitence did not strike true; she knew him too well. She knew his insincerity; his hypocrisy.

Her silence gave Clive confidence.

"Ross," he said, in a beseeching voice. "I've behaved rottenly but don't turn me down. I'm terribly sorry. Won't you forgive me, Ross?"

"I — will try to forgive you, Clive," she said in a slow voice. "If you're really sorry, it isn't for me to refuse forgiveness."

His fingers tightened over her arm.

"Can we begin again, then, Ross?" he asked eagerly. "Will you take me back — give me another chance? Oh, Ross, old girl —"

"Stop, please," she broke in. Her face grew hot and her eyes flashed. She wrenched her arm from his fingers. "You're making a great mistake," she added. "I am willing to forgive — as far as I can, but I'm not going to forgive to the extent of taking you back as my husband. I gave you that chance months ago and you simply threw it on one side. I shall never take you back again. I couldn't possibly live with you as your wife . . ." She shuddered and turned her eyes from him . . . "it's colossal impudence on your part to imagine that I would. No — you've made a great mistake, Clive, if you thought you could just come when it pleased you and get me back. It's out of the question."

Clive stood staring at her. He was sick with disappointment. His enormous conceit had led him to believe that he still had the power to move Ross, to get her back again. But he had failed — ignominiously. She would not take him back. Of course he might have known — she was infatuated with McCrayle now.

"So that's how you feel," at length he said, his voice thick. "You've lost every atom of love for me."

"Yes, every atom," she said, meeting his gaze squarely. "My love for you died — and *I* nearly died with the agony of it. But now it is buried, nothing can ever revive it again. My whole life is bound up in Bill, and I only live for the hour when I can marry him."

Clive uttered a rasping laugh.

"I see," he nodded. "Well, that hour will never come, Ross. I shall not give you your freedom!"

Her face whitened. She put a hand to her heart.

"You mean that, Clive? You can't be so cruel — so spiteful!"

"It's you who are mean," he said. "I'm ready to start afresh — to be a good husband to you — and you turn me down."

She shivered and looked away from him.

"You can't expect me to take you back — it is outrageous!" she said. "Besides, it isn't me you love — it isn't in you to love any woman. But you want all that I stand for — a comfortable home — an income!"

"Believe what you like," he said savagely. "I came here with nothing but decent thoughts and feelings today and you've simply chucked me on one side — because of McCrayle."

Ross drew her figure erect.

"Bill is a good, honest fellow. I admit my love for him—I'm proud of it," she said, with a bright colour in her cheeks, and a light in her eyes. "And if you refuse to free me, you will be vile and wicked — you'll add to a list of sins already too long."

Clive folded his arms on his chest.

"Well, I don't care. I'm not going to set you free. You're my wife, and my wife you'll remain."

"You coward!" she said, in a withering voice.

"Call me what you like."

"Oh, go — please go away!" she said, with a gesture of loathing. "I can't bear to look at you — to think that I ever demeaned myself by loving you — by living with you!"

"Anything else?" he asked with a laugh.

"Go!" she repeated, pointing to the door. "And never let me see you again."

He gave a savage laugh. Turning, he laid down his gun with a swift movement — then, before she realised his intention darted to the door, turned the key in the lock, put it in his pocket and faced her, his face white with passion, his eyes terrible.

Ross caught her breath.

"What are you doing? What do you mean —"

The next moment he had her in his arms and was holding her savagely against him.

"I'm going to make you sorry for all the things you've said to me," he said in a thick voice. "You're my wife — not McCrayle's yet, and by heaven, I'll teach you to turn me down in the way you have. I've locked the door — McCrayle can't get to you now. Take this — and this — and this —"

He punctuated the last words with kisses. She struggled with him desperately, her whole being revolting from the touch of his hands and lips.

"Let me go — you coward! Help, Bill — help!" she screamed at the top of her voice.

Clive — driven to madness — laughed and went on kissing her.

"My wife," he muttered. "Don't forget it — mine!"

"Bill! Bill, save me!" shrieked Ross.

Those piercing cries for help reached Bill McCrayle and roused him from the doze into which he was just drifting. He sat up, his heart beating jerkily, and rubbed his eyes.

"Bill! Bill!" came Ross's agonised voice.

McCrayle, who had been lying down fully dressed, rushed from his room across the living-room to Ross's door. He shook the handle violently, but found it locked.

"Ross!" he cried hoarsely. "What's the matter? Ross — open the door!"

"I can't," came her voice ... then silence ... and a man's insane laugh.

"Clive," said Bill to himself, his face paling. "Good God — it's Clive."

He put his full weight against the door — straining and kicking it. It was a frail lock and Bill was a big heavy man. The door soon burst open and he rushed into the room. He saw Ross in Clive's arms fighting against him. A red mist seemed to come over his eyes. He leaped at Clive and dragged him by the collar away from Ross.

"You," he said. "By God, you damned swine — how dared *you* come back?"

Clive swung round. Then — the two men were locked in a terrible grip, grappling with each other. Clive, half mad, dimly realised that this was his enemy — this was the man who stood between him and his wife. He tried to get at his gun — to shoot him — but Bill was powerful and he could not free his arms. The madness grew on Clive, giving him an added strength. The sweat poured down Bill's face, as he tried to overpower him. He looked up at Ross, who had sunk on to the bed, her face ghastly, her eyes wide with terror. She was rubbing her bruised arms, staring at the two men — half dazed.

"Ross is my wife — *my wife*, blast you!" Clive snarled at McCrayle. "I'll show you whether you can come between husband and wife — like this —"

"Are you crazy, man?" gasped Bill, struggling with him. "Stop it — stop it, I say!"

But Clive continued to fight with him — desperately, punching his face — his body. His eyes full of hatred.

"Ross is my wife," he repeated. "We'll fight for her. The winner has her — d'you see?"

"No — I don't see," panted Bill. "You'd better take care —"

He broke off abruptly. Clive had cunningly tripped him. The two men crashed down on the floor — Clive on top of the other man. Ross stared down at them, terrified, as she saw a trickle of blood on Bill's face.

Clive uttered a laugh that held the note of insanity.

"We'll see — we'll see! We'll see whose wife you are, my pretty Ross!"

He had Bill's arms pinioned. But the other man exerted all his strength and — freeing one hand — tried to get at Clive's throat.

For a moment the two fought in silence — a deadly silence that made Ross feel sick and faint with horror.

She stumbled towards them, but Bill shouted to her:

"Take care, Ross! He's out of his mind. Take care — I can hardly hold him — don't stay in here — fetch one of the boys to help me!"

Ross felt physically sick as she looked at her wretched husband. Shuddering in every limb, she turned and fled into the hall, calling for Fourpence, the house-boy. He was strong and agile. He could help Bill.

Scarcely had she got into the hall, however, before she heard a cry from Bill, followed by two loud reports.

She stood stock-still, the colour draining from her cheeks.

She turned and stumbled back to her bedroom, her face livid with terror.

"Bill!" she screamed. "Oh, Bill . . . Bill . . . *Bill!*"

She reached the bedroom and stared before her, her throat

dry, her knees sagging under her. She saw Bill standing by the window. He was rolling the sleeve back from his left arm. The arm was bleeding profusely. But Ross did not mind the blood. She only knew Bill had not been shot. He was alive. For one terrible moment, outside, when first she had heard the shots, she had been afraid that Clive had killed him.

Then her gaze swept to the figure of the other man on the floor. Clive lay face downwards, arms flung above his head. He was lying very still.

"Bill!" said Ross hoarsely. "What's happened?"

"He got the gun and tried to shoot me . . ." Bill's voice was unsteady. He was trying to bind a handkerchief about his arm. "He got me just below the shoulder – only a flesh wound. Don't look so scared, darling. But I'm afraid he is done for. I struggled with him – tried to get the gun out of his hand – and he fought like a thousand devils – then the gun went off – got him in the side!"

"Oh, God, how awful, Bill."

"Poor chap," said Bill. "He was quite off his head . . ."

He knelt down beside Clive and gently turned him over. Ross also went down on her knees. Clive's face was no longer hideous and contorted with mad passions. It was marble-pale. The fair hair was plastered down on his brow, damp with the heat. His eyes were closed. Ross felt sick as she looked at him. It was so much more the face of the old Clive who had been her young, handsome lover.

"Oh, Bill," she whispered. "Is he really dead?"

Before Bill could answer, Clive's lashes slowly lifted, and he gave a long sigh that was almost a groan.

"Ross —" he muttered.

She leaned over him. She supported his head on her arm.

"I am here, Clive," she said in a broken voice.

His eyes – their vivid blue dim, fast glazing – looked up at her compassionate face for a moment.

"Ross," he said again. "It was – my own – fault. Don't blame – McCrayle."

"Oh, Clive!" she said. "Why did you give way to such madness?"

"Perhaps it's – for the best," he gasped. "I – I've done for myself. You're – free now."

The tears rained down her cheeks.

"Clive – poor Clive," she said huskily.

His eyes closed again for a moment. A spasm of agony

contracted his face. Then, with an effort he opened his eyes and spoke again to Ross. He tried to grin at her.

"I've made a mess of things, haven't I? Try and forgive me, old girl."

"With all my heart, Clive."

"And you — Bill" — he turned his head slowly and painfully to the man who knelt the other side of him.

"That's all right, old chap." said Bill. "The whole thing's been a rotten mistake. Don't worry about it now."

"Ross," Clive's voice was growing weaker. "Kiss me — good-bye, sweetheart!"

The old lover's name for her. She felt suddenly heart-broken. Without hesitation she leaned down and kissed him. She couldn't speak. Her throat was choked with sobs.

Clive smiled ... then suddenly he gasped and a convulsion passed through his whole frame. His head fell back on Ross's arm. Bill took him from her and laid him gently on the floor. Then he put an arm around Ross and raised her to her feet.

"Come, dear," he said. "It's all over."

She went with him, her head bowed, her eyes blinded by tears.

CHAPTER XXIV

MANY months had gone by since the death of Clive Derrell. For eight months the little bungalow up on the tree-shaded kopje had had neither master nor mistress. It had been zealously guarded and kept in good condition by Twopence and his friend, Fourpence. The two faithful 'boys' had been left in charge of the farm during the temporary absence of the owners.

Now — while Autumn painted far-away England with gold and red and brown — it was the Spring of the Rhodesian year. The veldt was purple with exquisite heliotrope bell-clusters; sweet-scented water-lilies, golden arums, masses of pink sweet peas. Flowers of every colour blossomed and rioted over the rich red earth. The stream that bubbled down past the little bungalow seemed to be particularly clear and bright, singing its gay, riotous song. The sky was intensely blue. The whole air was filled with the gladness and freshness of the Spring.

Today, Twopence and Fourpence scuttled like a pair of black rats over the bungalow. Every room was swept and washed. Every pot and pan and vase and book was in apple-pie order. And the shining faces of the two 'boys' shone with a special delight. For this morning, the Bwana and the Missis were expected home. The shadow of sorrow, of sin, of death, had passed for ever, and in the golden glory of the Rhodesian Spring Bill McCrayle was bringing Ross home—as his wife—to a new, glorious life.

Soon after Clive's death, Bill and Ross had been very quietly married. They had gone to England for their honeymoon; having first made sure that Valmy Page was put on board a boat that sailed for home.

Neither of them saw Valmy. They did not wish to see her. But Ross sent her a generous cheque which would enable her to live in comfort until she got back to some kind of work in the old country. Valmy had written a passionate letter of gratitude and that was the last thing Ross was to hear of her cousin.

Ross, and Bill spent the honeymoon in Devonshire, by the sea-coast, that peaceful English summer. It was paradise for Bill and for the woman who had learned to love him. As a husband, Bill was still an adoring lover. In Ross, he found all the exquisite qualities which a man desires in his mate.

Now they had come back to their beloved Rhodesia; back to the little ranch in which they both wanted to settle and make their permanent home.

Ross, looking like a young girl in her white frock and hat, came up the kopje on her husband's arm, and answered the ecstatic greeting of Twopence and Fourpence, with tears in her eyes.

"Oh, Bill," she said, squeezing his arm against her side. "Isn't it all too wonderful? Our little ranch—our real home—at last!"

Bill put an arm around her and kissed the glowing cheek nearest him.

"My darling—I'm so glad you're happy," he said.

"Happy isn't the word for it, Bill darling. Our few months in Devonshire were lovely—but I'm glad to be back in Rhodesia —aren't you?"

"Why, of course," he nodded. "Rhodesia is home, isn't it, Ross?"

They found so much to do after their arrival. They walked about arm in arm like a pair of happy children. Together they inspected the farm; the cattle; the mealie land; the grinning Kaffir boys down in the kraals; and found everything to their complete satisfaction.

That night, when the sky was studded with stars, and a new moon silvered the veldt, Ross and her husband stood on the veranda looking at their little world. They found it exceedingly beautiful.

Ross leaned her head on Bill's shoulder.

"This is the first Rhodesian night that we've spent as husband and wife, Bill," she said dreamily. "My dear, I think if dear old Daddy could see us, he'd be glad."

"I believe he would, Ross."

"There's only one thing missing, Bill."

"What's that, Ross?" he looked at her almost anxiously. He did not want this cherished woman of his to feel that anything was lacking in their union.

Ross snuggled her brown head closer against his shoulder.

"Can't you think of anything you'd like on our farm — beside ourselves."

"No," he said emphatically.

"Think again, Bill."

She gave a laugh with a catch in it and made him look at her. He saw that her cheeks were like peonies, flaming and beautiful and that there was an expression in her eyes that he had never seen there before.

His heart gave a great twist.

"Oh, Ross," he said.

"Great stupid — don't you know now?"

"Is it — honest to God — are you sure?"

"I was sure before I left England."

"Ross!" said Bill McCrayle again — staring at her — a great dumbfounded fellow whose immense happiness robbed him of the power of expression. But his arms held her as though he could never let her go again and she could feel him trembling.

"It'll be nice," she whispered. "To have a small Bill — teach him to love Rhodesia — like we do."

"Angel," he said. "You darling angel." And put his flushed and awed face against her cool neck.

Ross stroked his rough curly hair and looked up at the

glittering stars. A little breeze brought them the rich scent of the veldt — of the spring night.

Then Bill lifted his head — kissed her very tenderly and put an arm about her.

"It's getting chilly," he said, trying to be matter-of-fact because he felt that he was going to burst with happiness. "You mustn't get a cold."

"How you do fuss over me, old silly," she laughed.

Arm in arm they walked into the warm, lamplit bungalow.

DENISE ROBINS

THE UNTRODDEN SNOW

Rowan's flight to Switzerland to start a new life coincides with the arrival of Ashley Moore, fresh from the success of a brilliant new musical show in London. Ashley is working on another musical in a chalet near the hotel where Rowan is working, and their paths seem to be constantly crossing — and meeting. But it is not until Fran Cottar, the beautiful wife of Ashley's best friend, arrives on the scene and Rowan finds her in Ashley's arms, that Rowan realises that for the first time in her life she is in love, passionately — and hopelessly.

'The magic lies in Denise Robins herself'
Barbara Cartland

CORONET BOOKS

DENISE ROBINS

LIGHTNING STRIKES TWICE

The first time the lightning of passionate love struck at Cressida was when she was an *au pair* girl in Rome, and fell in love with the fascinating painter, Dominic Miln.

But Dominic's vanity prevented him from returning this love and Cressida returned to England to try and start a new life. But the past would not leave her alone, and this unhappy love was to pursue her right through her subsequent marriage to another man, with tragic results.

'The Queen of Romance still reigns'

Daily Express

'Rarely has any writer of our times delved so deeply into the secret places of a woman's heart'

Taylor Caldwell

CORONET BOOKS

ALSO BY DENISE ROBINS IN CORONET BOOKS

☐	19479 0	The Other Side Of Love	50p
☐	01903 4	Betrayal (previously, Were I Thy Bride)	50p
☐	20654 3	Second Best	50p
☐	02474 7	Moment Of Love	50p
☐	02922 6	Loving And Giving	50p
☐	02920 X	Lightning Strikes Twice	50p
☐	01437 7	Nightingale's Song	50p
☐	12784 8	Restless Heart	50p
☐	20736 1	It Wasn't Love	50p
☐	14985 X	The Untrodden Snow	50p
☐	12792 9	Climb To The Stars	50p
☐	02435 6	Slave Woman	50p

All these books are available at your local bookshop or newsagent, or can be ordered direct from the publisher. Just tick the titles you want and fill in the form below.

Prices and availability subject to change without notice.

CORONET BOOKS, P.O. Box 11, Falmouth, Cornwall.
Please send cheque or postal order, and allow the following for postage and packing:
U.K. — One book 19p plus 9p per copy for each additional book ordered, up to a maximum of 73p.
B.F.P.O. and EIRE — 19p for the first book plus 9p per copy for the next 6 books, thereafter 3p per book.
OTHER OVERSEAS CUSTOMERS — 20p for the first book and 10p per copy for each additional book.

Name ....

Address ....

....